ALSO BY ALEXANDER McCALL SMITH
AVAILABLE FROM
RANDOM HOUSE LARGE PRINT

The Department of Sensitive Crimes

The Quiet Side of Passion

The Good Pilot Peter Woodhouse

A Distant View of Everything

My Italian Bulldozer

Chance Developments

Emma: A Modern Retelling

The No. 1 Ladies' Detective Agency

The Second-Worst Restaurant in France

The Second-Worst Restaurant in France

Alexander McCall Smith

R A N D O M   H O U S E
LARGE  **PRINT**

Published in the United States of America by Random House Large Print in association with Pantheon Books, a division of Penguin Random House LLC, New York. Originally published in hardcover in Great Britain by Polygon Books, an imprint of Birlinn Limited, Edinburgh, in 2019.

Cover design and illustration by Iain McIntosh

The Library of Congress has established a Cataloging-in-Publication record for this title.

ISBN: 978-1-9848-9043-6

www.penguinrandomhouse.com/large-print-format-books

FIRST LARGE PRINT EDITION

Printed in the United States of America

10 9 8 7 6 5 4 3 2 1

This Large Print edition published in accord with the standards of the N.A.V.H.

THIS BOOK IS FOR

Carole Turner-Record

The Second-Worst Restaurant in France

1

❧

Remarkable Cousin Chloe

It was one of Paul Stuart's friends who said to him, "I can't stress this enough, you know: breathing is important. Really important."

"I'd already worked that out," Paul replied.

"Oh, I know it sounds obvious . . ."

It does, thought Paul.

"But people forget. And they just breathe—you know, like this."

Paul waited.

"Whereas," his friend continued, "you should breathe like this."

In, out . . .

"I thought I already was," said Paul. "In, out. Like that?"

"Deeper. And hold the breath in for a while. Like this."

There was silence. Then the friend said, "And while you hold it in, think. That's the important thing. Concentrate your thoughts.

Think of the **present,** Paul. The right now. The actual."

"I'm thinking."

"Good. You need to be mindful, Paul. Mindful. In. Think. Out. Still thinking."

And he should also close his eyes from time to time, the friend said, and think about where he was and what he was doing, rather than about where he was going to be, and what he was going to be doing. And it was for this reason then that Paul, well-known food writer, celebrated cook, and a kind but slightly accident-prone man, now closed his eyes and took a deep breath.

He smelled coffee, and this was, he thought, a mindful sort of smell. In front of him, in the real world, was a freshly made, piping-hot cup of Brazilian coffee, its aroma drifting up to him on little wisps of steam. He loved the smell of that; a dark smell, a chocolate smell, but without chocolate's note of sweetness. The smell of coffee, really; that, he decided, was the way he would describe it. He opened his eyes and gazed out of the window.

He thought—as he took a deep breath— **Should I go?** He knew that was not mindful. He needed to think again, not about what he should do in the future, but about what he was doing now. But still the same question came back. **Should I go to France? Should I call Chloe right now and tell her: no France?**

He exhaled. He could still smell the coffee, which was now.

 𝒥t was late spring in Scotland and life was undoubtedly good—as was the view. From where he was sitting, in the kitchen of his flat, Paul could see in the distance, kissed by sunlight, the castle that dominated the city. Beneath it, the roofs and spires of the Old Town, with, here and there, those odd architectural spikes for which Edinburgh was so well known, sticking up as if to proclaim Scotland's ancient motto **Nemo me impune lacessit—Nobody challenges me with impunity.** Spikes placed on the tops of buildings, prickly thistles, the sharp-tipped antlers of Highland deer: these all played a major part in the iconography of Scotland, Paul thought; but so did the hills, those gentle, feminine hills; so did the waterfalls, and the light, and the cold blue sea; so did this city, that was like an opera set, on which at any moment somebody might fling open a window and start to sing.

Paul lived—in a part-time way, as he put it—with his girlfriend, Gloria, who was also the editor of his books, and with her two Siamese cats. It was living with somebody in a part-time way because Gloria kept her own flat on the other side of town, and still spent much of the day there. That was where her office was, where her mail was delivered, and where most of her clothes—a disorganised wardrobe, a riot of colour—were kept. It would have been easier, of course, if they had co-habited fully, but Gloria simply could not face sorting out the detritus of the years she had spent in that particular flat. It was just all too complicated; much simpler to leave things as they were. Besides, the arrangement gave both of them space, and space, she felt, was what every relationship—with anyone at all—required.

Paul and Gloria got on well. It had never been one of those passionate affairs, in which two people, in mutual intoxication, filled their waking moments with thoughts of one another. "It's not like that, with us,"

Gloria had said to a friend. "It's different with Paul; it really is. We're not like two love-struck kids, gazing into one another's eyes. We're . . ."

"Mature adults?" supplied her friend.

"Exactly."

"Oh well," said the friend.

It had its moments, though, and neither Paul or Gloria wanted or expected much more out of it. They were friends, as well as lovers, and that, they had both decided, was a good state to be in. To be a lover was easy enough; to be a friend required rather more. To be both was something not given to everyone.

There were disagreements, though—areas where a different view was taken of something that might not have been of great importance in itself, but was capable of disturbing the otherwise tranquil waters of their domestic relationship. Such as cats, and it was of these cats that Paul was thinking as he looked out from his kitchen window that morning.

Gloria was the owner of two Siamese cats, Hamish and Mrs. Macdonald. They were sleek, self-satisfied creatures, cuttingly arrogant and effortlessly handsome in a way in which lesser cats were not. They had light blue eyes that stared at you with a somewhat off-putting intensity. They had silky coats of a shade that a Belgian chocolatier might have taken years to perfect. They were vocal in a way that only Siamese cats can be, voicing their opinion in long-drawn-out cat-sounds that seemed to demand an instant response. They had several recognisable yowls: what Paul called an **asking yowl;** what he described as a **complaining yowl;** and finally, and more seriously, a **warning yowl.** The cats lived in Gloria's flat, amongst the books, papers, and colourful clothing. They had cat beds hooked onto radiators, and timed, battery-operated cat feeders that opened at set hours to reveal supplies of salmon and tuna within. They had everything, it seemed to Paul, that any cat could possibly want. And yet they always seemed to expect more. These cats, he said to himself, would never understand the virtue of moderation. **Do not want too much** did not apply to cats.

"How fond are you of those cats of yours?" he asked Gloria one evening.

This brought a surprised response. "What a question. Really, Paul! It's like asking a parent if she likes her children . . . or almost."

Paul did his best to explain. "Don't take this the wrong way, but those cats seem almost indifferent to you—or so it seems to me. The way they look at you—"

He now realised just how far he had strayed into sensitive territory. "Indifferent?" said Gloria, her tone now one of decided reproof. "Hamish and Mrs. Macdonald are **not** indifferent to me. How could you say such a thing?"

"I'm sorry, it's just the way they . . . Maybe that's the way cats are. I don't know much about these creatures—"

Again, he was cut short. "Hamish and Mrs. Macdonald are both very fond of me," said Gloria firmly. "In fact, they love me— actually love me." She intercepted Paul's look of incredulity. "No, don't be cynical. I'm absolutely sure of that. In fact, I positively bask in the love of my cats."

Paul had thought she might be speaking ironically, but now realised his mistake. Discretion might have prompted him to leave the matter there, but he persisted.

"I'm not sure that cats love humans," he mused. "Dogs do, of course."

Gloria shook her head. "Dogs . . . ," she began.

"All right then, dogs," Paul interjected. "How about dogs? Dogs will sacrifice their lives for their owners, if necessary. You know how it is—they'll jump into rivers to save a drowning child, tackle an armed burglar, that sort of thing. Whereas cats . . ." He looked up at the ceiling. "Is there any recorded instance of a cat doing anything unselfish? Feline altruism?" This, he felt, was the clinching argument. "An oxymoron?"

Gloria stared at him reproachfully.

"You see," Paul went on, "I have a theory that cats are perfect psychopaths." He had just thought of it, but it seemed to make sense.

Gloria looked doubtful. "You're making this up, Paul."

He smiled. She was right—but so, he felt, was his theory. "If you want to understand the psychopathic personality, look at a cat. They never experience guilt—unlike dogs, who look so guilty if they do anything wrong."

Gloria sniffed. "It might be that you don't

understand cats, Paul. Cats are not . . ." She searched for the right word. "They're not **obvious.**"

"Obvious?"

"Yes. You mentioned dogs, so let's go back to them. They wear their hearts on their sleeves. All that grinning and barking and slobbering." She gave a shudder.

"Whereas cats?"

Gloria was in no doubt. "Cats are effortlessly cool. Cats, one might say, have **it.**"

Paul knew that **it** existed, but was uncertain as to what **it** was. "I think we're going to have to disagree," he said. "Perhaps the world is divided into dog and cat factions, just as it is into those who like chocolate and those who like strawberries."

Gloria laughed. "Really? There are many—millions, I suspect—who adore both chocolates **and** strawberries. There are people who eat those strawberries covered with chocolate."

Paul thought about the taste wheel in one of his kitchen encyclopaedias; chocolate was earthy while strawberries were fruity, and he was sure that they were on different segments of the wheel. "Let me tell you,

Gloria, strawberry and chocolate do **not** go together. They just don't."

"Yes, they do," said Gloria. "I like them."

"I won't argue," said Paul.

She brightened. "Which reminds me . . . Taste, aesthetics, philosophy . . . The offer for the new book: Have you decided yet?"

As Paul's freelance editor, Gloria's job was to edit the highly successful books that he wrote on a wide range of culinary subjects. She had nothing to do with contractual matters, but she had an obvious interest in his keeping up the supply of the manuscripts she would read and knock into shape. Paul wrote well but tended to use long sentences that Gloria would have to chop into two, or sometimes even three, parts. She also arranged his illustrations, consulting picture librarians or engaging food photographers to ensure that Paul's reputation for lusciously presented books be preserved.

Paul was happy to abandon the subject of cats. He felt that he had somehow argued himself into an unwanted corner. He was not anti-cat—far from it—he was just being realistic about them. Cats were fine, but there was no getting away from their fundamental attitude. That was it, he thought: cats had **attitude,** whereas dogs . . . He stopped himself. It was time to address the offer for the new book.

He found that it was unnecessary to think for very long. Of course, he would accept. It was an extremely generous offer by any standards, the only drawback being that they wanted him to have the book ready within six months. Yet that was not impossible: he had already worked out what he wanted to say, and it would be refreshing to move away from his usual series—**Paul Stuart's Tuscan Table** being the latest title—and deal with something as broad and exciting as the philosophy of food. Paul had taken a philosophy course at university, but it was an introductory course that had spent far too much time on Hume, he felt, and had left many other philosophers untouched. Yet there was a clear role for the enthusiastic amateur, presumably even in philosophy, which was, after all, about things of concern to ordinary people as much as to experts. If he were to write about the philosophy of food it would be a personal statement, written from the heart as much as from the mind. The writing of it would not be a chore; rather, it would be a celebration, a meditation, an act of homage to a subject—food and its preparation—that had engaged him from the age of twelve. Unlike some of the chefs he wrote about, Paul was modest, but he felt that this book would be a good one. All he had to do, of course, was to write it.

It was on a Friday afternoon, when Paul returned from a trip into town, that he found Gloria waiting for him.

"Close the door behind you," she said. "As quickly as you can."

Paul complied, but was puzzled. "What's going on?"

"The cats are visiting," she said. "I don't want them to get out."

Gloria noticed Paul's face fall. "I hope you don't mind," she said, adding, before Paul had time to say anything, "I didn't think you would."

"Here in the flat?" he said. "Right here?"

"But of course," said Gloria. "I can't let them out just yet. Cats have to get used to new surroundings before they can go outside safely."

Paul thought for a moment. He did not want to appear unwelcoming, but cats destroyed things: they sharpened their claws on sofas, they tended to be sick if they ate too much, they shed hair on cushions and on any jacket they could find to curl up on. Some cats had fleas; some even had worms that could be passed on to people if the cats walked over your plates, which they did, on their way to drink milk from your jug or investigate your butter dish. There were many drawbacks to cats, and yet now Paul tried to look at it from Gloria's point of view. She wanted her cats to be happy, and of course so did he.

"Well, I suppose it's not for long."

Gloria nodded. "No, not for long. Just for . . ."

He waited. He hoped that she would say "Just for the day," but she did not.

"Just for a change of scenery," she said.

Paul was aware of something rubbing against his legs. Looking down, he saw Mrs. Macdonald, pressing against him, her back arched, her eyes looking up at him in guileless innocence.

"See!" exclaimed Gloria. "Mrs. Macdonald

is showing her approval. That's the way cats greet people they like. She's transferring cat pheromones to your trousers. It's the biggest compliment a cat can pay."

Paul looked down. Mrs. Macdonald was staring at him, as if challenging him to contradict what Gloria had said. "I'm not too sure about having cat pheromones on my trousers," he muttered.

Gloria disregarded this muted protest. "They have glands under their chins," she said. "That's why you see them rubbing their necks against things. It's their way of making their surroundings smell agreeable."

"You mean to them," said Paul. "Smell agreeable to them."

"Oh, we can't smell it," said Gloria. "We can't really penetrate their parallel world. That's the intriguing thing about cats—they lead these parallel lives, you see. We're not privileged to be part of all that."

Hamish had now appeared in the hall. He too was staring at Paul, as if unconvinced of his right to be there.

"It's all right, Hamish," said Gloria. "Paul will get used to you. Just give him a chance."

·   ·   ·

Paul did his best, even to the extent of being uncomplaining about the cats sleeping on the bed at night. "They feel more secure with us," Gloria said. "Mrs. Macdonald has nightmares, and it's much easier for her if she wakes up to find people around her." He emptied the litter tray without so much as a murmur. He filled the cats' food dishes with a breezy cheerfulness and plucked the cat hair off his clothing with a stoic insouciance.

Gloria complimented him. "The cats really appreciate what you do for them," she said. "They may not be able to express it, but they feel it nonetheless."

Paul did not want to be thought churlish. "I'm glad," he said.

Gloria looked relieved. "I knew you'd come round. Who could possibly resist Hamish and Mrs. Macdonald?"

For a few moments the question hung in the air.

Paul smiled. "They're certainly strong characters," he said.

He was tolerant, and would have put up with the two feline visitors had it not been for the difficulty he encountered in working in their presence. Hamish and Mrs. Macdonald did not like being shut in any particular room, and so they had the free run of the flat, including Paul's study. He tried closing that door, sequestering himself inside, but the two cats would simply demand entry, yowling in their voluble Siamese voices until he yielded. Once inside, they would prowl around, jumping up onto his table, walking across his computer keyboard, and rubbing themselves against the screen in an apparent effort to cover it with cat pheromones.

Paul found it impossible to concentrate. He had now started work on **The Philosophy of Food,** and although he had identified several good themes, he was unable to make much progress in getting them down on paper—at least, as long as the cats were in the room. After two weeks, he found that he had written no more than four pages that, on his reading through them, sounded disjointed and unconvincing. He scrapped everything he had done and began again; now it was even more difficult, as the ideas he had entertained before began to evaporate. This was not going well.

He would have to talk to Gloria. He had tried his best with the cats, but clearly the time had come to admit defeat and to ask her if the cats could possibly go back to her flat. He would have to get her to see it from his point of view: Gloria was normally a perceptive and sensitive person, but it seemed that when it came to her cats there was an uncharacteristic blind spot. In her eyes they could do no wrong, and it was inconceivable that anybody should find them less than unreservedly appealing. It was the same sort of blind spot, he thought, that people had about their children, and as such, it would require considerable tact.

It was while he was building up his resolve to deal with the cat question that he received an unexpected telephone call. This came from a distant cousin of his father's, who was known to him, and the rest of the family, as Remarkable Cousin Chloe.

"I shall be in Edinburgh the day after tomorrow," said Chloe, "and I wondered if we could meet for lunch at twelve thirty at the usual place. On me, of course—as always." She paused, but not for long enough to allow Paul to answer, before she continued, "I take it that you'll have nothing else on, you being unemployed."

"**Self**-employed, Chloe," said Paul. "Not unemployed—self-employed."

"Oh, of course, of course."

Paul accepted the invitation. He had a soft spot for Chloe, in spite of her high-handed manner and her tactlessness. Chloe was only in her early fifties, but she belonged, it seemed to him, to a bygone era, when people made tactless remarks and rarely apologised for what they were. Chloe, as far as he could tell, had never apologised for anything. She drank; she smoked small cigarillos— "But only in moderation, my dear"; and she preferred the company of men to that of women, especially if the men were in uniform. "I met a general the other day, darling—an actual, card-carrying general. He was just too divine to look at, and I must confess I went all weak at the knees. He noticed, I'm afraid, and asked me if I was quite all right. I missed my chance: I should have fainted in his arms, but one always thinks of these things too late, and the opportunity passed."

But now she was businesslike. "I have a great deal to tell you," Chloe said. "But I shall refrain from telling you until we meet. And vice versa, I hope."

"I won't tell you just yet about the cats that have invaded my flat," said Paul.

"Rats?" asked Chloe. "You've been invaded by rats?"

"Cats, Chloe. Cats."

"I look forward to hearing about it, darling. But until then, soldier on, as we all must. Happy days!"

It was the way she finished every telephone conversation, and Paul had never worked out what the appropriate response was, as immediately after saying **Happy days** Chloe would put down the receiver, cutting off any possibility of further conversation. Now he noted down the details of the engagement, sighed again, and returned to the fruitless task of trying to work while two Siamese cats, like opera singers limbering up for the performance, made their noisy presence felt.

Eating is an act, wrote Paul. **Like any other act, therefore, it takes place within the context of a moral past, a moral present, and a moral future.**

He sat back and read the sentence aloud

several times. At the end of this he sighed again, and deleted what he had written. Now he typed something quite different, a heart-felt triplet: **Why do voluble Siamese cats / Insist on screeching loudly / In other people's flats?**

He looked at these lines on his screen and smiled to himself. The sentiment, he decided, was authentic: this is what he felt. It was a **cri de coeur.** He needed advice, and the obvious source of advice was Remarkable Cousin Chloe. He had turned to her in the past, and her advice had been robust. She had a brisk way of dealing with problems, and that is what he thought he needed. He had not followed it, of course, as those who seek advice rarely intend to do what is advised, but this time, perhaps, he should listen very carefully to any suggestions she had to make. Time was running through his fingers; of the six months he had in which to complete **The Philosophy of Food,** three weeks had already elapsed.

2

❧

A Woman of Numerous Husbands

$\mathcal{P}$aul was immersed in the restaurant menu when Chloe arrived. Looking up, he saw her standing on the other side of the table, unwinding a silk scarf she had wrapped around her neck. He stood up, explaining apologetically that he had not noticed her coming in.

"No need to apologise," said Chloe, handing the scarf to a waiter who had appeared at her side. "Please hang this up for me, there's a dear." She flashed an appreciative smile at the waiter, who reciprocated. Noticing how the smile lingered, Paul thought, **Flirting with the waiter in the first minute . . .**

Chloe sat down. "Where do they get them from?" she asked, leaning across the table conspiratorially. "I mean, these positively edible young men who work as waiters in these places. Where on earth do they get them from?"

Paul shrugged. "I suspect that one's from France."

"I suppose some of them are actors," said Chloe. "Isn't that how actors keep the wolf from the door? Waiting in restaurants?"

"Possibly."

Chloe reached for a menu. "It's a miracle that we seem to have an endless supply of young men like that. Somebody, somewhere, is still producing them. Do you think it's on farms?" She waved a hand in the air, vaguely, but intended to convey an undefined rural hinterland.

"The problem, though," she continued, "is conversation."

Paul raised an eyebrow. "We haven't exactly . . ."

She raised a hand. "Oh, not us. Heavens no! You and I have never had any difficulty conversing. The problem is with young men—and their lack of conversation. They may look decorative, but try to talk to them about anything, and you pretty quickly plumb the shallows. They haven't lived, you see, and so they know nothing—or next to nothing."

"Well, some of them . . ."

"No, Paul, let me assure you—it's most of them. To have anything to say, you have to have **done** something, or at least **seen** something." She paused to look up from the menu. "Do you think I should risk the scallops?"

Paul encouraged her. "I think they'll be fine."

"Oh, I know they won't be off," said Chloe. "That was not what I was worried about. They'll be fresh enough, but will they be mostly water?"

Paul understood. "Most people don't know about that," he said.

"Well, I do, dear, and I believe I may even have learned it from you. Put a scallop anywhere near water, and you end up with twenty-five per cent scallop and seventy-five per cent water—or is it the other way round?"

"The other way round," said Paul. "One quarter water and three-quarters scallop. They absorb it very readily."

Chloe nodded. "Since you imparted that pearl of wisdom to me some years ago," she said, "I have assiduously avoided washing scallops. But the problem is: When you buy them already prepared, what's happened to them before? They're baptised, that's what—and the water's there. Frightfully convenient for the people selling them—they can charge the water at scallop rates."

"Just like bacon," said Paul. "Look at the water that comes out when you fry a rasher of supermarket bacon. You pay for the weight of that water too."

Chloe sighed. "Food is such a battle, isn't it? It's us against the big interests."

"Agri-business."

"Yes, precisely. And those people have an interest in having us eat as much of their salt- and sugar-laden products as possible. And pay for their added water while we're about it. They're very powerful."

Paul said that he agreed. He was sympathetic to the local food movement—to the natural products from the local farm. His books, he said, were written with that in mind.

"And well done you, darling, for making that stand," said Chloe. "But look at what those people are doing now. They're giving names to their ghastly products that imply that they're from the farm down the road—**faux** local. They're produced in factories in places like . . ." She waved a hand again, this time in the opposite direction from the last gesture. "And then they wrap them up and call them Old Lane Farm or something of the sort."

"With a picture of a bucolic farm setting," Paul said. "Contented animals in the field, the old farmhouse—that sort of thing."

Chloe shook her head in disgust. "I wonder about free-range eggs. Do you think the hens that lay these so-called free-range eggs are really allowed out?"

Paul sighed. "It's deceptive," he said. "The official definition of free-range eggs allows farmers to keep the hens in barns, as long as they have an outside run to which they can be given access. But there are no rules as to how often you have to let them use the run."

"And so they can spend most of their lives in the barn?"

"Yes. And in the barn the farm's allowed to keep nine hens for each square metre of floor space."

Chloe did a mental calculation. "But that's hardly any room at all."

"Exactly. They're cooped up together, shoulder to shoulder—or wing to wing, in their case. They get terribly stressed. There's nothing for them to do. Some of them end up going mad and start cannibalising the others."

"You know something, darling?" said Chloe. "I feel in the mood for the vegetarian choice. It's suddenly come over me."

Paul laughed. "The scallops had lots of room on the sea bed."

"Well, in that case, I might just manage a scallop or two."

$\mathcal{N}$ow, tell me," said Chloe. "Blow for blow— if that's not the wrong expression in what I'm sure must be a very loving relationship— how are things going with you and Gloria? I have a lot of time for her, you know. She's so much better than—" She stopped herself.

"Becky," supplied Paul.

"I'm sorry," said Chloe. "I didn't mean to be so direct. But I am a sort of aunt, after all, even if we're really . . ."

"Third cousins," supplied Paul.

"Exactement," said Chloe. "And in view of this relationship I feel that I can speak to you directly—without sautéeing my words."

"Mincing," said Paul.

"Perhaps, but mince is so rare these days—metaphors must keep up to date." She paused. "Does anybody eat mince any longer, Paul? You should know, I suppose."

"Some do. But not—"

"Not mince and tatties?" **Mince and tatties**—mince and potatoes—had been a staple of the Scottish diet for generations.

Paul said that he thought this was still eaten, but mince was probably now more frequently used to make spaghetti bolognese. "We've become increasingly Mediterranean," he said. "Except when we're eating chicken **tikka masala.**"

"Oh well," said Chloe. "But back to Gloria—do tell all."

The waiter arrived with mineral water. Paul took a sip from his glass. "There's not much to say," he began. "We get on very well together. We see things the same way, I suppose—which is important, isn't it? Imagine living with somebody who did not share your sense of humour."

Chloe rolled her eyes. "Very difficult," she said. "If not impossible. My first husband, I suppose . . ."

Paul waited. Chloe had had five husbands

so far—or five to whom she admitted—but Paul, along with the rest of the family, knew very little about them. She referred to them by numeral: husband one, husband two, and so on, although she never said very much about them. All of them had lived abroad and never came to Scotland, with the result that none of the family had ever met them. "Chloe is enthusiastic when it comes to husbands," Paul's father had said to him when he was a young teenager. And then, in a remark directed at Paul's two sisters, he had added, "She is not what I would call a role model in that department."

Now, in the restaurant, Paul felt that he might try to elicit further information.

"I'd love to know more about your husbands, Chloe," he said. "I don't want to press you about it, but you've never really told us, you know."

Chloe frowned. "Never told you? I suppose you're right. You were always too young."

"But that hardly applies now."

"Exactly how old are you, Paul?"

"Thirty-six."

Chloe looked thoughtful as she calculated

the gap between them: seventeen years. "Well, I suppose that's old enough to know. I didn't want to tell you when you were still impressionable—sixteen, seventeen . . . that sort of age. I'm old-fashioned when it comes to that sort of thing." She paused. "Corruption of youth—isn't that what they call it? It's what they condemned poor Socrates for. Corrupting the youth of Athens, for which the punishment was hemlock. Although, frankly, I doubt if he corrupted them all that much—he probably civilised them. It's terribly hard to corrupt young people, I always find—they're inevitably more worldly-wise than I am."

He wanted to encourage her. "I've been around a bit myself," he said. "I don't think you could shock me."

Chloe looked wistful. "Perhaps not," she said. "Yet it's rather sad to think that one has led a life that would fail to shock a younger cousin." She paused. "Do you really want to know about them, Paul?"

Paul nodded. "I do, I'm afraid. It's a part of you that I should know about and don't."

Chloe still looked reluctant. "I feel that it's

in somewhat poor taste to tell people about one's husbands. I think one has to assume a lack of interest, don't you?"

"No," said Paul, smiling. "I'd like to hear about them. I really would."

"After lunch, then," conceded Chloe. "I'll tell you over coffee. Now let's get back to you. You said something about cats over the phone. Tell me about these cats. They sound like baggage. Is that the problem— does Gloria have baggage?"

Paul told her about the cats and how difficult they were making it for him to work. She listened sympathetically, nodding and raising her eyebrows at appropriate points. Then, over coffee, Chloe began the story of her husbands. There was no regret in her voice as she spoke—if anything, there was a slight wistfulness. And Paul listened intently, without interrupting her with questions, and with no disapproving thoughts.

*M*y first," said Chloe, "or should I say my first **husband,** because he wasn't exactly my first lover, was an Italian called Antonio. He had the most beautiful surname, Gigliodoro, which means golden lily in

English. And he was, you know—he really was. We talk about gilding the lily when you try to adorn something that is already quite ornate enough, but I rather like the idea of a gilded lily, and believe me, Antonio was that, oh, my goodness.

"We were both barely nineteen when we met. You may recall that I was expelled from my convent school when I was just seventeen. Did your parents never tell you that? I suppose that's bowdlerisation for you, but there we are. It really was a most disagreeable place, and I was delighted to be expelled—it was something to do with a painting I did in the art class of the Mother Superior locked in an embrace with the then pope. The girls I showed it to thought it tremendously amusing, but the nuns did not like it, Paul—not one little bit. Except for one of the working nuns who was in charge of keeping the art room clean. She laughed out loud and muttered, 'That'll teach the old cow.' I thought I had done it rather tastefully—they were, admittedly, on a couch of some sort, but they both had one foot on the floor, which was the test of propriety that Hollywood used to employ, you know. You could stretch out on a couch with somebody as long as you kept one foot planted firmly on the floor—that was the standard of respectability. I made that point to the Mother Superior, but I'm afraid it didn't get through. She probably didn't hear anything I said—she was that shocked. So I said, 'Oh well, I suppose you'll be wanting me to leave,' and she said, 'Immediately. And you're not going into the dorm to get your things—they will be posted back to you.' I suppose they felt that my wickedness was somehow contagious and I had to be bundled out **tout de suite** without saying goodbye to any of my friends.

"Did I care, Paul? Not in the slightest. In fact, it was an immense relief, as I wouldn't have been able to take those nuns much longer. They were divided into two groups, you know: there were the teaching nuns, who had degrees and knew a bit about at least something, and then there were the working nuns, who wore slightly different habits and mostly came from obscure villages in Ireland. They did the washing and the cooking and all the other tasks that the teaching nuns were too grand to do, with their degrees and their teaching certificates. These working nuns had chapped hands, while the teaching nuns had soft hands and delicately manicured fingernails. The teaching nuns treated the working nuns as if they were inferior because they had only a basic education and were very superstitious when it came to pictures of saints and the sacred heart and so on. They were always crossing themselves and saying, 'Would Jesus, Mary, and Joseph all preserve us!' I can understand how the teaching nuns found that a bit tedious, with their degrees and all that, but they didn't have to look down on them quite so much. They struck me as being rather arrogant—snobbish, even—which is not an attitude that I like very much. I have always said, Paul, it matters not the slightest what bed you are born in—what counts is what you are inside, although there are some people, of course, who are quite impossible both inside and out.

"So there I was, thrown out of school at seventeen, much to the dismay of my mother and the secret amusement, I think, of my father. My mother was all for sending me to a finishing school in France, but I drew the line at that—on principle, I might add—and managed to persuade them to send me to Florence instead. They eventually agreed to this, but said that I could only go once I had turned eighteen, which in due course I did. I enrolled on an art course at a college in Fiesole, in the hills above Florence, and found myself living in a **casa dello studente,** a sort of student hostel, with a whole lot of other young people from all over the world. You can imagine the sense of freedom and the sheer exhilaration of my situation. Oh, it was bliss—perfect bliss.

"We were encouraged to haunt the Uffizi. They allowed us to copy some of the paintings—under supervision, of course— and we would also spend hours just soaking up the sheer beauty of the art. I gazed for hours at the Botticellis; I drooled over the Piero di Cosimos; I was permanently intoxicated with beauty. And then, one day after spending a full morning in the gallery, I was on a bus back up the hill to Fiesole when this boy came and sat down on the seat next to mine and we got talking. He spoke good English and looked as if he had stepped out of a Renaissance painting. We agreed to have dinner together that night—he said that he knew a restaurant where the manager was a friend of his father's and would let us eat for half price. Italy is full of such arrangements—top to bottom, it's the most splendidly corrupt country, bless them.

"That was Antonio Gigliodoro, and exactly a year later, when we were both still nineteen, we were married. Our parents did not exactly approve—mine on the grounds that I was only nineteen and he was Italian, and his on the grounds that he was only nineteen and I was a foreigner who spoke hardly any Italian and came from heaven knows where. My family did not come to the wedding, and he had only a few members of his there, all looking very sombre. But we were very pleased with ourselves and I suppose we were in love—in the way in which nineteen-year-olds tend to be in love.

"His family was wealthy and they rented for us a small flat with a view of the Ponte Vecchio, a wonderfully romantic place to spend your first days of marriage. Antonio was studying commerce at university and continued to do so—I carried on with my course at the art college. But then he failed his examinations and was thrown out of the university—with terrible results. In those days there was national service in Italy, and

Antonio received his call-up papers. He was to go into the army.

"His family was aghast. Apparently, they had paid a bribe to have him exempted, but the official taking the bribe had decided to make an example of him as somebody whose family did not pay a sufficiently large bribe, and his exemption was cancelled. His father was livid, and used all sorts of political contacts to get him off the list, all to no avail. So they decided to consult a cousin who was a prominent psychiatrist. He examined Antonio—whom he knew well, anyway— and declared him insane, which of course he wasn't, even by Italian standards. He gave him a certificate to prove this, but the army didn't seem to care. They said they had a special regiment composed entirely of lunatics and he could do his national service in that. So Antonio had to go in after all.

"I must admit I was secretly relieved. We had married too young, I decided, and when I raised it with him, he confessed to feeling much the same way. I plucked up my courage sufficiently to go to his family and ask them whether they could use their connections to have the marriage annulled on the grounds of Antonio's insanity. They were delighted, of course, and gave me a handsome payment to mark their gratitude. Antonio was fine, by the way: he did rather well in the lunatics' regiment and was eventually given a commission and some sort of medal. Perhaps the medal was for being sane—I really don't know. Of course, practically everybody gets medals in Italy, sooner or later, but I'm sure his was well deserved."

ᒉ felt that I had had enough of Italy, charming country though it undoubtedly was," Chloe continued. "So I went off to Madrid, because I had friends who had gone there and they had invited me to come out and see them. And that is where I met my second husband—about whom I shall tell you in due course, but perhaps not now, because we need to talk more about you and your problems—to which, by the way, I think I have the solution."

Paul looked at Chloe with heightened interest.

"My problems?" he asked.

"Yes, Paul, yours. And now I shall tell you exactly what I propose."

3

❧

Chicken Kiev and Its Ramifications

*P*aul sat with Chloe in her car, parked in front of the tenement block in Gladstone Terrace where Chloe owned an empty flat. Very little persuasion had been required to convince Paul that it might be the ideal place to work without feline interference, and they'd come to view the apartment.

"Such solid architecture," said Chloe, looking up at the buildings. "Thank God for the Victorians, Paul. They were an awful bunch of prudes, of course, and rapacious as hunting dogs, gobbling up half the world for their empire."

"But they built to last—you have to give them that."

"Oh," said Chloe, "I'd give them much more. They built plenty of schools and hospitals, and they believed in education, I suppose, and in drainage, just like the Romans.

They loved making drains too—it's a sort of sewer mentality, in the nicest possible sense. But Victorians were so miserable in other ways. Unhappy people."

"Why?" asked Paul. "Why the unhappiness?"

Chloe did not hesitate. "Because they were pre-Freud."

Paul raised an eyebrow. "Freud was the watershed?"

Chloe smiled. "Freud changed everything. Released us from all sorts of suppression. Sex, my dear. He explained it. Shone a light on it." She paused, and the smile turned to a look of regret. "The Victorians were just a little too early for all that. So they put all their energy into repression."

"Oh well . . ."

"Of course, they were presided over by that monstrous dwarf, Victoria." Chloe shuddered. "She cast a real shadow."

Paul protested, weakly. "She wasn't that bad, surely."

"Oh, she was, Paul. Poor woman. As a child she was held prisoner, you know. Locked up in Kensington Palace and not allowed to play with other children. She was watched by an adult all the time—and I mean all the time.

No wonder she looked so unhappy." Chloe shook her head. "Unhappiness persists, you know, Paul. Somebody who's unhappy today is probably paying for the misery of his grandparents."

Paul looked doubtful. "That's a bit deterministic, surely."

Chloe was unperturbed. "But that's the whole point, darling. We **are** determined. Parents and grandparents—they're the problem."

She paused for a moment. "Cousin Annabel," she said. "Remember her?"

Paul remembered a tall woman with a Roman nose. He had met her a few times as a boy, but she lived in Malta and was rarely in the country. She had died a few years ago, still in Malta, where she had been running a small hotel with her Maltese husband.

"She spent her life trying to prove something to her father," said Chloe. "She was his only child, but he had set his heart on having a boy and he couldn't conceal his disappointment that she was a girl."

Chloe looked at Paul. "The worst mistake a parent can make," she said. "Not to love a child for what she is."

"Yes," agreed Paul. He had been loved

by his parents and he found it difficult to imagine what it must be like to be denied that love. The world would seem all wrong; just wrong.

"So she felt she had to prove something to him," Chloe went on. "She had to prove that girls were as good as boys. It was as simple as that. He didn't expect her to do what a son would have done, and so she tried and tried to show him that he was wrong. And when she herself had children, she bent over backwards to encourage her daughter—and discourage her son."

Paul groaned. "He's the one who got into a spot of trouble . . ." He tried to remember what it was; something sufficiently serious to involve the police.

"Yes," said Chloe. "But, you know, Paul, you can't really blame him for what he did. It can't have been easy being Annabel's son."

"And the daughter? What was her name? What happened to her?"

Chloe looked sympathetic. "Anastasia. Poor girl. She was burdened with that name—on top of everything else. Did you ever meet her?"

Paul shook his head. "Not that I recall."

"I saw quite a bit of her," said Chloe. "She

tried to get people to call her Nancy, which sounds a little bit like Anastasia, but people who knew her as Anastasia simply couldn't remember to make the change. She married a man called Flip."

"Flip?"

"My thoughts exactly. How can you be remotely **serious** if you're called Flip?"

"It would be difficult," said Paul.

Chloe continued, "Annabel disapproved, largely because she disapproved of all men, as far as I could make out. Flip didn't stand a chance—he was undermined from the word **go.** As for the son, he ran away to somewhere in the Caribbean—Antigua, I think it was—where he bought a yacht and took people for cruises round the islands. St. Kitts and Montserrat—places like that."

"Well, some would say an enviable life—"

Chloe interrupted him. "Yes, possibly. These cruises, though, were naked. Everyone—naked."

"I see."

"Except when they came into port," added Chloe. "Apparently, they're a bit straitlaced on these Caribbean islands. Very churchy people, many of them. They like people to wear clothes."

Paul suddenly felt sorry for the son. What made anybody go off to Antigua and start running naked cruises? "Do you think his choice of . . . career was anything to do with his mother? Was he fighting her?"

Paul had not been serious, but Chloe was. "Very probably. He wanted her attention. And he eventually attracted it—but not in a way of which most mothers would approve." Chloe looked thoughtful. "You see toddlers doing it, don't you? They deliberately drop their food on the floor and then look at you to see what your reaction's going to be." She paused; she was looking up at the building. "I must get the windows cleaned. Remind me, Paul."

"I could do it myself," offered Paul. "It's the least I can do—you're letting me use the place, after all."

Chloe patted his arm. "You're such a sweetie, Paul." She opened the driver's door of the car and started to get out. "Let's go and check that everything is going to be all right. We have a cleaning lady who goes in from time to time, and I asked her to make sure that it was all up to scratch after the tenants left."

As they made their way towards the entrance to the common stair, Chloe remarked, "I mentioned Montserrat. You know I went there myself some years back—before the volcano erupted."

Paul vaguely remembered the Montserrat volcano and the images of the islanders fleeing from their homes.

"They were the most engaging people," said Chloe. "Friendly. Courteous. The police chief was a charming man, I recall. He'd been a senior policeman in Jamaica, you see, and had ended up there. He wore a corset. Yes, a corset, to make him look thinner—he wouldn't leave the house without it, and the problem was that if he was called out on any emergency there was always a delay while he got himself into his corset."

Paul laughed. "And the islands' criminals knew that response might be a bit slow—as a result of the corset?"

Chloe looked thoughtful. "Yes, it must have been awkward at times. But do you think many men still wear corsets?"

"If they ever did," Paul answered.

Chloe agreed. "I think very few do," she said. "But perhaps more should—for aesthetic reasons. Men do tend to develop those stomachs, don't they? Corsets would address the problem."

"Possibly," said Paul. They had reached the door. He thought of the police chief on Montserrat, imagining him in his room with a fan overhead and luxuriant vegetation visible through the window. He saw red flowers on the shrubs and heard the screech of insects. He saw the corset laid out on a chair, ready for use, and he heard the resigned sigh of its owner.

The flat was on the first floor of a four-storey Victorian tenement on the edge of the Meadows. It was an attractive and well-kept terrace, clad in the honey-coloured stone of which vast swathes of Edinburgh were built. There were, in fact, two terraces, facing each other across a wide street, on either side of which, marching up a gently rising slope, was a line of elm trees, now in the full leaf of summer, and as tall as the buildings themselves. There was an air of quiet satisfaction to the place, and this made Paul think, **Yes, I can work here.**

From the entrance hall, a stone stairway,

worn down by the tread of feet over a cen-
tury and a half, gave access to the landings.
Each landing had two flats off it, the front
doors of which were painted the same dark
blue as the street door below. Light filtered
down the stairwell from the glass cupola
three floors up. The air was cool, with that
slightly dusty smell that old stone will have.

Chloe struggled with her keys. "I meant to
sell this place," she said as the lock turned.
"But I never got round to it. It produces a bit
of an income. Students like this part of town."

They gained entrance to the hallway, and
then into the airy main body of the flat.
Paul was impressed with the brightness of
the rooms—the product of generous-sized
windows. He could not work in depressing
conditions, but there was no doubt as to this
flat's suitability.

Chloe gestured to a desk in one corner of
the living room. "Could you do your writing there?" she asked.

Paul crossed the room to stand at the desk.
From where it was positioned he could look
out at the elm trees. It was, he said, perfect.

"This is so generous of you, Chloe."

She smiled. "I wasn't going to get new

tenants until at least the end of September. I don't like short-term summer lets. They tend to be groups of actors for the Fringe, and the like. Thespian tenants are . . ." She trailed off.

"Difficult?"

"Destructive. They hold parties." She pointed to one of the living-room walls. Strange, semicircular marks ran up and down it, as if placed by an eccentric interior decorator. "I found out that those were made by a juggler. He practised against it."

"I see," said Paul.

"And in one of the bedrooms," Chloe continued, "there were footprints on the wall. How they got there . . ."

Paul laughed. "Best not to enquire."

Chloe pointed to the kitchen door. "I can show you what's what in the kitchen."

"I suspect I won't be cooking here," said Paul. "I'll just use it during the day, if you're all right with that. And I'll pop out to that corner deli for my lunch."

"A good choice," said Chloe. "It has a literary name, doesn't it? Proust's, or something like that."

Paul corrected her. "Victor Hugo, I think."

"I knew it was something like that. Proust's would be a good name for a deli, though. Everything would be described in long sentences."

"And they'd sell madeleine cakes," Paul offered.

"And lose your order in the mists of time."

There was a sudden thumping noise from the ceiling above. Paul looked up. In the room immediately above them, somebody had put music on at full volume. But it only lasted for a few seconds, before silence returned.

"Students," muttered Chloe. "The last tenants complained, but I think the students went away after their exams."

"It sounds as if they're back."

Chloe nodded. "If they're troublesome, go and complain. The other neighbours will generally back you up. Nobody likes students." She paused. "Except their mothers, perhaps—and other students."

Paul smiled. "It could be worse," he said. "I lived in a flat once where my neighbours had dogs. Six of them. They barked."

"As dogs will."

"It nearly drove me insane."

Chloe looked sympathetic. "It's one of

life's great privileges," she said, "not to have too many neighbours. People get needlessly sentimental over community."

Paul thought about this; Chloe might be colourful, but she tended to utter the first thing that came into her head, and then wrap it up in philosophical language. "Loneliness?" he said.

"Perhaps. Perhaps." Chloe brightened, changing the subject. Her philosophical ruminations seldom lasted long. "So, will this work for you, Paul? Will this help you finish this book of yours? What was it about again?"

"The philosophy of food."

She looked at him with interest. "Yes, of course. But tell me, darling, is there all that much one can say about that?"

He told her that volumes had been written, great tracts, and she smiled. "Well, Paul, you obviously have something to add, and this might be just the place to add it."

"You're too kind, Chloe."

She smiled at him once more. "I'll give you the key. It's all yours." She reached into her bag to retrieve the key. "Yours **pro tem,** that is."

. . .

$\mathcal{H}$e explained the arrangement to Gloria.

"I need a place to work," he said. "Chloe's flat will be ideal. It's quiet. No disturbances."

Gloria frowned. "I thought you worked best at home. You told me once . . ." She did not finish the sentence. "It's nothing to do with me, is it?"

He assured her it was not. "I like having you around," he said.

"But you can't work when I'm here? Is that it?"

He chose his words carefully. "No, you're fine. But I can be disturbed from time to time by . . ."

She could tell what he was about to say. "By Hamish and Mrs. Macdonald? Is that what you're saying?"

He nodded, uncertain what her response would be. She shook her head, as if with regret. "Such a pity."

"What's a pity?"

"That you won't give yourself the chance to get to know them better." There was a wistful note in her voice now. "If only you'd meet them halfway."

He tried to imagine how one met a cat

halfway. "I've tried to be friendly," he said. "I really have. But somehow, they've rebuffed me."

Gloria looked concerned. "I hope you don't feel you're being driven out."

"No, I don't. But the cats are a bit of an issue."

"An issue?"

Paul sighed. "I don't actually dislike them, I suppose, but I don't want them to interact with me all the time. It seems that those two have some deep interest in involving themselves in my life. They want to join in, but the trouble is . . ."

She waited.

". . . well, the trouble is that they're a different species. They lead their lives and we lead ours. I don't really have much to say to cats."

He saw that she had looked away from him and was now staring thoughtfully at the floor. "I shouldn't have assumed," she said. "It was just too much."

"Well, there we are. I know it's not a big issue—not in the cosmic scale of things—but it's been difficult for me." He reached out to touch her. She looked at him reproachfully.

"I feel bad," she said.

"You don't need to."

She hesitated. "Do you want me staying here with you?"

He answered immediately. "Of course I do. Of course."

He kissed her, and she looked up at him. He felt protective of her, as he always did when they kissed. A kiss was a surrender—and a promise; and it was the promise that made him feel protective.

As they drew apart, she said, "Because sometimes I feel . . . well, I feel excluded. It's as if I'm trespassing on your space."

He felt a momentary pang of vague, un-articulated guilt, that familiar feeling that comes when somebody reproaches us in a way that is perfectly justified and appropri-ate. And he defended himself in the way in which we all defend ourselves in those circumstances—by denying the unwanted truth. "No, no. You're not . . ."

"Would you tell me if I were?"

"Yes. Yes."

She looked away. He wanted to apolo-gise, but he did not know what to say. He would try to get on better with the cats.

He would try, because he did not want to hurt Gloria in any way. That was not in his nature. He would try.

Two days later, Paul used Chloe's flat for the first time. Equipped with a small bag of books and papers, along with a coffee percolator, he let himself into the flat and settled down to work. He did not use the desk he had seen on his first visit. When he had come to inspect the place with Chloe, he had noticed that in one of the rooms at the back there was a table close to the window. This was the place he chose to work; the view was not as good as that from the front of the flat, but he told himself that he was not there to contemplate the trees in the street below, but to write another chapter of **The Philosophy of Food.** This chapter—" The Otherness of Food"—was proving difficult. He had already identified and explored the central idea: that the act of eating is an act of **incorporation** in which we take food into ourselves, we put our stamp upon it in the way in which we prepare and present it, and yet we want it to remain something other than us—something which still has an identity of its own. Was that clear enough? Paul thought so. Possibly. He would have to give examples of the naming of food and the way in which the name established a separate identity, sometimes an exotic one, for what was otherwise familiar. By naming a dish we could give it a history, and a place too. This made something that was mundane and without much to it into something that could have a colourful identity. Once named, food could have a hinterland of associations with a culture or with a place. Yes, that was it: the acculturation of food; that was exactly it.

He thought of Chicken Kiev. That was a dish on which he had already done his research, and he had the sheaf of notes with him. He began to write.

The humble Chicken Kiev . . . He stopped. Was Chicken Kiev humble? No, that was not quite right. Chicken Kiev was common . . . but that, too, was the wrong word. **Common** suggested a certain simplicity and lack of anything but basic preparation. An unmarinated steak was common in that sense, as was fried fish, a grilled lamb chop, or a plain omelette. Chicken Kiev was

widespread—that was the word, he decided;
a widespread dish was one that cropped up
frequently, on all sorts of menus and in all
sorts of situations. Chicken Kiev was like
the prawn cocktail that used to appear at the
beginning of every golf club dinner, or on
the Saturday-night menu of every three-star
hotel trying to inject a bit of style into drab
surroundings. Paul smiled as he thought this.
What a social burden for a prawn to bear . . .

He began again. **That widespread dish
Chicken Kiev is a good example of the
exotically named dish that injects an
element of glamour into a meal.** Kiev . . .
**the word is suggestive of a world beyond the
borders of Europe, a Russia that is not part
of the West, that . . .** He stopped once more.
Kiev was in Ukraine, and not in Russia at
all. And yet it had been bound up with
Russia, had it not? That had been the case
under the rule of tsars and then the Soviet
Union, and its emergence as a modern in-
dependent state was quite recent. Of course,
there were some Russians who considered
it part of Russia and would have it back in
the blink of an eye. Those same Russians,
he imagined, would call Chicken Kiev a

Russian dish, and might be quite offended if the Ukrainians claimed it as their own. And then there were some historians of food who took the view that the roots of Chicken Kiev were to be found in French cuisine, the characteristic way of preparing chicken in this style having been imported into Russia by French chefs engaged by Russian aristocrats. This view would give the credit for the invention of Chicken Kiev to the French, specifically to Marie-Antoine Carême, who founded **haute cuisine** and who visited Russia during the reign of Tsar Alexander I.

But then he remembered something else. Somewhere in his scribbled notes was a reference to the Pozharsky Cutlet, a fried chicken dish associated with the Pozharsky family of innkeepers. French chefs took this cutlet from the Russians, rather than the other way round—or so the Russians claimed. This, they argued, was the precursor of Chicken Kiev.

Paul stared up at the ceiling. The scope of **The Philosophy of Food** was going to be broader than he had imagined. It was going to be about history, ownership, pride, and national identity—and food, of course. One rich seam of enquiry would lead to another, and yet here he was still scratching the surface of the subject, hardly penetrating what was revealing itself to be a mass of debate and disagreement. He returned to his notes. Did he really have to say something about Pozharsky Cutlets? Did it really matter whether these cutlets preceded or succeeded the making of Chicken Kiev? Not really, he thought, and yet the fact that people would actually hold strong views on the subject said something about the power of these food associations.

The music above his head started very suddenly. He was surprised at how loud it was, and how its resonances seemed to be amplified as they travelled down the wall from the flat above. And then, while he was reflecting on this, he heard several people, it seemed, jumping up and down on the floor above. This was followed by laughter—also transmitted down the wall with extraordinary clarity—and the sound of exuberant shouting.

The music stopped, but only for the few seconds needed for a change of tune. Now came something with deeper bass, thumping with that headache-inducing beat of heavy metal, sending vibrations into the very fabric of the building. Paul put his hands over his ears, but that did little to keep out the sound. It became louder now as a singer joined in, vociferously protesting about some injustice, some mistreatment or indifference. **I knew you never cared,** complained the disembodied voice. **Never cared, never cared . . .** Songs, thought Paul, are mostly about being head over heels in love or not being loved enough. There were no songs—as far as he knew—about simply being content, about merely **liking** somebody else. He liked Gloria, but if he wanted to sing about his feelings—and he did not—then he would be hard-pushed to think of any songs that expressed the way he felt.

Paul rose to his feet. Chloe had told him to complain, if necessary, and he would. He was not being unreasonable, he told himself. This was the morning, after all; surely people were entitled to be able to hear themselves think during the working day. He was as tolerant as the next person—even more so, he told himself—but this level of noise was insupportable. It was selfish too: unless, of course, those who were making it were unaware of the fact that sound travelled so easily. But that, he felt, was unlikely. They would know that others could hear them, but would simply not care.

He would be polite. He would say, "You know, I hate to complain—I really do—but I wonder if you could turn things down just a little. Not a whole lot, but just enough so that I can work downstairs." A reasonable approach like that—not a blunt request to turn everything off—could hardly be rebuffed.

He left the flat door open and went up the stairs to the landing above. The door, with its chipped paintwork, spoke of the landlord's neglect. Beside the bell a list of six names confirmed what Chloe had told him: this was a student flat. It also reminded Paul of his age; how many years ago was it that he had last shared a flat with more than one person? When had he last put butter or cheese into the fridge and wondered whether it would still be there when he next looked? For a moment or two he hesitated. He was the adult now; the adolescents were inside. His knock on the door—the bell looked broken—would for those inside be an announcement of the adult world—the world of parents and authority and the spoilsport. How could it be anything else? If you were nineteen, or whatever age his neighbours were, you simply would not have the empathy required to see the situation from the other point of view. He toyed with the idea of putting up with this. It would not last forever, after all: they would get tired; they would go out; they might even—remote possibility that it was—remember that they were students and do some studying. But then he reminded himself that it was summer. Students tended not to study in the summer months, in which case they might have jobs—some restaurant or hotel somewhere might be waiting for them to start their shift, unless parents were paying the rent and everything else, and there was no job to go to.

He suddenly felt annoyed. These kids— because that is what they were—could sit around playing their music because somebody else had worked to make it possible, and that person was still working. Every moment of leisure cost somebody, somewhere, the effort of work. Nobody lived on air.

He knocked loudly, thumping the door

with his fist in his growing irritation. He pressed the button of the bell too, but this wobbled uselessly under his finger. He resumed his knocking, hoping that it might be heard under the rising throb of the music inside.

As his fist was about to descend with another thump the door suddenly opened. Just inside the hall, a young woman drew back in surprise.

Paul dropped his fist. "Sorry," he said. "I wasn't . . ."

She grinned. "I didn't think you were going to hit me. You were knocking—obviously."

"Yes," he said lamely.

Then she asked, "Are you from downstairs?" She answered her own question. "Yes, you are, aren't you? Oh my God, I told them. I told them the music was too loud."

Paul nodded. "It is—a bit. I was wondering if you could . . ."

"Turn it down? Of course. I'll ask them, although . . ." She looked over her shoulder before turning back to face him and saying, apologetically, "Keith is . . . well, he sometimes doesn't . . . if you see what I mean."

"It's just that I'm trying to work." And

then, finding that he wanted to explain himself, he added, "I'm writing a book, you see, and it's hard to work if there's a din."

She looked over her shoulder again. Then she stepped forward, indicating that they should stand on the landing. "Sorry— I could hardly hear you. Can we talk outside? It's easier."

She smiled at him. In a room behind her, somebody inside shouted something at somebody else and there was laughter.

"Look," she said, "could we talk downstairs?"

Paul hesitated. He had not intended to engage beyond making his request, but this young woman was obviously trying to be helpful.

"All right," he said.

She seemed pleased. "You don't have any coffee, do you? I'm dying for a cup and we've just run out. In fact, we ran out yesterday and nobody could be bothered to go and buy some. They're lazy." She paused, and then added, "And noisy. But you know that, don't you?"

She closed the door behind her. "There, that's better." The music, anyway, had abated slightly. They had heard his knocking, she said, and had assumed it was a complaint. "They're not too bad," she said. "Everyone except Keith is reasonable enough. He leads us astray, I suppose."

They took to the stairs. She walked ahead of him, and he found himself looking at her. She was tall, almost Paul's own height; she had light sand-coloured hair; she was, he thought, in her early twenties. He had thought they would be younger.

"I'm Alice," she said as they reached the landing below.

"Paul."

She waited for him to push his door open. "I didn't think anybody lived here," she said.

"They don't," said Paul. "Or not really— I'm just using it during the day. It belongs to a cousin."

He found himself doing a quick calculation. She could be twenty-two or -three—in which case there were only a dozen or so years between them. He blushed at the thought; was this how it came to you—the growing awareness that youth was behind you? Did you know that once you started calculating, as he had just done?

They entered the flat. From upstairs, the

music could still be heard, even with the door closed behind them. Alice stopped and looked up at the ceiling. She turned to Paul, and he saw that she was visibly embarrassed.

"It is loud, isn't it?" she said. "I never thought."

He saw the look of apology, but he saw something else too. She was looking at him with interest. It was not very obvious, but it was there—the look that showed that this, for her, was not just a routine encounter with a neighbour, but was something more. For a moment he felt unnerved, but the feeling quickly passed. She was just the way people of her age group were: there was a frankness in their manner that could be disarming.

She was looking across the hall and into the room where Paul had been trying to work. The table before the window was strewn with his books. He could see the piece of paper on which he had made his notes about the Pozharsky Cutlet.

She turned to him. "Is that your book?" she asked, pointing to the table.

"It's part of it."

Her eyes shone. "What is it? Fiction? A novel?"

He shook his head. "Food. I'm a food writer."

She smiled. Her cheeks were dimpled—not deeply, but it was noticeable. Her eyes, he saw, were hazel—at least in this light. It was a lovely face, he thought; pretty: innocent in a guileless way—which was the best way for innocence to express itself. It was not a face that went with the heavy metal music now being pumped out by the sound system upstairs.

"That's what I do," Paul said. "I write books about food. But what about you?"

She did not answer his question, asking instead, "What sort of food?"

Paul pointed to his desk. "I was just saying something about Chicken Kiev. And something called a Pozharsky Cutlet."

She looked incredulous. "But how much can one say about Chicken Kiev, or the Poz . . . Poz . . ."

"Pozharsky Cutlet. Actually, quite a lot—or so I was discovering."

"I'm impressed. I've never met anybody who's written a book, I suppose." She looked thoughtful. "Or a book that anybody might want to read—might actually go and buy.

One of my tutors at uni wrote a couple of books, but nobody read them."

He asked her what she was studying.

"Studied," she replied. "I graduated two years ago."

He asked her what she had studied.

She waved a hand in the air. "Oh, English literature." The hand gesture was odd, but rather appealing. It suggested that English literature was something light and airy—the sort of thing one might toy with for a few years while doing many other important things. And prefacing English literature with an **Oh** underlined the implicit suggestion that English literature was not a subject about which one should get too concerned. You could achieve the same effect with other things too. **Oh, physics** put string theory in its place. **Oh, civil engineering** made it sound as if the strength of materials, the building of bridges and so on, was nothing much to be exercised about.

"It must be very enjoyable," said Paul. "Reading novels and poetry and . . ."

She shrugged. "Yes, it was . . . sometimes. I did a course on the Victorian novel. I loved that. I couldn't stand the early stuff. **Sir Gawain and the Green Knight** and so on. Ghastly. Not for me."

"I don't blame you. I had to read Chaucer at school."

"Oh, Chaucer," she said.

He thought: **That's Chaucer dismissed.**

"I didn't mind Chaucer too much. I read him a bit at high school." She remembered something. "We weren't allowed to read 'The Miller's Tale,' of course. That was discouraged. Have you read it?"

Paul shook his head.

"Deemed unsuitable," she said. "Sex."

"Oh, sex," said Paul.

She glanced at him.

"Chicken Kiev," she muttered.

He looked at her quizzically. "What about it?"

"Well, you're the one who seems to know everything about Chicken Kiev. You're writing a book about it, after all."

He laughed. "Not a whole book. There's a section in which I—"

She cut him short. She reached out and touched him lightly on the forearm. "Make it for me. Go on."

His surprise registered. She touched him again.

"It was just an idea," she said. "You could teach me how to make Chicken Kiev."

"Right now?"

She glanced at her watch. "Well, it is lunchtime, isn't it?"

He looked at his desk. He needed to work, but what harm would there be in taking an hour or two off?

"I suppose I could." He paused. "Although, you know, it's not something I usually make. Chicken Kiev has become something of a cliché."

Alice frowned. "Just because too many people like it? Isn't that a bit snobbish?"

He realised that it was. "Yes, I suppose it is. I didn't mean it in that way. What I said . . . It's just that there are some things that strike one as being rather too popular. We get bored with them."

She saw what he meant. "I suppose you're right. Spaghetti bolognese—boring old spaghetti bolognese. That sort of thing."

The music up above suddenly became louder. They both looked up at the ceiling.

She was embarrassed. "That's Keith," she said. "I'm going to speak to him."

She said something else that he did not catch. He looked at her and wondered if he was reading something into this encounter that simply was not there. His uneasiness returned.

She repeated her question. "I said: How do you make Chicken Kiev? Is it complicated?"

He shook his head. "We can go and get what we need from the deli."

She asked whether the deli sold chicken. They did, he said. There was a fresh meat section. "They have everything."

"Good." She turned, and as she did so, she brushed against him. It was inadvertent, he thought, but then she turned again, and it happened once more.

He put on his jacket.

"I like that," she said, admiring it.

"Linen," said Paul.

"I love linen."

He reached for his keys. "So do I. Linen's . . ."

"Cool," she said. "In every sense."

They made their way out of the flat and into the street below. He could not help but watch her, his eyes drawn to her. Then, round the corner, they went into Victor Hugo, the deli that Chloe had recommended. Inside, he pointed to a bowl of marinated olives. The olives were outsize and green—he thought they looked luscious. There was an invitation to sample them—a plate displayed a selection, neatly sliced, glowing with oil.

He said, "Look at those."

She smiled, and pointed at the samples. "Let's."

"Yes," he said. "Let's."

She picked one out with her thumb and forefinger and made to feed it to Paul. "Specially for you," she said. "I'm Eve with her olive."

Her words hit him with an almost physical force. "You mean apple," he stuttered.

"Olive. This is the modern version."

Paul drew in his breath. Mindfulness. Then he thought: **What's happening here?** He wanted to turn away, to free himself of this sudden advance, but he felt flustered. He should not have offered to make Chicken Kiev. Chicken Kiev was all wrong . . .

He began to turn his head away, to reject the intrusive gesture, but she reached out with her free hand, gently pressing it against his cheek. "No. Here," she said. "Eve's olive."

Then Gloria walked in and picked up a baguette from a basket near the door. She looked up and saw Paul and Alice. She saw her touching his lips; she saw her hand against his cheek. She did not see the olive.

She said nothing, but turning his head to escape from Alice, Paul spotted Gloria. He started to speak, opened his mouth to say something, but could think of no words. Gloria stared at him for a moment, and then looked away. She left.

Paul muttered an excuse to Alice and began to pursue Gloria, who was walking away swiftly. He caught up with her, and grabbed at her blouse to stop her.

She looked at him. Her expression showed her sorrow. "Let go," she said. "Just let go."

"You won't believe me," he said, trying to stop her.

"No," she said, "I won't."

"She's one of the people from upstairs. The noisy ones. I was talking to her about Chicken Kiev and she said that . . ."

Gloria shook her head. "Oh, Paul, come on . . ."

"No, it wasn't anything. It really wasn't."

She was staring at him. "You were virtually kissing her."

He protested his innocence. "I wasn't, Gloria. It wasn't a kiss. She had an olive."

"An olive?"

He nodded, but rather shamefacedly. It sounded unbelievable—as the truth often sounds. "She picked up an olive, you see, and was making a joke about Eve and her apple."

He realised immediately that he had made it sound infinitely worse.

He attempted to correct himself. "I don't think she was talking about temptation." He paused. "It was an olive, not an apple."

And then he said, "Oh, Gloria, I'm so sorry. This really was nothing. I offered to make this girl Chicken Kiev. You know—Kiev's in Ukraine—and Chicken Kiev . . ."

Gloria was staring at him.

"She saw me writing about it, you see, and . . ." He swallowed. "I'd just met her, you know, and she saw that I'd been writing about Chicken Kiev. In the flat. It was on the table. I was writing about Chicken Kiev at the table and then—"

Gloria cut him short. "She was in the flat? She was?"

He felt miserable. "I'm sorry. I really am. All I can say is that there was nothing between us. Nothing. On my side . . ."

"And hers?"

He looked down at the ground. "I don't know. She's a bit . . ."

"A bit what?"

He looked up. "I said I'm sorry—and I am."

For a few moments Gloria was silent. Then she said, "I don't think it's working all that well, Paul."

He frowned. "Us?"

Gloria looked sad. "Yes, us. I've been thinking about it. I should have discussed it with you. Before this . . . this Chicken Kiev nonsense."

"But all that was true. There was Chicken Kiev—or would have been. I was going to buy some things here."

He could see that she was no longer listening. She had become calmer. "I think we need to take a break. Maybe for a while."

"No," he said. "We shouldn't. We could try. I'll try. I'll . . ."

"I don't think so."

He searched her face, but saw only resolve.
"You really mean it, don't you?"

She said she did.

"Do you think that we just . . ." Paul searched around for the right way of putting it. "Do you think that we just persuaded ourselves that it would work out? We were in Italy, after all, and that's pretty romantic."

She was not sure. "Possibly."

"People often fall in love in places like Paris or Venice. It just seems the right thing to do." He smiled. "And yet, friends and lovers are different. Perhaps you shouldn't sleep with friends."

"No, perhaps not. And we never talked about it, did we? We didn't discuss our relationship."

Was that a mistake? he wondered. The discussion of a relationship rarely fostered romance. Relationships just **were.** You could not generate lightning.

He reached out to touch her. "Friends?"

"Of course." Then she added, "The cats will miss you."

He began to say, "And I'll miss them," but could not. He could not lie. So he said, "They'll be pleased to get back home."

She nodded. "Cats are creatures of habit, you know. They like their familiar territory."

"Don't we all?"

She leaned forward and kissed him. The kiss, he realised, was the kiss of a friend, and not that of a lover; it was a distinction that could not be missed. But one that was oddly reassuring nonetheless.

From the corner of his eye, he saw Alice emerge from the deli. She was looking in his direction. She hesitated, and then walked off.

Chloe called round at Paul's flat two days later. He told her about Gloria's move back to her own flat.

"We're going back to how we were," he said. "So that's it. But it was by mutual agreement. We're still friends."

"You poor boy," she said. "You poor, poor darling."

"And I don't think I'll be using your flat after all," Paul continued. "Not only have I got my own place back, but there was just too much noise upstairs."

"Did you speak to them?"

"Yes," he replied. "I did. They made a bit of an effort, but not much."

"Well, at least you have your own flat again, now that the cats are away."

"Yes."

She was studying him with a look that suggested she was planning something.

"You know, I'm going to France," she said. "I'm renting a house for a few months."

"Why?"

"Because the spirit moves me. I feel the need for France. It's a yearning, I suppose." She paused. "You have your book to finish, don't you?"

"I do."

"And didn't you go off to Italy to finish the last one?"

Paul nodded.

"Then come with me to France. As my guest."

He hesitated. He had to finish the book, but he still felt raw over Gloria's move. He was missing her, and he had thought about trying to get back to where they had been. He had decided, though, that the time was not right. Perhaps in the future he would do something, but not now.

"Do you mean it, Chloe?"

She wagged an admonitory finger. "Of course I mean it. Absolutely." She looked at him with mock reproach. "Don't **you** always mean what you say?"

"I try to," said Paul.

"So?" Chloe said. "France? It's not all that far from Poitiers. A small village. The house looks all right from the photographs—rather nice, in fact. Easily big enough for the two of us—and visitors."

He thought of what the alternative would be. He did not want to be by himself. Chloe was entertaining; she made things happen. And he longed for France too. Whenever he thought of France, he longed for it.

He hesitated.

Chloe smiled. "Well, think about it. And now, tell me, were you seeing somebody else?"

"No," said Paul. "But I suppose I was tempted . . ."

Chloe made a gesture of resignation. "Who isn't?"

"Tempted?"

"Yes. Temptation is a universal thing, Paul. It's like gravity. It's always there."

"But if you're happily involved with some-body, should you feel tempted?"

Chloe laughed. "**Should you** is a differ-ent question from **do you.** The real issue, of course, is whether you act on tempta-tion. You can be faithful to somebody in the flesh and yet mentally . . . well, you may do all sorts of things. Especially if you're a man."

Paul protested. "Why single out men?"

Chloe's reply was robust. "Because men **are** different, Paul. Men are by nature always ready to be tempted."

Paul grinned. "How would you know about that, Chloe—not being a man?"

"These matters are universal. Men think we don't know what they do, but we do. We know very well what men get up to—and what they think about."

He nodded. "Ah." And then, "I was very fond of her."

"There has to be more to it than that, Paul," she said.

"I know."

"Poor boy." Chloe sighed. "You need to have an affair, Paul. Have an affair that revitalises."

"I don't think so."

This seemed to amuse Chloe. "If anybody says he doesn't need an affair, then he needs to get away. He needs to go to France." She paused, and looked at him conspiratorially before adding, "Have you ever looked at the French, Paul? I mean, really looked at them?"

He did not answer. It was a strange, almost absurd question. Had he looked at the French?

"There's something about them," Chloe continued. "They occupy space in a different way, for a start—they seem to **belong.**"

Yes, thought Paul. **They belonged.**

"And then their attitudes are chalk to our cheese," Chloe continued. "They're more passionate; they have more fun. They're more intense—in an open, demonstrable way. Look at their body language."

The gestures, thought Paul; the expressive use of the hands; the shrugs and pouts.

"And it's infectious, you know. That's what people don't realise until they go there and get under the skin of the place. Then you find out."

"Really?"

"Yes, even we can be changed—just by being there. Our northern, Protestant culture, our essential Scottishness, can be shed so very easily."

But then Chloe seemed to think of something else, and her expression changed. "Cheese," she said dreamily. "**Jambon sec. Terrine. Confiture. Tarte.** Not to mention . . . how many different wines? Virtually uncountable?" She smiled at him. "How about it?"

He did not argue. France could be a solution, to many things, perhaps, but mostly to the book. He had to finish the book. "Yes," he replied.

She smiled. "As in **d'accord?**"

"Yes."

4

❧

Wilde's Last Words

Chloe arrived in France ten days before Paul. He caught the high-speed train, the TGV, to Poitiers from Paris, and she was waiting for him at the railway station when the train drew in. She was in the middle of a knot of people, some of whom were ready to board the train, while others were there to meet those arriving. He spotted her immediately, even before the train had come to a complete halt; the straw hat she was wearing, a wide-brimmed floppy construction, singled her out—no French person would wear such a quintessentially eccentric hat—as did her complexion, that pale, almost translucent skin, so different from the sun-burnished tones of the French on their summer holidays.

He had resolved to travel light, but had failed, and had with him two bulging suitcases that he succeeded in getting off the train only with some effort.

"Largely books and papers," he said apologetically, as Chloe tried to help him.

"My dear," said Chloe, flinging her arms around him. "You're going to get so much done. Everything is prepared: the house, the desk in the house, the view from the window in front of the desk. **Tout. Tout.**"

They began to make their way towards the car park. A placard beside a newsagent's stall announced the latest rail strike, and Chloe gestured to this. "You've arrived in the nick of time. We're about to be cut off. Plant courgettes against the revolution, I always say." She laughed. "I've lived through two revolutions, Paul. I must tell you about them one of these days, but I do tend to get them a bit mixed up. One was a bourgeois revolution against a socialist government; the other was the other way round. Both ended up with the same people being in power, but pretending to be different." She stopped briefly, to get her breath. "Generally, I preferred the socialists to the bourgeoisie. They were more fun, I thought, and were surprisingly ready to recognise that although one was bourgeois oneself—and we are, I'm afraid, Paul, whether we like it or not; in spite of that, the radical socialists were very ready to forgive one's origins—provided, of course, one was vocal enough in one's self-hatred. They loved you if you were prepared to excoriate everything in your past. They loved that."

They entered the car park. "I managed to negotiate a car along with the house," Chloe explained. "It's one of those old Citroëns. I suspect it shouldn't really be on the road any longer—but it has a great deal of character and seems to start every time I ask it to. It's a very bourgeois car, of course, but one should never despise anything that gets you from A to B."

She was right about the car, he felt. It was one of those low-slung saloons with the swept-back rear that looked nowhere better than being parked in front of a prosperous country house. This car, an extraordinary lilac of a shade more or less never encountered in a vehicle, was beginning to show its age. The paintwork was faded—the lilac might have started life as something a bit stronger—and the leather seats within were covered with a network of cracks and blisters.

Paul's luggage loaded, they began their journey.

"Chloe," Paul ventured as they left the car park and swung out onto the main road, "one does drive on the right in France, doesn't one?"

It took Chloe a few moments to react. She was about to explain the car's suspension system—which she found quaint—but stopped herself. "Possibly," she exclaimed, swinging the car into the correct lane. "There's so much that one has to remember." And then she sounded forth on the subject of suspension. Paul looked out of the window, struggling with his nervousness. To go anywhere, with anybody, was an act of faith. You trusted in the other's judgement, navigation, and sense of what they were doing. What did he know about Chloe? Very little, he realised, other than that there had been a succession of husbands, that she had a mind filled with enthusiasms of one sort or another, and that she had a tendency to act on impulse. Yet he had placed himself in her hands and now he was in France—a foreign country, after all, with a different way of doing things—as her guest, having thrown his fate in with that of an eccentric older relative whose life thus far had consisted of a series of scrapes, near-misses, and peculiar dalliances.

"We're going to have such a time," Chloe remarked, as the road snaked out of town. "Such a time. Look at that, Paul. France."

She took a hand off the wheel to point out the landscape that had opened up before them. Crops of wheat and barley stretched out to a distant horizon of low curves; here and there, small forests, irregular in shape and extent, interrupted the sweep of the land, making for dark patches against the lighter green of the fields. Lanes, almost too narrow to admit a car, hemmed in by exuberant hedgerows, ran off the main road at unpredictable angles, marked by white metal signposts bearing the name—inevitably a long one— of some tiny village. The position of those villages was given away by a church spire poking up in the middle distance, or by a cluster of red-tiled roofs. "You could get lost so easily," observed Chloe. "You could wander around for weeks, and end up nowhere."

She turned to him briefly. "But don't worry, Paul, I know exactly where we're going."

A tractor, towering on impossibly high wheels, a spraying mechanism of some sort attached to its rear, lumbered towards them, taking up most of the road.

"Entitlement," muttered Chloe, as she slowed down and edged onto the road-side verge.

The tractor driver glanced at them dismissively as he passed.

"Well, I suppose he's been living here for hundreds of years," said Paul. "That makes a difference."

Chloe nodded. "It's very reassuring being a peasant," she said. "You must feel utterly secure. You belong. You're it. You don't have to apologise to anybody."

Paul wondered whether anybody still used the term **peasant.**

"Oh, the chattering classes don't," said Chloe. "They subscribe to the notion that we're all exactly the same. But that doesn't wash with the peasantry. They don't need to be condescended to. And they're not embarrassed by being who they are. Why should they be? Their life consists of looking after the cows and getting the potatoes in, and so on. They understand the importance of such things."

"Whereas we . . . ," Paul began.

Chloe took over. "Whereas we lead our urban lives with a slight sense of superiority. We admire all the wrong things—and the wrong people. We worship money. We think those who manipulate money are to be handsomely rewarded, ignoring the fact that those money changers—for that is what they are, Paul—couldn't lift a crop of potatoes if they tried, nor milk a cow, I suspect." She shook her head in disbelief. "No, give me these people any day of the week. At least the life here is honest."

Paul suppressed a smile. He suspected that Chloe needed a theme—some central narrative that dictated what she would do and think. Perhaps that was what this trip to France was all about: the discovery of a rural lifestyle, governed by the seasons, uncomplicated and natural. That had been all but lost in so many other places, but survived with a Gallic stubbornness in France. Small-scale French farmers—that tractor man and his like—took instructions from nobody, least of all from the authorities in Paris. Perhaps this was what motivated Chloe—a romantic, rural idyll.

He thought of Marie-Antoinette and her fake peasant village, her **hameau,** in the grounds of Versailles.

"Marie-Antoinette—" he began.

Chloe cut him short. "Marie-Antoinette never dressed up as a milkmaid," she said firmly. "That's a **canard** that has been repeated time and time again, but is absolutely untrue. She wore comfortable dresses when she was there, but she was **never** a milkmaid."

"I wasn't going to accuse her of that," said Paul. "I was just thinking about how one might romanticise the countryside." He paused. They were passing a farmyard just off the road; a goat was tethered under a tree; an open barn door gave a glimpse of stacked bales of hay within; an ancient cart was abandoned next to the barn, its wheels at an angle, its shaft resting on a pile of bricks.

"She had a working farm," said Chloe. "She had a Swiss guardsman who looked after it. They bred rabbits, chickens, pigs. She used the produce herself."

"So that's where she got the eggs for her **brioche**," said Paul. **"Let them eat cake . . ."**

"No," snapped Chloe. "No, Paul. You should not perpetuate that gross calumny. She **never** said that—there's not one shred of evidence. That was Rousseau's fault. His **Confessions** are full of invention, and one of them was about somebody—and he did not name her—who made such a remark. Marie-Antoinette's enemies then attributed the words to her. It was very unfair. She was not like that at all, you know."

Paul was surprised. "She had a social conscience?" This seemed to him to be unlikely. Marie-Antoinette represented, in his view, the **ancien régime** in all its powdered wastefulness. The tumbrils took things too far, but what could the aristocracy expect?

"Believe it or not, she did, Paul. She was concerned about the suffering of the poor when she came across it. There's evidence, but of course people don't always want to look at the evidence." She gave him a discouraging glance, causing the car to swerve. "Once they decide on something, people are usually very reluctant to take a fresh look."

With mock-seriousness, Paul assured her

that he would reconsider his attitude towards Marie-Antoinette.

"So you should," said Chloe.

Paul looked out of the window. They had crossed a low-level bridge and the road now followed a gentle incline. Fields of sunflowers flanked them on either side, painting the landscape yellow.

"Are you a monarchist, Chloe?" The question seemed to follow naturally from the discussion of Marie-Antoinette. Yet, he thought, you could be a monarchist and still disapprove strongly of somebody like her—if that is what she really had been like. And he thought, for all that Chloe had defended her character, she was like that. All of them were.

Chloe took some time to answer, initially repeating his question as if to tease out some unspoken nuance. "Am I a monarchist?"

"Yes."

"It depends, I suppose, on the context."

He waited for her to explain.

"You see," Chloe continued, "there's the principle, then there's the practice. You might approve of the idea of monarchy—of constitutional monarchy, shall we say—

and yet disapprove of a particular monarchy. As far as that monarchy is concerned, you might not be a monarchist, but you may approve—possibly quite strongly—of other monarchies."

"Or you could reject the whole notion," said Paul. "You could reject it as being fundamentally undemocratic."

"Yes, you could." Chloe paused. She slowed the car. "We're getting close. It's the next turning on the right."

She returned to monarchy. "I rather like the Scandinavian monarchies. And our own, I suppose, subject to some qualification, of course. They do a good job, by and large—rushing round opening things and encouraging people."

She laughed, and sounded the car's horn, perhaps for emphasis.

"What tedium for them," she continued. "And they provide people with a sense of tribal identity, which I think people need, deep down. But then you get some other monarchies that are definitely not to my taste. Monaco, for example. I can't bear the place. Did I tell you I spent a month there once? All expensive flats and glove shops and so on. But there was one of their princesses who really was very colourful."

They were approaching the turning now, and Chloe slowed down further. "I have had more than one husband, Paul, as you know, but that princess—well, I'm not in her league. She's wonderful—positively inspiring for the rest of us. She had some very remarkable companions—a Corsican bartender, for example; a Belgian bodybuilder; and then, as you must already know, she ran away with a famous elephant tamer from a circus. One could not make that up, Paul. Such colour. And all in the Royal House of Grimaldi—good for her. What **chutzpah**!"

They were now on a narrow lane that twisted and turned unexpectedly. "One has to be so careful on these roads," said Chloe. "I almost hit a motorcyclist yesterday. He was travelling at terrible speed. His fault entirely, of course, but what's the point of talking about fault after you're both dead? None, I'd say."

Paul agreed. "No need to hurry."

"Precisely," said Chloe. "And then there's Zog. King Zog of Albania. That was his real name, you know. Delicious, isn't it? The ultimate Ruritanian monarchy. He more or less appointed himself—he had been some sort of tribal chief, rather like those clan chiefs we have in Scotland—and he was promoted to king. He built a palace in Tirana that wasn't very grand at all—a sort of large suburban villa, in fact—and installed himself in that. Toy soldiers at the gate—that sort of thing." She paused. They were passing a small field of pigs. "Look at them. Look how utterly content they are. They don't like the sun, though, you know. Pigs can get sunburned. They love shade. Shade and mud. That's what a pig wants out of life."

"King Zog," Paul prompted.

"Oh, him. Yes, there he was. He was a rather melancholy-looking man—not entirely happy with his lot, I suppose. And he had a mother and four or five sisters. Four, I think. The sisters lived with him—all of them—and he dressed them in naval uniforms. I've seen photographs of Zog's sisters, all kitted up in white uniforms—caps, the lot. They put a big sofa out on the lawn and the sisters sat on it in their uniforms and had their photograph taken.

"Nobody invited him anywhere, apparently.

He waited and waited, but received no invitations at all. All the other royal houses were far too snooty to recognise him properly, and eventually he had to leave the country. He ended up in the Ritz hotel in London, poor Zog. But I suppose if you need temporary quarters, you can do worse than the Ritz."

They were approaching a village. A sign by the road announced **St. Vincent de la Colline** and beyond it a hand-painted notice, at a slightly drunken angle, advertised **Oeufs, Pommes de Terre, Fruit,** an arrow pointing in the direction of a farmhouse just off the road.

"We're here," said Chloe. "Or almost. We're on the other side of the village."

"Saint Vincent de la Colline," muttered Paul. "Who exactly was he?"

"Oh, some local saint," Chloe replied. "Of great obscurity—I doubt if anybody knows anything about him any longer. There are any number of these saints. France has hundreds and hundreds of them. There are no real hills around here, so I suppose he must have come from some other hill altogether. But he must have done something. If he existed, of course." She smiled. "Perhaps he produced a hill out of nothing. It might have been one of his miracles—and quite enough, I would have thought, to get one canonised. **You want a hill, dear people? Voilà!"**

"**De trop,** in fact," muttered Paul.

"Saints really are a bit much. Dreadful company, I imagine. One would be so tempted to say to them, 'You are so, so apocryphal!' And so many of them are, you know. Some of these saints are **distinctly** apocryphal. I read the other day about a Corsican saint called Saint Baltazaru of Calvi, who performed the miracle of changing wild boar into sausages without benefit of a **charcutier.** Apparently, he just had to touch a wild boar and it would become sausages—just like that."

"A real miracle," said Paul.

"Yes," said Chloe. "How comfortable it must be to believe in miracles, Paul. And to believe in saints and angels, too. The very idea that there is a community of benevolent figures watching over us, ready to intervene on our behalf."

A duck was crossing the road ahead of them, followed by an erratic line of ducklings. Chloe brought the car to a halt, and they watched the small procession.

"Of course, there might be angels, for all we know," said Chloe. "Why should we imagine that the only things that exist are the things we can see ourselves? Doesn't that sound somewhat solipsistic to you?"

Paul watched the ducks. The mother, anxious over the welfare of the stragglers, was urging her brood across the road.

"Those ducks," mused Chloe, "don't know that Paris exists, but that doesn't mean it doesn't."

"I've never really thought much about angels," said Paul. "I know that some people are keen on them, but they don't do much for me."

"That's because Scotland is bereft of angels," said Chloe, putting the car back into gear. "You haven't been brought up with them. Angels inhabit southern climes, I imagine. Italy in particular. They love Italy. And France, I suppose—particularly southern France."

Paul said that he thought they might be indifferent to surroundings. "If you're incorporeal, I'd have thought it didn't matter all that much where you were."

"No," said Chloe. "Saints are very sensitive

to their milieu. They love gentle landscapes—hillsides covered with olive groves, canyons in mountains, where the air is scented with thyme and rosemary. Mountaintops in Greece."

"You speak as if you've seen them," said Paul.

Chloe sounded regretful. "Alas, I haven't. But I may have felt their presence." She pointed out of the driver's window. "Look. That's the house—over there."

They had passed through the village—it did not take long—and were now at the start of a poplar-flanked driveway. Just visible, behind a cluster of fruit trees, was a solid-looking stone house, its windowsills and doors painted light blue.

"That's it," said Chloe.

She half turned to face Paul. "Well, what do you think of that? A **maison de notaire,** all to ourselves."

Paul replied that he thought it charming. He glanced at the ground that surrounded it—at the stand of fruit trees and the riotous bougainvillea against the fence. Above the house, the sky was a high expanse of singing emptiness. He caught his breath. He foresaw days of warmth and languor, fading into one another; he foresaw the quiet growth of his manuscript—twenty pages, thirty, forty— uninterrupted by telephone calls and the vague worries of daily life; he saw evenings of half-light and dipping swallows returning to nests under the eaves; he saw tables spread with ripening cheeses and olives and bottles of local wine.

"Oh goodness," he muttered.

"Yes," said Chloe, turning the car onto the drive. "You know what this makes me think of? Renoir."

Paul thought of **Luncheon of the Boating Party.** "Yes," he agreed.

"Renoir was vigorously opposed to France changing," said Chloe. "He wanted it to remain the same—to remain real."

Paul gazed at the house. He saw details now: the white-painted shutters of the three first-floor windows, pushed back flush against the wall; the stone pediment surrounding the front door; the irregularity of the two wings added to the house, afterthoughts both; the gravel of the final section of driveway, onto which the lilac-coloured Citroën now glided with such a satisfying crunch.

"Renoir would have liked it here," said Chloe.

They were in front of the door. Chloe switched off the engine and turned to Paul.

"I feel that something quite significant is going to happen, Paul," she said. "I don't know why, but I have that sense."

The engine silenced, there was quiet: cicadas, perhaps, but only faintly audible; the rattle of dry leaves in the stirring of a breeze; birdsong somewhere.

"But it seems so peaceful."

"That's why," said Chloe. "There's something about to happen here—something I can't quite put my finger on, but which we shall, no doubt, discover in due course." She opened the door on the driver's side.

Paul struggled with the first of his outsize suitcases. He looked up. "How do you know?"

Chloe was in what appeared to be a yoga position beside the car, stretching her arms high above her head. She complained that sitting at the wheel of a car gave her cramp. "Know what? That something's about to happen?"

"Yes. That."

She lowered her arms slowly. "Do you know what makes for a good still life? I'll tell you: it's when the painter manages to convey a sense that something is about to happen. The objects in the painting all look immobile, but as you contemplate them you begin to feel that at any moment there could be movement. Somebody might come into the room. A storm might blow up outside. The wind will move the curtains. All of these things **might** happen."

"And that's what you feel here?" Paul gestured to the garden, and the village beyond.

"Yes," answered Chloe. "Just look."

A bed of lavender, edging the driveway, moved in the breeze, the stems creating a ripple of purple. In the village, there was no sign of movement; but then a window was opened in the front of a house and a forearm appeared, tiny at this distance, struggling with the outside shutter.

"There you are," said Chloe. "Just look."

She came to Paul's help, heaving the second case from the car.

"I'll come back for that," Paul said. "Don't worry."

Chloe smiled at him. "You forget something, Paul. I was a member, you know, of the East of Scotland Ladies' Weightlifting Club." She paused, consolidating her grip on the handle of the case. "Or did you not know that?"

Paul laughed. "I'm afraid I didn't."

"Not surprising," said Chloe. "Considering that I have just made it up."

He laughed again, but thought: **Is this true? Is any of it true? The husbands? That business about the Corsican saint who changed wild boars into sausages?** Had he inadvertently stepped into a play—with a fantasist as director? The French created the theatre of the absurd, he reminded himself: Ionesco and his rhinoceroses; Anouilh; Beckett . . .

As they made their way the short distance to the front door, Chloe asked: "What were you thinking about? Back there—a moment ago?"

"Drama," said Paul. "French drama."

At the front door, Chloe put down the case she was carrying and fished a large, old-fashioned key out of her pocket. "Do you know something?" she said. "There's a house in the village with one of those nice old mailboxes. The postal horn in iron relief. I walked past it the day I arrived and couldn't help but notice the name. Godot."

Paul smiled.

Chloe fumbled with the key. "When I mentioned it to Annabelle—you'll meet her tomorrow—she said, 'Oh, that house belongs to some people from Paris. They bought it, but never arrived.'"

"So!" exclaimed Paul. "They were called Godot. I see! Art imitates life."

"No," continued Chloe. "Not so obvious. No Godots ever lived there, apparently. These people were called Beckett. So **Godot** was ironic—the sort of joke that Parisians would appreciate." She paused. "Paul," she continued, "Oscar Wilde said, 'Life imitates art far more than art imitates life.'"

"Did he?"

"Yes, he did. He coined so many **aperçus.** And, broadly speaking, he was right, I think."

Paul sighed. "I'm tired, Chloe. I can't think about all of this . . ."

"Of course you are, darling. Who isn't these days?" She pushed open the door. "One last thing, though, while we're on Wilde. His last words—do you remember them?"

He shook his head. He wanted to sleep. He had not slept the night before, as was often the case when he was about to embark on a journey. It was early evening now, and he was looking forward to an early dinner and then bed.

"Wilde was in his hotel room in Paris, dying. Apparently, he thought little of the interior decoration and declared: 'Either the wallpaper goes or I do.'"

"Marvellous."

Chloe looked rueful. "If only he had actually said it."

5

❧

Liberté, Egalité, Fraternité

When Paul awoke the next morning he felt the momentary disorientation that sometimes comes with being transported, too quickly, from one world to another: the discovery that the windows, and the light they allow through the chinks in the shutters, are in unexpected places; that the usual sounds of the morning—the slight hum of traffic, the occasional voice drifting up from the street below, the familiar creaks and sighs of even the most solidly built house—either are absent or sound different. That morning in the unfamiliarity of his new surroundings he heard only silence, broken suddenly by birdsong, a sudden chorus triggered by some little avian injustice in the twigs and branches. He imagined himself still asleep; he was confused, but in a second or two it came to him that this was France, and that when he opened the shutter he would see the expanse of unkempt lawn he had noticed through the dining-room windows last night; beyond the lawn would be the stream and its bounding fields; and there, under their uneven tiles, would be the roofs of the village he had planned to explore that morning.

Once out of bed, he opened the shutters of his window. He had been tired when he eventually turned in the previous night, and had paid no attention to where he was. He had forgotten that he was on the ground floor and was looking out not over the lawn, but onto a courtyard at the back of the house. Chloe's car had been driven through an archway in one side and was parked up against the rear wall of this courtyard, directly opposite his window, while against the wall to his left a climbing rose, riotous with dark red blossoms, sent tendrils almost to the height of the gutters. The ground was paved with uneven white stone—limestone, by the look of it—that here and there had cracked, allowing clusters of grass to establish themselves. A couple of sizeable stone troughs, rough-hewn and covered in lichen, were immediately below his window, and had been planted to provide a source of herbs for the kitchen. He could tell from above that these had been little tended or picked—in one, rosemary was edging out the less robust herbs; in the other, the purple flowers of rampant mint obscured Sweet William, thyme, and chives. He could smell the herbs and could touch them, too, if he leaned out over his windowsill.

Chloe had mentioned that she breakfasted late, and he should not expect to see her until at least nine. "I read in the small hours," she said. "A biography of Renoir at the moment."

"That's why you said Renoir would have liked it here?"

"Exactly. Renoir is on my mind. I feel that he's something of a companion. Anyway, that justifies my getting up late. If you are up and about earlier . . ."

"I shall be very quiet," promised Paul.

"No, it's not that. I sleep through anything, so don't bother to creep about. Had I lived in Pompeii, I suspect I would have been one of those found fast asleep in bed, turned to stone under blankets of stone."

She smiled at Paul. "The way to leave this life, I always say: some sudden, cataclysmic disaster and whoosh, you're propelled into the next world—or oblivion. One might take one's pick."

"Or remain open-minded."

"Yes, as long as one can exclude reincarnation. That's such a bleak prospect, don't you think? Imagine having to do it all over again . . ."

To have another five husbands, thought Paul.

". . . and to have to go through adolescence," Chloe continued, "with all its agonies. Or to be reincarnated as something else altogether—something lower down the food chain—an antelope or something like that, having to worry at every moment about being pounced upon by a lion."

"That would certainly be unpleasant."

"Although have you ever noticed," Chloe asked, "how in those wildlife films that people like to watch, when you see some poor creature disappearing into the jaws of a predator, the expression on the face of the soon-to-be-consumed is one of calm resignation? **Oh well, so I'm being eaten. Pity.**

That's what it is, you know—a sort of re-signed acceptance. Do you think that is because the animal in question has no idea that it is going to die?"

Paul shrugged. "I hadn't thought about it."

"Well," said Chloe, "no animals think that, you know. They don't know they're mortal. Animals have no reason to believe that they will not simply go on forever. That's not the case with us, unfortunately. We know exactly what's coming, and we don't like it."

She had gone on to suggest that if he were up early, he could entertain himself with a walk to the **boulangerie** in the village.

"I've already paid my respects there," she said. "You'll meet Monsieur André. He's stout, as befits a baker, and his hands are covered in flour, or have been whenever I've seen him, which is also quite befitting. I like people to dress appropriately."

"Oh yes?"

"Bank managers, for instance, must wear ties—if they're men, of course."

"And if they're women?"

She smiled. "They should wear the things that women bank managers wear. You know the sort of thing." She stifled a yawn. "But let's not think about bankers. You could pick up a few of his croissants and a couple of baguettes to see us through the day. I can't resist French baking. It is one of life's most exquisite temptations—along with men." She lowered her eyes. "Although perhaps I shouldn't say that. And men are, after all, quite easily resisted, no matter how delectable they may be. Croissants aren't. Nor those tarts the French make with all the different fruits on them. Heaven. There are some men of whom one might say **heaven,** but not all that many. Not after a few days." She paused. "You must stop me, Paul, if I become too **outrée.** I shall never take offence."

Paul let himself out of the house. The sky was clear and the early June sun had already floated well over the line of trees to the east. The air, which was still, had about it a promise of impending languor: it was going to be a warm day. Scotland, as usual, had been bracing; May had been a disappointment, as it often was, and temperatures had rarely reached the point at which sweaters and jackets could be put away. Scotland's problem was the sea: it was never far away, however far you retreated inland. France was different. Here you were part of a continent, with the warmth that could settle on a continent.

He looked about him, savouring the feeling of being on the point of exploring a whole new place. Then, following the driveway, he continued to the short stretch of road leading directly into the village. He did not have far to walk—about fifty yards further on, he reached the village outskirts, marked by a collection of small houses, each surrounded by a patch of garden. There were a few rickety and unprepossessing outhouses—garages and sheds—and behind them a stagnant pond, thick with reeds. There was a general air of neglect to this part of the village; the houses were clearly lived in—there were cars parked beside them—but none of the doors or window frames looked as if they had been painted for years. Here and there an effort had been made in the garden—a row of beans, a line of cabbages, a display of flowers did its best—but for the most part nature seemed to have been left to its own devices.

In the village itself, the buildings appeared in better shape. There were several well-kept villas—**maisons de notaire,** like the one that Chloe had rented—and the public buildings—the **mairie,** the school, and the church—appeared to be well looked after. A tricolour adorned the **mairie,** beneath it the symbols of the Republic in stone. **Liberté, Egalité, Fraternité** were inscribed under a figure of Marianne, France's guardian. Wearing her Phrygian cap, she stood defiant and confident in her republican values. He looked up at the stone motto and wondered how anybody could reject any of them. And yet all three of them, it seemed to him, were, in one place or another, under siege. France, at least, professed their value, just as it tried to keep alive culinary authenticity. The pleasures of the table were sacred in France, where people were deadly serious about their food. He stopped himself. Should one be serious about culinary traditions, about recipes, about gourmet matters, in a world where for many the main issue with food was simply getting enough to survive? Should he be ashamed of devoting his time to something as mundane as how we prepared food? His book would have to confront these fundamental issues of want and satiety; one could not write a book on

the philosophy of food without considering a number of uncomfortable truths. And
yet, the facts of scarcity should not inhibit
all pleasure in taste: the simplest dish, the
most basic bowl of rice or potatoes, could be
dressed up, could be made more palatable by
the use of everyday flavourings, by giving the
dish a name. There was nothing wrong with
that, and the French, as a nation, understood
it. He looked again at Marianne, so self-
assured, so protective; no, culinary matters
were not beneath her notice—she might be
as sympathetic to **la cuisine** as to **la raison.**

The bakery was just off the main square,
tucked away in a narrow lane, too thin to
admit cars. The window-front bore the
name of the business in fin de siècle script,
Boulangerie Alphonse André. Dimly,
through the semi-opaque glass, he spotted
the form of M. André within, moving behind his counter, outlined by a light shining
from further inside the shop. As Paul pushed
open the door, he saw that several customers
were already there, early birds like him.

M. André was serving a middle-aged man,
wrapping loaves in thin tissue paper, while
a woman at the other end of the shop was

selecting bread rolls with a set of tongs. Paul's arrival brought the conversation between the man and the baker to an end, eliciting a polite greeting from the baker and a nod from the man. The woman looked over her shoulder in frank appraisal—strangers in the village were a rarity, and curiosity was justified.

Paul pointed to a tray of croissants behind the counter and asked for four. As the baker put them into a bag, he enquired after Chloe. "Your friend, monsieur—I take it she is well?"

The woman at the back of the shop waited. Paul understood the baker's strategy.

"My cousin," Paul said. "My father's cousin, actually. Yes, she is very well." It was no surprise to him that they should know who he was; a small village, anywhere, is no place for secrets. People wanted to know—and usually did what was necessary to find out.

"You're very welcome here," said the baker. "We hope you like our village."

The man he had been serving had not yet left the bakery. Now he joined in. "Town," he corrected.

"Village," said the baker emphatically.

"We're very small, but then, who would live in Paris these days?"

"Not me," said the man.

Now the woman spoke. "Paris!" she said, her voice full of disgust.

Paul smiled tactfully. "Big cities," he said. "They're not for everyone."

"Yet that's where everyone wants to live," said the baker. "Talk to the young people. Talk to them. It's all Paris, Paris, Paris."

"You're right, Alphonse," said the man. "Not me, though."

"They wouldn't have you, Henri," said the woman.

Henri laughed. "Nor you, Diane."

"We have everything we need," said the baker, dusting the flour off his hands. "A **mairie**—you will have seen it, I imagine— and a very good school, even if it's very small. And we even have a restaurant. Have you been there yet?"

"I've just arrived," said Paul. "Yesterday."

"Ah yes," said the baker. "Your cousin, Madame . . . Madame . . ."

"Chloe."

"Yes, Madame Chloe said you would not be coming until a bit later."

The woman at the back now moved up to the counter, placing her bag of rolls on top of it. "Not everyone likes our restaurant, Monsieur André. I don't think we should boast about it."

The baker smiled. "No, you're right. You know what they say about it? They say it's . . ."

"The second-worst restaurant in France," supplied the man. "How about that?" He laughed. "The second-worst . . . some would say **the** worst. Not me, of course, but others would."

"They do their best," said the woman. "And if it weren't for Annabelle and Thérèse, it wouldn't survive."

The baker looked at Paul. "You've met the twins?" he asked. "Your landlords?"

Paul looked blank, and the baker explained. The twins, he said, were the two women who owned the house that Chloe was renting. They had a good bit of property in the vicinity, and this included the restaurant. They had never run it themselves, but had left that up to a man called Claude Renard. They had a soft spot for Claude, who had worked for their parents, and because of this he paid only a token rent for the premises.

"Even so," said the baker, "he can't make a go of it. The problem is . . ."

The woman supplied the rest. "The problem is that he can't cook. He just can't."

"I'm afraid that's true," said the baker. "He is no cook, monsieur—and that's putting it charitably." He shook his head sadly. "Poor Claude."

Paul listened sympathetically. "That's a pity," he said at last. "A restaurant always helps a town, doesn't it? It brings visitors, business . . ."

"Not this one," said the baker.

Paul was interested to find out why it was called the second-worst restaurant in France. "Where is the worst one, then?"

"They say it's in Marseille," said the man.

"No," the woman disagreed. "It's in Nantes. That's what people say, anyway."

The baker pointed out that the place in Marseille probably deserved the title because of the mortality rate amongst those who ate there. "They lost two diners in one night a few years ago," he said. "Food poisoning. The police were involved."

"That's not good," said Paul.

"No," said the baker. "The chef went to prison, I believe."

"And worked in the prison kitchens, no doubt," said the man, with a chuckle.

The baker grinned. "Possibly."

This banter came to an end when the door was pushed open and a noticeably pregnant woman came in. She was tall, her long blonde hair straggly and unkempt. She looked in her late twenties or thereabouts, thought Paul, and had a soft Madonna-like face, rather at odds with the rest of her appearance. Her clothing was garish—the sort sold on the bargain rail in supermarkets.

Paul felt the temperature drop. The amiable discussion silenced, the man who had been standing near the door nodded briefly before slipping out. The woman, fishing in her purse, extracted a banknote and proffered it quickly. The baker glanced at the new arrival and then turned in a business-like manner to the counting out of the woman's change.

The woman muttered something under her breath. It was not intended to be heard, but Paul picked it up. He gave a start. **Harlot.**

Nobody else heard. Paul looked at the woman, who met his gaze defiantly before she moved towards the door.

Paul was not quite sure what he had witnessed, but it was something significant. He was sure of that.

$\mathcal{A}$ croissant," said Chloe, as she welcomed Paul back to the house, "is exactly what I need right now. Exactly."

She took his bag from him and extracted the neat parcel the baker had made. "Look at this, Paul. Just look. He's wrapped them up so beautifully. That sort of thing wouldn't be done in the Anglosphere."

Paul smiled at the term. "The Anglosphere?"

"Oh, it exists all right, Paul," Chloe continued, unwrapping the rolls. "A world in which people speak English, think in English, and behave in an English-speaking way."

Paul laughed. "I'm not sure what English-speaking behaviour is like."

"It lacks elegance," said Chloe. "Put it beside Japanese-speaking behaviour, or French-speaking behaviour, and you'll see the difference. We don't wrap things up like the French. We don't bow to others all the time like the Japanese. Of course we don't push and shove like the Russians, nor invade our neighbours as they do—at least not any longer." She paused. "Of course, people don't understand the Russians. I had a boyfriend once who was a colonel. I love colonels, by the way—they have just enough authority to be interesting without being dull, as generals tend to be. Mind you, a colonel has to be tall."

She went on to explain the relevance of the colonel. "This colonel friend of mine used to be attached to NATO headquarters. And he said they sat around in there and talked about the Russians. He said that he understood how jumpy the Russians were and how they didn't like having NATO forces on their borders, because Russians have always felt threatened by the West— they just have. They're paranoid about it and you have to be very careful not to make their nightmares any worse. You keep your distance. But he said some of his counterparts didn't see it that way. They said that it was better to go eyeball-to-eyeball with them. I don't think it is."

Paul sat down. He was hungry too; the

croissants were still slightly warm from the oven and exuded a rich and tantalising smell. Baked dough—one of the great smells . . . He stopped himself; that was the sort of pronouncement that Chloe made, and he must avoid becoming like her, or he would end up making sweeping statements about Russians, just as she did.

"Why can't a colonel be short?" he asked. "What about Napoleon?"

Chloe raised a finger. "Napoleon was a marshal, Paul—a marshal. That's different."

"But he must have been a colonel on the way up."

Chloe shrugged. "Very possibly, although most dictators don't go through the normal **cursus honorum.** They skip the middle ranks and end up at the top. There's no such position as **assistant** dictator, I believe. Nor deputy assistant dictator."

She joined Paul at the kitchen table and began to butter her croissant. "Of course, croissants have lots of butter in them already and some would say . . ." She reached for a small jar of dark jam. "And some would say that adding butter to a croissant is to pile Pelion upon Ossa." She glanced at him, uncertain as to whether he had taken the reference. He had: somewhere in the recesses of Paul's mind the voice of his Latin teacher at school came through: **Two mountains in Greece, you see: Virgil refers to piling Pelion upon Ossa as a metaphor for adding one very large thing to another—going too far, in other words.**

"There's nothing wrong with butter," said Paul, reaching for the butter dish. "It's been rehabilitated—along with eggs. We can eat eggs again, thank goodness."

"I never stopped," said Chloe, licking a dab of butter from the tip of a finger. "Eggs, butter, cheese. Red meat. Everything. I never stopped—and I'm still alive, I believe."

Paul suggested one should not boast about survival. "Nemesis lurks, Chloe. She has her radar switched on and she picks up people who talk about having beaten the odds."

"I shall offer her a buttered croissant if she calls for me," Chloe retorted. And then, "Did you pick up the paper?"

Paul had called in for the newspaper at the

small **maison de la presse** next to the bakery. "I did." He reached into his bag. "Here it is, but it's yesterday's. I only noticed after I had left the shop."

Chloe took the paper, glancing cursorily at the front page. "So it is. But that's what happens here—I should have told you. The morning paper comes in at midday, and so most people are a day behind. Or at least those who like to read the morning paper over breakfast are. They catch up the following day."

"Why wait?"

It was as if everybody should know this. "Because one **feels** different at midday, Paul. One feels more tolerant, more accepting. At breakfast one is more impassioned and can **react** to the news—which these days is inevitably so provocative."

She tapped the front page with her index finger. "You see. Read this at breakfast and you'll splutter. That loud fascist politician— you know the one—has been whipping people up in Lyon. Look at the picture. Look at him. Telling everybody that their whole way of life is being imperilled by a few thin people clambering off a boat from North Africa."

"I suppose every country has a loud fascist politician," said Paul.

Chloe agreed. "They're like tropical storms," she said. "They come along and rant and rave and then suddenly they run out of steam. They veer out to sea and dissipate."

"Not all of them."

"No, not all of them." Chloe put the paper aside. "I shall read it a bit later. Then I'll buy today's edition this afternoon and read it tomorrow at breakfast. In strict order, of course, like those two men in Burma. Or was it Malaya? Somewhere out there."

"What two men?"

"Two Englishmen. Or one was an Englishman and the other might have been Australian—or vaguely Australian. There wasn't too much of a distinction in those days. One of them got the papers sent out from London . . ." She looked at Paul. "I should explain. Somerset Maugham—it's one of his Far Eastern stories. He wrote these wonderful, atmospheric stories of people living on rubber plantations in the jungle. One of them was about these two colonial officials— **colons,** as they call them here. One was very grand, and a crashing snob. The other, the younger one, was very ordinary, a bit rough around the edges. The senior one dressed for dinner every evening—way out in the jungle—while the other one didn't bother. The older one happened to understand the locals and their sensitivities. The other one didn't, and abused the young local who kept his house for him. That's often the case, you know: people who have never previously had people working for them don't know how to treat those they employ. People who have always had some authority do know, and are much better liked as a result. I've seen that myself."

"The newspapers?"

"Yes, the newspapers—they came out from London, but were about six weeks out of date by the time they arrived—in a large bundle of a month's worth, or whatever. So the senior man stacked them up and read them one day at a time—in order. But six weeks out of date, of course."

"Like reading a history book?"

"Exactly. And he was very careful about not opening the next one to find out what happened. He waited for the next day to find out about the outcome of things—or the day after that, as the case may be."

Paul waited.

"The older man," Chloe continued, "had to go off up-river. While he was away, the younger man—the rough diamond—opened the newspapers and read them all. When the senior one came back he noticed, and was livid. The young man said that he didn't think he'd mind, but he said, 'I mind very much.' Just that. 'I mind very much.' Imagine somebody saying that to you—icily—'I mind very much.'"

"People do," observed Paul. "They mind very much about all sorts of small things."

Chloe smiled. "You may read the paper, if you wish. Before me. I won't mind very much." She paused. "And then you must go and write this book of yours until eleven o'clock, when we are bidden—you and I—for coffee with Annabelle and Thérèse. They own this house, and they've invited us for coffee. They've already inspected me, and now I think they want to take a look at you. People are very inquisitive in these small places."

· · ·

Shortly before eleven they made their way to the house occupied by the two sisters, Annabelle and Thérèse. It was no more than half a mile away, a short walk along a path that skirted the houses in the main street.

"They're twins," said Chloe as they approached the high garden wall behind which the house sheltered. "I haven't seen much of them, but they've been very welcoming. When I arrived they let me into the house, of course, and they called round the next day with a basket of fruit and vegetables. They were wearing identical clothing—I noticed that. Rather old-fashioned dresses, pretty enough in their way, but just somehow, well, of another time. The sort of dress worn by a maiden aunt tucked away in the country. The sort of dress that signals that you aren't really in touch, that you aren't really **au courant.**"

"I suppose they must have been used to being dressed in the same outfits when they were children," said Paul. "Parents do that with twins, don't they?"

"Some," said Chloe. "But sometimes it's the twins themselves. They can be very dependent on each other. They want to look the same."

They opened the gate and made their way along a shaded path that led, round a cluster of bushes, to the front door. The house was larger than the one they had rented, although it was recognisably the product of the same architectural imagination. The blue woodwork, such a striking feature of their house, was present here too.

"Very Catholic," whispered Chloe. "Marian blue." She smiled at Paul. "Do you think the Virgin Mary really did wear blue?"

"I doubt it."

"I sometimes wonder what she was like—in real life. I take it she was a historical person?"

"Probably."

Chloe sighed. "Such great mysteries."

It was, Paul thought, something of a theological statement, and as theological statements went, **Such great mysteries** had something to recommend it.

Chloe rang the bell. From within the house there came the sound of a door slamming, followed by the turning of a lock.

The door was answered by a woman in

what Paul judged to be her early fifties. She had an attractive, open face, with wide, almond eyes. He noticed her skin; it was clear and of a striking tone, the colour of porcelain.

"I'm Thérèse," said the woman, turning to Paul. "And you must be Paul. Chloe said you speak excellent French."

"Hardly excellent," said Paul. "But I try."

"He's being modest," Chloe interjected. "He speaks Italian too. And Spanish, I think . . . or is it Portuguese?"

"I envy you," said Thérèse. "I should speak English better than I do, but you know how it is." She made an apologetic gesture.

Her sister appeared from the hall behind her. "And this is Annabelle," said Thérèse.

Paul looked at the sisters. He searched for some feature that would enable him to distinguish them, but found none. The hair was the same, the dresses were the same—even their shoes, which might have provided a means of distinction, were of the same colour, with the same small bow on the toecap.

The sisters ushered them into the hall and then into a formal salon. This was a large room, high-ceilinged, looking out onto a stretch of lawn. The furniture had that

particular quality of bourgeois French draw-
ing rooms—several large armchairs, in the
straight-backed, uncomfortable style, dominated the centre of the room, while an outsize Louis XIV sofa, worked in needlepoint,
was backed up against a wall. The sofa's tap-
estry showed a hunting scene, with slavering
dogs attacking a stag while minstrels entertained the huntsmen with music. On the
walls there were ornately framed pictures,
all by the same hand and in the sentimental
style of Jean-Baptiste Greuze: a boy reading a
book, a child playing with a kitten, a woman
looking wistfully up at the ceiling.

Coffee was served in porcelain cups, so
thin as to be almost transparent. There were
madeleine cakes, neatly arranged on a deli-
cate china plate.

"Madeleines," said Chloe, helping herself
to one of the cakes.

"Proust," said Paul.

"Ah," said Thérèse. "Proust."

Chloe sipped at her coffee. "I find him so
funny," she said.

Thérèse frowned. "I don't think he meant
to be funny."

Annabelle, reaching for a madeleine,

nodded her head in agreement with her sister. "Proust was very serious about everything. He was very grave."

Chloe shrugged. "Well, I find him amusing. All those ridiculous people he wrote about and their affectations. The **comte** de this, and the **duc** de that. It's all terribly funny." She paused, taking a sip of her coffee. "And as for Albertine. She was really a boy, you know. Proust changed her from Albert into Albertine, but she was really a boy."

Thérèse waved a hand airily. "We could talk about Proust forever. He inspires very long conversations." She turned to Paul. "We hear you were at the baker's this morning."

Paul smiled, recalling Chloe's remark about local inquisitiveness. He glanced at Chloe, and his glance was intercepted by Annabelle.

"Yes," she said. "We are very interested in what happens here. Normally, you see, nothing happens. Days and days go by with absolutely nothing happening. A fox kills a chicken, perhaps, or there is a peal of thunder, but rarely anything of the remotest significance. So when people come to stay in our midst, or somebody's car drives into a ditch, we're naturally very interested in it."

This brought nods of agreement from Thérèse. "That's true," she said. "Although there have been moments in the past when things happened. And even now, of course, there are things brewing up."

Annabelle finished the explanation. "It's just that they take some time to happen. That's the difference."

"It's flattering to be noticed," said Chloe. "Attention is always better than indifference."

Thérèse addressed Paul. "You met Monsieur André? We're very proud of him. It used to be that every small village in France had its baker. He was very important—almost as important as the local priest. Nowadays . . ." She shrugged.

"Monsieur André would never desert us," said Annabelle. "He's had his offers, but he turns them down. He was even approached about a job in Paris, would you believe it? One of the Parisians who comes down here in the summer thought he could take Monsieur André back with him. Some fancy cake shop up there."

Thérèse became animated. "And he said no. He refused point blank. Refused the money, the status, the lot. Refused."

"Very fortunate," said Chloe. "I've been buying his croissants. They're delicious."

The compliment seemed to please both sisters. "We're very proud of them," said Annabelle.

"People say that he makes his dough with holy water," said Thérèse. "He gets the priest to bless it and then he uses it in the bakery."

Annabelle laughed dismissively. "People say all sorts of things. Little of what they say is true." She turned to Paul. "Audette was there, I gather."

Paul looked blank.

"That young woman," Annabelle prompted. "The pregnant one. With the . . ." She pointed to her hair. "Untidy up there."

Paul nodded. "Yes, she was."

"She lives at the bottom of our garden," said Thérèse. "Not **in** the garden, of course, but at the far end. It used to be part of the stables for this house. Now it's a cottage. It's not very nice."

Annabelle looked embarrassed. "We charge her very little rent."

"Which she hardly ever pays," added Thérèse.

Annabelle shook her head. "She has a cash-flow problem, poor girl."

"The least of her problems."

Chloe frowned. "There's no man?"

Annabelle made a face. "I wouldn't say that. There were, if anything, rather too many men."

"But none at the moment," explained Thérèse. "No man when one is required. The usual story."

Chloe sighed. "Men," she said.

There was an immediate response from Annabelle. "Yes, men."

Chloe looked at Paul. "Paul is a man, of course," she said. "Not all men . . ." She left the sentence unfinished.

The sisters both turned to Paul. "Please forgive us," said Thérèse. "We are, in general, in favour of men, and there are many . . ."

". . . many agreeable men," interjected Annabelle.

Chloe agreed. "Many," she said.

"Exactly," said Annabelle. "Unfortunately, Audette became involved with an unsuitable man."

"Profoundly unsuitable," added Thérèse.

"And when her . . . her condition became apparent, he was off like a shot."

"Men," muttered Annabelle.

Chloe put down her coffee cup. "Poor girl."

"She works part-time in the supermarket," said Thérèse. "She does a few hours in the mornings. She steals most of her food from there. They all do, apparently. I met one of the managers and he told me. He said that every supermarket in France just has to accept that their employees steal from them. And they can't fire them because of this country's labour laws. You can't lose your job in France."

"They all try to change that," Annabelle explained. "All the politicians, one by one, promise the Germans that we'll change our laws, and the Germans believe them. The Germans run Europe, as you probably know. They deny it, but we all know they've never really given up on that particular ambition. It's been around for a long time— the Holy Roman Empire was all about that. So the French government has to report to them, so to speak, and it reassures them that everything is going to change and France will become a bit more like Germany—

well run and efficient and so on. But then nothing happens, because we French will not accept any interference in our lives. We have our way of doing things and we won't put up with people who want to reform everything. So everything remains the same and the supermarkets have to continue to feed their staff."

"We pay, of course," Thérèse pointed out. "They add the cost to our bills."

Annabelle brought the conversation back to Audette. "She's not too bad, actually. She's rather a sweet girl who had a bad upbringing. Mother was a simple-minded creature who saw the Virgin Mary appear in a potato field one day. She made a big fuss about it and the Church sent people down from Paris to investigate it."

"The Virgin Mary," muttered Chloe.

Annabelle made a gesture of resignation. "Yes, the Virgin Mary. You'd think she'd be too busy to appear in potato fields to rather simple country women. Why not manifest yourself on the Champs-Élysées if you're going to do it?"

"Good question," said Thérèse. "Of course, they dismissed the whole thing and the priests went back to Paris. Anyway, that was her mother. Our parents sometimes gave her work in the kitchen, but she wasn't very good at it. The father was in the army. He was a brute and he used to terrorise them. Eventually he went off to somewhere in West Africa and was shot, I think. Audette's mother did her best with her, but it was difficult to keep her on the straight and narrow, and I think she gave up. She died about five years ago, leaving Audette to look after herself. She was just about twenty then, I think, and had moved in with a motor mechanic in Poitiers. He was a sort of Hells Angel. Awful."

Annabelle took up the story. "Then she came back here and we let her stay in the cottage. She took up with a farmer for a while, and then—"

Thérèse interrupted. "She met a young man with only one eye. He came from quite a good family, actually. We called him Polyphemus, like the Cyclops. He rode a motorbike and always sat on it at a bit of an angle, so that he could see the road ahead with his one eye. It was very disconcerting."

"He had an accident," said Annabelle. "And he went away. Audette seemed very upset by that one, and for a few months there were no men."

Thérèse corrected her. "Except for that plumber."

"Him!" snorted Annabelle. "He was married and had six children. Six children!"

"Men," said Chloe.

"Then she took up with the man who everybody thinks is responsible for the baby," said Thérèse. "He was called Bleu and he lived in the village, in one of those small houses in a row that you've probably walked past."

"Bleu," said Annabelle with disgust. "What a ridiculous name. Bleu."

Thérèse remembered something. "It transpired that he was an electricity thief. We would have imagined many things of which he might be guilty—many unspeakable things . . ."

"Unspeakable," agreed Annabelle.

Chloe's eyes widened. She enjoyed hearing about unspeakable things, thought Paul. It was all grist to the mill.

Thérèse continued, "But we would not have imagined that he was stealing electricity—on top of all those other things . . ."

Chloe leaned forward. "These other things?" she said. "What exactly—"

"Unspeakable," Paul cut in. "Therefore, not to be spoken about."

Chloe shot him an irritated glance, but Thérèse was happy not to speculate. "Heaven knows," she said. "Men like that . . ." She took a sip of coffee. "I was astonished, quite frankly. I'd never heard of anybody stealing electricity, but that's just what he was doing."

"Oh, I've heard of it," volunteered Chloe. "It's a common pursuit in Naples, where they are very ingenious in inventing new forms of dishonesty. You can buy—quite openly, apparently—specially adapted meters that criminal electricians install in your house. These register only one-tenth of the power that you're actually using. They save a vast amount on electricity bills, but it's straightforward theft, isn't it?"

Bleu had not interfered with his meter, Thérèse said. "He didn't steal electricity from the electricity company, he stole it from his neighbour. Their houses were joined together, you see, and he drilled through a common wall into his neighbour's garage. Then he connected the wiring, so that his house ran on power from next door."

Chloe wondered how he was discovered.

"The neighbour's bills were sky high," said Thérèse. "Twice, if not more, what they should have been because Bleu was using a lot of power for a small sawmill he had in his back garden. He made planks out of fallen wood and then sold them on to a timber merchant in Montmorillon."

"Fallen wood **and** chopped-down trees," corrected Annabelle. "He cut down some of our trees, I'm sure of it—that wood beyond the **étang.** Those trees were perfectly healthy. Bleu cut some of them down."

"So the neighbour investigated?" asked Paul.

Annabelle answered. "Not before he himself was investigated. The electricity people report to the police if somebody is using too much power. They suspect that this will be for cannabis growing. They force the plants in old barns and places like that. You need lots of power for the heat lamps."

"He was raided," said Thérèse. "We told you that nothing happened here, except sometimes. Well, this was one of those occasions. It was quite the biggest thing round here for a long time, as you can imagine. Ten policemen, most of them armed to the teeth and wearing those unflattering bullet-proof jackets."

"The only fashionable bullet-proof clothing is Italian," interjected Chloe. "The Carabinieri have some very flattering armoured outfits. Just the thing."

They all looked at her. She smiled. "I lived in Italy, you see. I was married—all too briefly—to an Italian."

"This raid," said Paul. "Did they find the wires?"

Thérèse shook her head. "No. They turned the place upside down, but it was soon apparent that there was nothing to hide. The police were disappointed—I heard some of them talking about it in the street. It seems they'd been hoping for a shoot-out, because they hadn't had one for years and yet they still had to dress up in those heavy flak jackets."

Annabelle explained that the neighbour had come across Bleu's wires quite by chance. "He was moving a workbench in the garage when he bumped it against the wall. A bit of the plastering came away and he saw the wires behind it. All was revealed.

"He reported Bleu to the police. They came down and had a word with him. There were difficulties with proof, though, as by the time they came he had taken all the wiring out."

"So that was the end of that?" asked Paul.

Thérèse replied that it was not. The neighbour, it transpired, had been a civilian clerk in the Foreign Legion barracks in Corsica. He had plenty of ex-legionnaire friends, and one of these lived not far away. "They give them French citizenship, you see. After five years in the Legion you can become a French citizen. This **mec** was from somewhere in the Balkans, Montenegro, I think, and he had been in the Legion for years. I saw him once in Montmorillon, at the market, buying mushrooms with his wife. She's French—a local woman—and quite petite. He's a real bruiser, and has that typical Balkan male head. They all look as if they've been hit on the back of the head with a shovel. He had that."

"The brachycephalic skull," said Chloe.

"Anyway, this neighbour—Georges—had

a word with his ex-Balkan friend in town and told him about Bleu's stealing his electricity. He said that he had been swindled out of fifteen hundred euros because of it and he saw no prospect of getting it back. The Balk was outraged for his friend—you know how they hold grudges down there—and he said that he'd come and talk to Bleu about it. Well, he did, and lo and behold Bleu came round to apologise. He also brought a cheque for fifteen hundred euros. He had difficulty in saying much, though, as the Balk—ex-Balk—appeared to have broken his jaw for him."

"Ah well," said Chloe. "Balkan men can be so **decisive.**"

There was a brief silence while this remark was absorbed. Paul saw Thérèse and Annabelle exchange glances; they approved of Chloe—he could see that—because they were of the same type. Chloe had found her French counterparts. He smiled inwardly; one Chloe was enough to cope with, but **three** . . .

Thérèse broke the silence. "Very." She paused. "I must say, Chloe . . . if I may call you that . . ."

"Of course."

"I must say that you're refreshingly direct in your observations. We've become so used to people being afraid to say anything about anything for fear of offence. You seem to be unaffected by all that."

Paul groaned inwardly. Chloe needed no encouragement. "Well, the truth is the truth, and denying it doesn't make it any the less true," she said.

He sighed. "I'm not sure if we should be talking about the shape of people's skulls." He paused. "It's not helpful." He thought: **I sound so pious, but Chloe can't expect not to be contradicted.**

Chloe made an insouciant gesture with her hand. "It happens to be true. Should you just ignore it? Pretend that people don't have heads that are flat at the back? It's no disgrace to look as if you've been hit on the back of the head with a shovel—it's not an insult. It's rather fetching, in fact."

Thérèse seemed keen to paper over the cracks. "Well, be that as it may. That was the business with the electricity. Then, when Audette revealed that she was expecting a baby and intended to keep it, it all became too much for him. He found a woman from a well-known family of horse thieves round here—people called Manistrol, a dreadful bunch—and went off with her in a caravan. The Manistrols steal caravans as well; in fact, more caravans than horses these days. That was Bleu."

"And good riddance," added Annabelle.

Thérèse poured more coffee. "Poor Audette," she said. "We rather like her, even if her situation is somewhat hopeless. Mind you, she has Claude on her side. He's very protective."

"I think he sees her good qualities," said Annabelle. "There's a kind side to her. When Thérèse was ill, she brought her soup every day."

Thérèse nodded. "Stolen from the super-market, I think, but delicious nonetheless." She looked at Chloe. "And what can you do when somebody brings you stolen soup? Decline to eat it?"

Chloe sympathised. "One has to eat the soup that people bring you. I've never turned away soup—never."

Thérèse smiled at Chloe. Irony, thought Paul. Did the French do it in quite the same way as the British?

"No," said Annabelle, after a short pause. "One should not turn away a gift—of soup or anything else, for that matter."

"And she's a hard worker," added Thérèse. "The baby's due any day, but she carries on working. She has another job, you know."

"She's the waitress in our local restaurant," Annabelle explained. "Have we told you about that place? We're actually the owners, Thérèse and I; of the building, that is—we don't run the restaurant, of course. You must go there."

"They were speaking about it in the bakery," offered Paul.

Annabelle and Thérèse exchanged glances. "What do they know?" said Annabelle dismissively. "They laugh—but what do they know?"

Paul did not mention the baker's comment.

"We're very proud of what Claude does with it," said Thérèse. "There's a little room for improvement, of course, but there always is, isn't there?"

"You must go there," said Annabelle.

"Do we need to book?" asked Paul.

Thérèse nodded. "It can get quite busy. There's an important road not all that far away, you see. There's a sign beside the road that says **Highly Recommended,** and so they stop."

"You'll like Claude," said Annabelle. "Salt of the earth. He's the chef. His nephew, Hugo, is his sous-chef. Claude is a bit hard on him, perhaps, but who are we to interfere? They get by."

"Yes," Thérèse said quickly. Paul felt that she did not want to talk about Claude. "You must go there."

Chloe was decisive. "We shall. We shall go tomorrow evening."

"I'll warn them," said Thérèse. She laughed nervously. "We'll not warn them in **that** sense."

Annabelle corrected her. "Inform them, rather than warn."

"Yes."

6

❧

Moules

If Paul had been concerned that progress with his book might be slowed by Chloe's distracting conversation, then his fears proved to be misplaced. Rather than divert his attention from the task in hand, Chloe turned out to be something of a hard taskmaster, insisting that he be at his desk by nine each morning. There he should stay, she said, until lunchtime, unless, as on that first day, an important social engagement required his presence elsewhere. "And in the afternoon," she said, "I suggest that you work between two and five. This will leave you time for a walk, if you are so inclined, before dusk and dinner, which will be at eight sharp."

He did not resent this somewhat high-handed structuring of his day. He had come to France to work, and it was only through turning his back on temptations and closeting himself in his room that **The Philosophy of Food** would be written. He knew that, and yet he also knew that he could so easily be caught up in other activities; and if that happened, the pile of paper that represented his manuscript so far would remain stubbornly the same size. He needed somebody to keep him at the task, and Chloe, notwithstanding her tendency to go off at a tangent, seemed single-minded when it came to work.

"I'd never suggest that you work all the time," she said to Paul. "All work and no play makes Jack a dull boy, as the saying goes." She paused, and looked dreamily out of the window. "I was married to a Jack once," she said. "He was my American husband, bless him, and he was in so many respects the ideal husband. Immensely good-looking—oh my goodness, you should have seen him. He was like Apollo. People were dazzled by him. And generous by nature, which I think always goes so well with considerable assets. It's all very well being generous if you have nothing to give away—anybody can be generous in such circumstances—but it's much harder if you have an awful lot of money—and an awful lot of stuff. Being generous then is much more praiseworthy."

Paul thought about it. He was not sure whether Chloe was right. She liked to coin aphorisms, but when you examined them they were either downright wrong or, at the most, half-truths. Surely what mattered with generosity was the intention behind the gesture and the extent to which a gift involved a sacrifice. What did they say about the widow's mite? The widow gave up something to make her small gift; the rich man would barely notice his much larger transfer.

"Largeness," said Paul, as he thought this through, "is measured on the inside rather than the outside."

He looked at Chloe. She appeared uncertain, but then she nodded her head. "You're right," she said. "That's quite true, Paul."

Paul did not say anything further on the subject. He suspected that what he had said was nonsense, or at least so enigmatic as to be practically useless.

"This husband of yours," he said. "This Jack: you've never spoken of him before."

Chloe closed her eyes. "Too painful," she

said. "I still miss him, you see. I can't really say that I miss the others, but Jack was somehow different. If he were to reappear and ask me to marry him again, I'd do so like a shot."

Paul looked disbelieving. "But you divorced him," he said. "There must have been a reason for that."

"Overwork," said Chloe. "On his part. He was always working. He made money, you see, and once you start making money, it's difficult to stop. People always want more."

She smiled ruefully. "I'll tell you more about Jack some other time. You must get down to work. A **magnum opus** will not write itself, Paul." She glanced over his shoulder at the papers before him on the desk. Then, transferring her gaze to the screen of his laptop, she read the title of his chapter: "Food as Political Gesture: The Case of Italian Futurist Cuisine—and Others."

"Paul!" she exclaimed. "What an intriguing chapter title! I love Italian Futurists, even if they're now a bit passé." She looked regretful. "I suppose Futurists never think they'll be old hat, just as gilded youths never imagine they'll be forty and a little bit flabby round the waist."

"No, I suppose they don't."

"Being able to imagine one's older self is a real challenge," Chloe continued. "And yet, ask anybody to whom the future has already happened whether it took place quickly, and they'll say, 'It happened in an instant.' Life passes in an instant."

She took a step back. "I'll leave you to it, Paul. Tell me about your Italian Futurists some other time."

"They were very ephemeral people," said Paul.

Chloe looked wistful. "But such fun," she said.

$\mathscr{S}$everal hours later Paul read what he had written. **Filippo Tommaso Marinetti, the author of** The Futurist Cookbook, **set out the objectives of Futurist cooking at a famous dinner in 1909. The menu at that dinner included such creations as ice cream on the Moon, Consumato of Roses and Sunshine, and Roast Lamb in Lion Sauce. The names of the dishes reveal the playful nature of Futurism, but the movement had a more explicitly political, nationalist purpose. The Italian** people, Marinetti believed, had to be weaned off their unhealthy diet if they were to fulfil their historical destiny and gain their rightful place as a dominant nation. A bad diet, the Futurist cooking manifesto argued, had made the Italian people sluggish and unadventurous. In particular, the consumption of pasta had had this effect, and it was only through the eschewing of pasta that the nation's creative energy would be released. "It may be," suggested Marinetti, "that other nations owe their success to their cheeses and salt cod, to their sauerkraut. Italians succeed regardless of their bad food. Look at the Neapolitans. They have been passionate, generous, and intuitive in spite of their fondness for pasta, not because of it." Macaroni, in particular, was the object of Futurist scorn. Marinetti wanted all references to it removed from literature and conversation. "We can easily get rid of macaroni," he wrote. "Nobody will miss it. Nobody will shed a tear for the glutinous substance, even if they are in the habit of eating it morning, noon, and night. All references to macaroni in literature and in

art must be purged. Publishers must recall all their books in which mention is made of macaroni . . ." The campaign against macaroni was a failure. Pasta, whatever its alleged negative effects on creativity and energy, remained an important part of the Italian diet, much to the chagrin of the Futurists.

There was more, and by the time Paul left his desk early that evening, the chapter was almost complete. He stretched his limbs and crossed the room to the window. In the courtyard outside, an ancient tabby cat, its ears half bitten off in a hundred territorial skirmishes, was caught in a shaft of buttery sunshine. Paul watched the cat as it followed a fly. The cat's head moved in sudden, jerky attentiveness as the fly buzzed about; and suddenly, unexpectedly, the cat struck out with its paw. The fly, as skilled in its way as a highly trained fighter pilot, darted out of reach and resumed its buzzing.

He thought of Hamish and Mrs. Macdonald, whose world seemed so different from the life led by this French cat. Those two Siamese had never had to fight for anything, he imagined; unlike this cat, with its battle scars, like the wounds of some old Homeric warrior keen to get back to Ithaca but taking a long time to do so. The thought saddened him—not because the cat's life was a hard one, nor because his unsuccessful swipe at the fly spoke to the failing of his powers, but because it led to further thoughts, and these were of Gloria. All that could have been so different; they might still have been together, and she might be here with him in France. She would love the bakery and M. André's croissants. She would delight in the wide skies, and the sleepiness of the village, and the sense that a lot of history had taken place here, but all of it a very long time ago. Yet that was not to be; now there were different saliences in his landscape. He had **The Philosophy of Food** to write; he had the challenge of an eccentric, if not somewhat outrageous, cousin to deal with; he had dinner at the second-worst restaurant in France ahead of him.

He was disturbed by a knock on the door. When he opened it Chloe was there, balancing a small tray of tea things. "You can stop now," she said, placing the tray on his table. "Satisfactory progress?"

Paul nodded. "I finished what I wanted to say about the Italian Futurists. And I've started on the other examples."

"Of what?"

"Of food and politics. Patriotic food, for instance. The Americans serve that on the Fourth of July. It tends to be red, white, and blue."

Chloe was interested. "Lin Yutang," she said.

Paul waited.

"A Chinese essayist. He wrote a book called **The Importance of Living**—a fairly self-evident title, I would have thought, but there we are. But he said something about patriotism that I've always remembered."

"And that was?"

Chloe smiled. "I feel I'm always telling you things. I must try not to. One should not address one's cousin as a public meeting." She paused. "That was Queen Victoria, I think. She said it about Disraeli and about how he spoke to her."

"You don't," Paul reassured her. "I like listening to you, Chloe. I'd like to hear more about your husbands, for example. That Jack . . ."

Chloe's voice was low, barely above a

whisper. "Oh, please don't let's talk about him—or any of my husbands right now. I miss them all, you know. I say I don't and that I only miss Jack—and maybe one or two others—but I really do, you know. I miss my boys. I miss them so much."

Paul stood quite still. You can misjudge somebody like Chloe, he thought. You can think of them as galleons in full sail, breezing through life, expounding their theories with such confidence, whereas all the time they're sorrowing inside. He reached out and touched her gently on the forearm. She looked down at his hand, and then up at him. She smiled, and then moved away, slightly, almost imperceptibly. But she moved away. Paul wanted to say: **Chloe, I don't mean it that way.** But he said nothing, because it was just inconceivable. Chloe was his older cousin. She was more of an aunt than anything else. Surely she could not imagine that he was interested in her in that way. No.

Chloe's tone became brisk again. "Lin Yutang said something very perceptive about patriotism. He said: 'What is patriotism but love of the good things one ate in childhood?' That's what he said, and . . ."

Paul laughed. "May I use that?"

"Of course. It's his thought, not mine. By all means use it." She paused. "Even if it isn't remotely true."

They walked to the restaurant. The evening sky, at that point in the summer, had not yet darkened and was filled with a soft blue light that would in half an hour or so shade into the velvet of night. The village might have been quiet, but it was filled instead with activity. A man worked in his vegetable garden, sucking on a cigarette as he did so, the smoke rising in a tiny, brief cloud above his head; a woman tended a vine on a slice of communal land beside the **mairie;** the bakery van reversed and M. André emerged to unload a hefty sack of flour from the back.

"I don't know what to expect," said Paul. "Do you?"

Chloe shook her head. "I suppose when we go to restaurants we usually go on a recommendation. A review, perhaps. As long as it's good. Would you ever go to a place that you were told is simply bad?"

Paul replied that he would not. "Reviews never say **Dreadful place—do go.**"

Chloe was firm. "This won't be dreadful."

"The conversation in the **boulangerie**?"

"These small places are full of waspishness," Chloe answered. "Envy stalks. It always does in a village. There's envy everywhere you look."

They had reached the restaurant, a small, self-contained building at the far end of the village. It was typical of so many rural French restaurants, with its air of quiet assurance, a sense of being what it was and nothing more. It was built of the honey-coloured stone common to the area and had a creeper, slightly undisciplined, growing up the front wall. There were window boxes, the paint peeling, spouting red and orange nasturtiums; shutters, painted light green, were fixed back against the stonework; a large board sign advertising the name of the restaurant, La Table de St. Vincent, filled the space between the two windows of the building's second floor. The day's **prix fixe** menu, written in coloured chalk on a small blackboard, was displayed beside the door.

The restaurant's dining room was larger than might be imagined from the outside. A dozen tables, covered with faded blue gingham cloths, occupied most of the floor space, although there was still room for a large sideboard on which stood a line of bottles of wine, like soldiers on parade. The prints on the walls, in thin oak frames, were Vuillard and Bonnard interiors: a young girl arranging flowers; a domestic scene of two women sewing; a stout, black-suited French paterfamilias presiding over a meal.

"Nothing wrong with all of this," whispered Chloe appreciatively.

There were several diners already there, and they could hear more arriving in the small car park at the side of the building—the crunch of car tyres on the gravel, followed by the slamming of doors. They had been wise to book, as the tables were filling up.

The chef greeted them. This was Claude, a man in his late forties, thought Paul. He was well built, with that solidity that stopped just short of fat, and he had tattoos on both exposed forearms: a rose on one, and on the other what looked like a masonic symbol. He was wearing a white neckerchief, tied loosely, which lent a slightly raffish air to his appearance.

"The ladies told me about you," he said,

wiping a hand on his apron before extending it first to Chloe, and then to Paul. "My name is Claude. I'm the chef and **patron.** Everything, in fact. You're very welcome."

He led them to their table. They had obviously been given the best one in the house—right up against the front window. As they sat down, Claude asked them whether they would like an aperitif while they perused the menu. "We go for a limited menu," he said. "Being short-staffed, we find that's best."

"It certainly is," said Chloe. "Those places that offer forty or fifty choices—how do they manage it?"

She had said the right thing. Claude raised his eyes. "Exactly. They can't. Better to have a small choice—one of three dishes per course, perhaps, because then you know it'll be properly prepared."

He turned to Paul. "Monsieur, I hear that you write books about food?"

Paul made a self-effacing gesture. "I try. But I am not much of a cook myself."

Claude nodded. "And you're writing about our cuisine here—in this part of France?"

"Not really," said Paul. "I'm working

on a book on the philosophy of food. It's more theoretical."

"But he does write about actual dishes," offered Chloe. "His last book was called **The Tuscan Table.**" She paused. "And don't listen to him when he says he isn't a good cook. He's one of the best."

Claude seemed impressed. But then a shadow passed over his face. "You're not a critic, are you? You don't review?"

Paul was quick to reassure him that he did nothing like that. "Don't worry—I'm not going to write anything about you."

Claude took this in. "We had a reviewer in once," he said. "A very arrogant man. He wrote a review for one of the local papers. It was very unfair."

"They can be," said Chloe, exchanging glances with Paul. "I think that reviews of restaurants should be written by chefs, not by journalists. The same goes for the stage. Actors and directors are the most suitable people for that, because they know how difficult it is to stage anything. Armchair experts may have no idea of how to do the very thing they're criticising."

"You're so right," said Claude, looking

appreciatively at Chloe. "But now you must excuse me. There's a party of people outside and I must show them to their table. Audette will come and take your aperitif order shortly." He handed them each a menu and went off to settle his new guests.

"Charming fellow," said Paul **sotto voce.**

"My thoughts exactly," agreed Chloe. "People are so unkind, aren't they? He's obviously very proud of this place, and why not? This is what France is all about—small, **real** establishments. Local food. Local ambience. Not great, characterless barns serving standardised fare."

They looked at the menu.

"It's pretty short," said Paul.

"No bad thing," Chloe countered. "And what more could one want: starter—**Moules marinières**—well, I'm fine with that. Soup—onion soup, if you want it. I love that—always have. And then a choice from three entrées. Nothing wrong with **Gratin de pommes de terre aux anchois.** I love anchovies—and **pommes de terre,** too, of course. **Navarin printanier,** which is . . . well, what is it, Paul?"

"A lamb stew with spring vegetables. And it's summer, isn't it?"

"Don't be so pedantic. Spring and summer are states of mind."

Paul laughed. "They're seasons, actually."

"Well, I'm sure it will be delicious, even if the chronology is a little bit dodgy. And look, **Boeuf bourguignon.** No cause for complaint there."

Paul agreed that **Boeuf bourguignon** was usually delicious.

"And then," continued Chloe, looking down the menu, "**Quatre fromages**—four cheeses. That's generous. You must admit that. Sometimes you only get two. Four here. Four. Followed by a custard tart. Custard! I adore custard, Paul—I adore it. I'm sure you do, too. You like custard, don't you?"

"If it's made well," muttered Paul. "It has a rather school-lunch feel to it, though. It has the wrong associations for me."

"Perhaps, but perfectly adequate."

"I'm not saying it isn't," said Paul. He felt that Chloe was trying to make him look churlish. But she, in his view, was being gushingly enthusiastic. This restaurant, in spite of its bad advance publicity, was probably perfectly acceptable—a comfortable, rather run-of-the-mill country restaurant—but not much more than that. Chloe seemed keen to dictate his opinions, and he resented being told what to think. "But it's a bit pedestrian, isn't it? **Moules marinières** are okay but not . . . how shall I put it? Not very imaginative. There are so many other things you can do with mussels."

Chloe seemed surprised. "Really? I don't think I've ever done anything other than **Moules marinières.** That's how people eat mussels, surely."

Paul explained. "Actually, there are hundreds of ways of doing them. The French are very inventive when it comes to mussels." He reeled off a short list. "**Moules à la moutarde de Meaux, Tian de moules aux épinards, Moules farcies . . .** I could go on."

"Gracious," Chloe exclaimed. "That's me put in my place."

Paul softened. "I'm sorry. I didn't mean to . . ."

"No, you shouldn't apologise—I should. I can't help myself. I go on. I know I do.

Here's me sounding off about mussels when I know so little and you know so much. You know everything, it seems, that there is to be known about mussels."

He felt regret. This extraordinary woman, with her enthusiasms and tangential observations, was fundamentally good-natured. There was no call for him to seek to put her down. And she was lonely, he sensed; she was lonely and her loneliness made her gush.

"You don't go on, as you put it, Chloe. I like listening to you. I like what you say."

She looked at him gratefully. "Do you? I don't overdo it?"

"Not in the slightest. I may not agree with everything you say, but—"

"**Mais ni moi non plus,** but I don't either," she interjected.

They both laughed. And then Audette appeared through the swing door that led to the kitchen. She was carrying a tray, moving slowly in her advanced state of pregnancy. She glanced over at their table and nodded in acknowledgement of the smile Chloe gave her. "I'll be with you," she said. "One moment."

Now she stood beside their table. "Claude said you wanted a drink?"

"Could we order wine now?" asked Paul. He looked across the table at Chloe. "Would that suit you? Rather than something else?"

"We'll go straight to wine," said Chloe, giving Audette a barely concealed look of appraisal.

Audette took a folded piece of paper from the pocket of the apron she was wearing. "This is the list," she said. "But some of those are finished. Numbers two, three, five, six, seven, and nine are finished."

She handed the list to Paul, who looked at it. He frowned. "Since there are only ten, that means there are only one, four, eight, and ten."

"That looks like it," said Audette, as if the whole matter had nothing to do with her.

"Of which only one—number one—is white, and the rest are red," continued Paul.

"Could be," said Audette, placing her left hand on the protruding bulge of her stomach.

"When's the great day?" enquired Chloe.

"Three days ago," replied Audette. "But I knew he was going to be late—I always knew it. I don't want it to be too late. I had a friend who let it run for two weeks and it was awful, just awful."

Paul gave an involuntary shudder. He looked away. Chloe, though, looked sympathetic. "How dreadful," she said.

"There was blood everywhere, she said," Audette continued. "All over the hospital bed. Blood. I can't take blood—I just can't. I don't like the smell of it. Some people say they can't smell it, you know, but I think it has got a smell. Definitely. It's a sort of metallic smell, I've always thought."

Paul tapped the list. "What shall we have? Are you going to choose mussels?"

Chloe nodded. "Yes. Definitely."

Paul pointed to a selection on the list. "Then we'd better have number one," he said to Chloe. "It's a Chablis. We could have that and then choose a half carafe of the house red."

"You can't go wrong with Chablis," Chloe said.

Paul said nothing. You **could** go wrong with Chablis, he thought, and if anybody could do it, he imagined that the second-worst restaurant in France might do just that.

Audette pencilled a note in her book. "Number one. Good. Then?" She suddenly gripped her stomach. "Oh. He kicks. How he kicks."

"Oh," said Chloe.

"It's getting really sore. He wants to come."

Chloe raised an eyebrow. "Perhaps you should sit down."

"It's worse when I sit down," said Audette. "Being pregnant can give you haemorrhoids, you know."

Chloe gasped. "You poor thing . . ."

Audette spoke loudly enough to be heard at neighbouring tables. The restaurant suddenly became silent, apart from the sound of cutlery on plates.

"You ever had them?" Audette continued.

Paul took control. "I'm going to start with mussels," he said. He looked across the table at Chloe. "And you, Chloe? Mussels?"

Chloe looked at the menu. "Yes, I shall have mussels too."

"Good," said Audette. "Local. Very good."

Paul gave a start. "The mussels? Local?"

"From over there," said Audette, waving vaguely in the direction of the window.

"Mussels come from the sea," said Paul. "We're pretty far inland here, aren't we?"

Audette shrugged. "And then?"

Paul waited for Chloe. "**Navarin printanier** for me," she said.

He followed suit. "Likewise. And then, custard tart."

"And for me," said Chloe.

Audette made another note in her book, and then sighed before moving away, ponderously, towards the kitchen door.

"Well!" whispered Chloe.

"Yes," said Paul.

"Have you ever been talked to **quite** like that by somebody serving you in a restaurant?"

Paul shook his head. "No," he replied.

"Mind you," said Chloe, reflectively, "there are few conversational restraints these days. Anything goes, doesn't it?"

"People are frank," Paul said.

Chloe's eyes lit up. "Perhaps everyone should wear a button on their lapel," she suggested. "The equivalent of those warnings they slap on films. **Contains explicit language. Some violence and nudity.** That sort of thing—but for people. That way you'd know what sort of person you're about to talk to."

Paul laughed. "Chloe, you're ridiculous."

"So our friend Audette would wear something that said **May speak about intimate personal problems.**"

Audette was in the kitchen for no more than a couple of minutes before she reappeared, now bearing a bottle of wine.

"May serve Chablis warm," whispered Paul. "Another possible warning."

Chloe glanced at Audette, approaching heavily across the room. "Poor woman," she said under her breath. "People shouldn't have to work when they're that uncomfortable."

Audette reached the table. The trip from the kitchen appeared to have exhausted her. "Is this what you asked for?" she said, showing Paul the label on the bottle.

"It looks like it," said Paul. "I'll taste it first."

Audette frowned. "You buy it the moment I take the cork out," she warned. "Those are the rules. You can't change your mind."

Paul raised an eyebrow. "But all I want to do is see that it's not corked."

"It has a cork," said Audette. There was a

strong note of resentment in her voice. "All wine has corks."

Paul shook his head. "Well, not all, you know. And corked is a way of saying **rotten.** I want to check it's not rotten."

Grudgingly, Audette applied a corkscrew and then poured a small amount of wine into a glass, offering it to Paul. He raised the glass and sipped. He frowned.

"Not quite as chilled as one might like," he said.

Audette said nothing, but glowered at him, as if challenging him to reject the offering.

"I suppose so," said Paul.

Audette poured a full glass for both of them—full almost to the brim.

"Goodness," said Chloe. "I shall have to be careful not to spill."

Paul raised his over-full glass to Chloe, carefully, but still transferring a small amount to the front of his shirt. "This is definitely an unusual restaurant," he said. "But to your health, Chloe, and thank you for inviting me to France."

She raised her glass in response, and despite her steady hand the warm Chablis dribbled over the tablecloth. "We must give it a chance," she said. "I've taken to the twins and I want to like their restaurant."

Paul understood. He, too, had taken to Annabelle and Thérèse, and hoped that after an unpromising start with Audette things would get better. You did not judge a restaurant solely on the conduct of a single member of staff, nor on her over-filling of a glass, her ignorance of the fact that mussels came from the sea, nor her inappropriate talk of intimate complaints. These were superficial matters—what really counted was the food, and they had yet to try that.

Their wait for the mussels was a long one, but they entertained themselves by talking about Paul's book and the doings of the Italian Futurists.

"Italy is such a marvellous country," Chloe pronounced, "and we all love it dearly. Romantic poets went there to die, which was just the right thing to do."

"To die? The right thing?"

"Yes. If you're a poet, Paul, you shouldn't hang around too long. Best to write a bit of poetry and then expire while still young and romantic. Look at Keats—he was twenty-five. Shelley was twenty-nine. And there was Rupert Brooke, too—such a romantic figure, who chose a wonderful place to die. The island of Skyros, where you can be buried under an olive tree. An olive tree, Paul!"

"Stands the church clock at ten to three? And is there honey still for tea?"

"Well," Chloe said, "Brooke expresses it all, doesn't he? He expresses England so very succinctly." She paused. "Those lines almost make me cry, Paul."

He was surprised. "Why?"

"Because of what has been lost, perhaps. The gentleness. The quiet. Honey for tea. That sort of thing. As you know, Paul, I'm half English and half Scottish. Well, with a bit of Irish thrown in there somewhere. But the English bit, which comes from my mother, responds to all that—to English understatement, to English reticence. To a cricket match, where nothing happens for hours. To people drinking tea together politely and not saying a word. To Morris dancing, even—have you seen much Morris dancing, Paul?"

Paul said that he had been in Oxford once on May Day and seen the Morris dancers in their white outfits, bells at the knees, dancing their strange stick dances.

"It's extremely affecting," said Chloe. "Pagan, really—that comes through very strongly. All that business about the Green Man and the renewal of spring. And the sight of men dancing together—that always moves me, Paul, because it makes the men look gentle, which is what men can be if encouraged. If only men would dance together more, rather than snarl at one another, as they're slightly inclined to do." She paused. "But let's not discuss England, or Scotland, even. We're not there at the moment, and you're busy writing about Italian Futurists and their odd ideas about food. Let's talk more about the Italians and why they're such wonderful people and make such magnificent friends."

The conversation about Italy continued until the mussels arrived—carried, with further effort, and grimaces, by Audette.

"Two mussels?" she announced as she reached their table.

"Two mussels would be too few," said Paul, with a smile.

Audette looked at him. "What?"

"I was just joking," said Paul. "You see, two mussels would be no more than an amuse-bouche—and a small amuse-bouche at that."

Audette shrugged. "Two mussels," she repeated. "Here."

Two bowls were placed before them and Audette retired to the kitchen. A wisp of steam and mussel rose from each plate. Paul sniffed at the air. "I love these things," he said, dipping his spoon into the thin sauce in which the mussels were half submerged. Using a fork, he prised flesh from one of the shells and popped it into his mouth.

"I'm thinking Proustian thoughts," said Chloe, as she took her first mouthful. "The coast of Brittany, and I was thirteen, and there was a boy staying in the same hotel, and he was a year or two older than me and the kitchen at the hotel served mussels every night. The boy had freckles and he used to look at me from the table he occupied with his parents near the window, and I used to look back at him. And we never spoke for the entire ten days we were there—not once. And I was achingly—achingly—in love with him."

Paul was frowning. He used his fork to spear another mussel. This one he raised to his nose and sniffed at.

"I'm not sure they're all that fresh," he said.

"They're all right," said Chloe. "Mussels always taste a bit shellfishy. They're fine."

Paul ate a few more. "They're marginal, I'd say. You have to watch these things. We're a long way from the sea here. Have they been properly refrigerated? That sort of thing."

Chloe put down her spoon. "Do you want to send them back? You might say, 'These mussels are corked.' That would give them something to think about."

Paul shook his head. "I said: they're marginal. I'll eat them."

"Good," said Chloe. "Because I'm rather enjoying mine."

On the way home they saw fireflies— tiny points of light in the velvet of night. Chloe said, "I'm happy to be in France. I'm truly happy."

"So am I," said Paul.

"And I don't want this to end."

Paul agreed. "Neither do I."

There was a brief silence. Somewhere

in the night a dog barked; a reproachful voice brought the barking to an end. "Bonaparte! Quiet!"

"Bonaparte!" said Chloe. "It's a common dog's name in France, you know. Médor, though, I'm told, is the equivalent of Fido. There are plenty of Médors."

They reached the house. Chloe had left a light on to welcome them back. As she fumbled with the keys, Paul had the first message of misgiving from his stomach. It was not pronounced at that stage—no more than a slight feeling of unease. There was a distant gurgling sound.

"Are you all right?" asked Chloe. "Some tea?"

He shook his head. "I'll probably turn in straightaway."

"You've had a long day. How many pages?"

"Oh, I don't know. I haven't counted. Six, maybe. Seven."

As he went upstairs, he felt his stomach churn. He undressed and slipped into bed. There he felt the first sensation of real nausea. **Mussels,** he thought. **Moules marinières.**

7

✣

Le Deuxième Mari

The doctor, a cousin of Thérèse and Annabelle, stood beside Paul's bed. He had not closed the door behind him, and Paul was vaguely aware of the presence of Chloe and the twins in the corridor outside his room. The doctor, a thickset man in his late fifties, with heavy grey eyebrows, peered at Paul before reaching out to check his pulse.

"You have not been very well, monsieur."

Paul, who had woken up only a few minutes before, felt the dampness of the T-shirt he had worn to bed. The material was sticking to his skin; he had been sweating.

"I think I've had a fever. I ate something, you see."

The doctor took a thermometer out of his pocket and placed it under Paul's tongue. "Where?" he asked.

Paul struggled to speak. "La Table . . ."

The doctor sighed. "La Table de Saint Vincent?"

Paul nodded.

The doctor waited until he had extracted the thermometer before asking, "What?"

"I think it was the mussels," said Paul. "I thought they might be a bit off. But I ate them. It was my own fault."

He remembered that Chloe had also ordered mussels. "My cousin outside," he said. "She had them too. Is she . . ."

"She's right as rain," said the doctor. "She told me that you and she had exactly the same things."

"So maybe it was something else," said Paul. "Something I touched, perhaps."

The doctor looked dubious. "No, it was probably the seafood. People react to toxins or bacteria in different ways. It depends on the flora of the digestive tract. Some people can eat virtually anything—others can't. And sometimes it can just be in one mussel and not in all of them." He paused. "You're taking fluids?"

"Yes. I'm thirsty now."

"Not too much. But keep yourself hydrated. You'll be better in a couple of days, I think. If not . . ." He shrugged. "If not, I'll come back and see if we need to give you something."

The doctor moved away from the bed. "I'll have a word with them," he said. "This is a public health matter. It's not the first time I've had to speak to our restaurant."

"I don't wish to cause difficulties for them," said Paul.

The doctor raised an eyebrow. "You're very considerate. Most people—outsiders—would be up in arms about something like this."

"I'm not," said Paul. "I know how difficult it can be to run a restaurant."

The doctor seemed relieved. "Claude has his enemies. Some people around here don't like him for historical reasons. But he's a good man and a lot of us are very fond of him. We don't want him to fail."

Paul said that it would give him no pleasure to see any rural restaurant fail. "If those people give up, then the fast-food set-ups take over. Hamburgers . . ."

The doctor took on an expression of disgust. "Them!"

"And if France throws in the towel on that battle, then all is lost."

It was just the right note, and the doctor beamed with pleasure. "Exactly, monsieur! This is about France. This is about what we believe in."

"Still," said Paul, "they need to watch the freshness of their seafood."

"But naturally," said the doctor. "I'll have a **quiet** word. I won't report this further up the line. In the meantime, you rest and don't exert yourself. Don't eat anything just yet."

"I'm never going to eat again," said Paul. "Never."

The doctor laughed. "Monsieur, you are very amusing. I hope that we shall meet again." He started towards the door, but stopped. "Monsieur Stuart, may I ask you: how did Claude do the mussels last night?"

"Very simply," replied Paul. "**Moules marinières.** The usual thing."

The doctor shook his head sadly. "There are so many better ways of doing mussels. **Moules dijonnaises,** for instance—with a mustard sauce. I'm particularly partial to those. Have you tried them?"

Paul felt the nausea rise in his stomach. **The hair of the dog that bit you . . .**

"Or **Soupe de moules safranées,**" the doctor continued. "What about that? That comes from the Loire, where they grow a lot of leeks. It has leeks, of course, and saffron. The husband of the local midwife makes that, you know. He's from the Loire."

Paul smiled. "I need to visit the bathroom," he said.

The doctor made a gesture of acceptance. "It's tactless of me to discuss mussels—please forgive me."

"It's nothing," said Paul.

"I wish you a quick recovery," said the doctor. "But, on second thought, I'm going to confine you to bed for four days. You must remain where you are in order to give yourself a chance to recover. Your system will have had a bad shock."

Paul protested. "But it's just a touch of food poisoning."

The doctor shook a finger. "Monsieur, I've had patients who say just that and then— **pouf**—the next day they're dead. **E. coli** is very deadly. Very."

Paul did not argue. There was a sharp

pain in his stomach and he needed the bathroom more than ever. He nodded his assent and went out into the corridor, past
Chloe and the twins, who were scurrying
away, embarrassed at being caught eaves-
dropping on a medical consultation.

When Paul returned to his bedroom, he
found Chloe awaiting him. Seated in the easy
chair beside his bed, she looked at him sympathetically as he eased himself back under
the duvet.

"I couldn't help but overhear what the
doctor said," she began. "We must follow
his instructions. Four days."

"I doubt if it's necessary," said Paul.
"Usually these things are over in a day
or two."

"Be that as it may, you really must do as
he says. The twins speak very highly of him.
They say that he's one of the best doctors
for miles around, and he hasn't charged you
a bean. He's their cousin, you see, and he
never charges them."

"I'm very grateful," said Paul.

"And as for the restaurant," Chloe continued, "Thérèse and Annabelle are most
concerned about that. They've spoken to

Claude, who's devastated. He's refunded the cost of our meal and he's insisting on visiting you. I suggested tomorrow—when you're a bit stronger."

"It's not his fault," said Paul. "I won't hold it against him."

Chloe was clearly pleased by this. "They are very attached to him," she said. "And I can understand why. I spoke to him this morning and he's utterly charming."

"Good," said Paul. "However, I'm not sure that his restaurant is all it might be."

"They say he tries terribly hard," Chloe said. "He works at it, but . . ." She looked sad. "Poor dear, he doesn't seem to get anywhere with it. And his nephew, who helps him in the kitchen, is no better, I was told."

"And then there's Audette."

Chloe groaned. "Yes. She needs a little instruction, I'd say. Serving people in a restaurant is a bit of an art."

Paul closed his eyes. He did not want to think about restaurants or food. The pain in his stomach had abated, but he still felt weakened and shivery. He thought about the damage that a few quite invisible bacteria could wreak on the human system. We were Goliath and the bacteria were a tribe of tiny Davids, and they could lay us low within hours.

"How about tea?" asked Chloe. "There's nothing like tea to restore you."

Paul accepted, and in a few minutes Chloe was back with two mugs.

"You don't have to talk if you don't want to," said Chloe. "I'll keep you company for a while, and then perhaps you can sleep."

"You do the talking," said Paul. "I'll just lie here." He took a sip of his tea. "Tell me about your husbands."

Chloe affected reproach. "You'd think I spoke about nothing else," she said.

"You only told me about your Italian," said Paul. "And you mentioned the American, but just mentioned. He was called Jack, wasn't he? I would like to hear about—"

"It would be best to do them **seriatim,**" Chloe interrupted. "Jack was number four, in fact, so we can talk about him some other day. We have plenty of time."

"So who was number two?"

"Well," began Chloe, "after dear Antonio Gigliodoro I was still in what I might describe as a Mediterranean mood. After

you've been . . . been **involved** with a man
from those latitudes, northern men seem
a bit, well, insipid. There's a lot to be said
for Latins, you know. They have a certain
vigour, shall we say."

Paul smiled. "You put it so delicately, Chloe."

"And so I should. If there's one thing one
should **not** talk about, Paul, it is the secrets of
the bedroom. That is of no concern to anybody else, and it is **very** bad taste to disclose
what happens there." She paused. "That isn't
to say that you can't talk about what **other**
people get up to in that department—that's a
matter of great interest to all of us—but you
shouldn't talk about yourself in that way."

Paul pretended to be chastened. "Of
course not."

"Good. Well, after dear Antonio was con-
scripted into the Italian Lunatics' Regiment,
or whatever it was, we drifted apart, as I think
I told you. The Pope was so understanding,
and the annulment came through in record
time—Antonio's family were connected with
the old Roman black aristocracy, as they're
called. They pulled strings and those strings
were attached to the Pope's right hand. He
signed the papers and that was that—as far

as the Church was concerned, we'd never really meant to get married and the whole thing could be put aside. Such a sweet pope.

"I was free to go. Antonio's family had been generous and I received a large sum intended to tide me over for a few years. In fact, they were used to living pretty highly and they miscalculated how much I actually needed. They gave me enough to live on for fifteen years, perfectly comfortably. I think they may have got their decimal places mixed up, but they could well afford it and I didn't want to embarrass them by pointing out the error. It would have been tantamount to accusing them of being bad at maths, which I would never do, Paul."

Paul nodded. "Of course not. Tactful you."

"I needed to get away, and so I went off to Madrid. I had a friend there who was working as an au pair for a Spanish family before she went off to do a degree, and she invited me to come and stay with her. The family was apparently happy for her to have guests, and so she asked me to join her for a few weeks. She could get me work with one of the family's friends, she said, if I wanted it. Or I could help her look after her family's two children, one of whom suffered from anger issues—at the age of four—and needed a lot of supervision.

"I liked the family, and even the four-year-old with anger issues was not too bad. I discovered that you could calm him down by throwing a bucket of water over him. That worked, although you'll find that nowhere in the books, Paul. People are reluctant to take on these little monsters, you know, the tantrum-prone two-year-olds and so on. But I wasn't, and it really worked. I've told people about it, but they don't believe me. They've all read these dreadful books telling you to negotiate with two-year-olds, but that's a waste of time, in my view. A bucket of cold water thrown over them stops them in their tracks, and they generally behave themselves after that. Or at least I have no trouble with them."

Paul's eyes widened. "I'm not sure these days, Chloe . . ."

"Oh, don't give me **these days,** Paul. Children haven't changed, and the way to deal with bad behaviour down amongst the toddlers hasn't changed either. A firm response is what's required. Anyway, that's not the point. The point was that I was there in Madrid and I met Octavio, who was ten years older than I was. I was just twenty, then, Paul, and . . ."

"Twenty," muttered Paul. "You can't be blamed for anything you did at twenty."

Chloe smiled. "How kind of you. Yes, it's a headstrong time—a romantic time, too. And I had this tendency to fall in love, I suppose. Some people have a weakness, and mine is to fall in love."

"If it's a weakness."

Chloe thought it was. "It makes you vulnerable. Very strong, very determined people are able to resist such impulses. They're above all that."

"But think what they're missing."

Chloe shook her head. "I'm not sure being in love is always a positive feeling. It's a state of enhanced awareness, I suppose, that may be exciting at times, but I was . . . I was . . ." She searched for the right word. "I was **disconcerted**—I always have been when I first tumble—and that's the word I should use, perhaps, rather than **fall.** You tumble in love . . . or stumble in love, perhaps. Trip, too. We trip in love, which might describe more accurately what happens to you." She paused and looked quizzically at Paul. "How much of a classical education did you have, Paul? I forget the details."

He made a sign—the distance between barely separated finger and thumb. "Not much. I had a Latin teacher who didn't exactly inspire. He loved Horace's poetry and kept going on to us about Horatian odes. He said that we should aspire to being like Horace with his Sabine farm and his rural melancholy, which is ridiculous when you're talking to sixteen-year-old boys. We were more interested in Catullus and the spicier bits."

"Who wouldn't be at sixteen?"

"So not much of a classical education."

"No." Chloe waved a hand airily. "I had tiny fragments. But some of it stuck, I suppose, and I still know who Homer was, although he possibly didn't exist, you know. He was a sort of committee, I believe—a committee whose job it was to remember vast screeds of poetry, all made up by the committee in the past. And there's far too much fighting for my taste—rather like the Old Testament. Dreadful bad behaviour there—smiting and so on. Quite a lot of begetting, too, which is infinitely better than smiting. But lots of grudges. Anyway, I picked up some Latin at school and take great pleasure in using it if I have half a chance." She sighed. "Which is so rarely these days. People look at you blankly when you start quoting Latin to them. Even the Catholics, who used to get a bit of Latin here and there, but no longer. They've lost so much, haven't they? Latin, Purgatory, indulgences—all that baggage. And what are they getting in return? Guitars and happy clapping—that sort of thing. Anyway . . ."

Paul was silent. The room was warm. If it were not for the queasiness in his stomach he might have drifted off, lulled into sleep by Chloe's monologue.

"What I was going to say to you, Paul," Chloe continued, "is this: **Ira furor brevis est.** Anger is a brief madness. It's a Latin proverb. But you can change it so easily into **Amor furor brevis est**—love is a brief madness. So apt."

Paul reminded her. "Octavio?"

"Yes," she said. "I met him in a coffeehouse. They have those in Spain, you know—those rather plush places where people sit and read newspapers and drink strong coffee. I had wandered into one of those when it was looking rather full and I was about to go out again. But there was Octavio, and he signalled to me that there was a place at his table and I could sit down if I wished. He was by far the most interesting-looking man in the place, because all the others were at least forty, and at twenty, forty is positively ancient.

"So I sat down and Octavio called the waiter over and ordered for me. He could tell that I couldn't speak Spanish—there's a look about people who can't speak Spanish—and his English was quite good. So he introduced himself and I fell in love with him there and then. It took two minutes, at the most. It was like getting an anaesthetic. You start counting backwards from ten and you're out by the time you get to eight. Bang. Love."

Paul stared at the ceiling. He wondered why this had never happened to him. Had he been in love—ever? Or had he just been in something less—**in friendship**? Was love no more than that, just intense friendship? Or intense friendship plus sex? Or was that thoroughly reductionist—cheap, even—because love was something far greater than that: a cherishing, a valuing, something not far removed from **agape**? You could love somebody passionately and yet not want the physical . . . Or could you?

"Octavio asked me all about myself. He was one of those people who do that—he was always interested in you, not just himself. That's the big distinction, Paul—people who are interested in themselves and people who are interested in other people. And you can always tell. The people who are interested in themselves never ask you anything about you. They just don't. It's a very simple test. Count the number of uses of the first-person-singular pronoun and then tot up the number of mentions of the second-person singular. If there are more of the first than the second, you have your answer. Self-obsessed. Watch out: selfishness ahead.

"We talked for over an hour that first time. It was as if I had known him forever—you'll have met people like that, won't you? They're so sympathetic you feel as comfortable with them as if they were old friends. Then he invited me to meet him for dinner, and for lunch the next day, and dinner too. And then, after about two weeks, he proposed to me and I accepted on the spot. I think I probably even said yes before he had finished his sentence, but that sometimes happens. Apparently, it happens a lot in Germany, because German puts the verbs at the end, as you know. The poor girl sits there waiting for the verb to come along and says **yes** before he finishes because she just can't bear the strain. That's not a problem in more succinct languages, like English."

Paul looked at Chloe. She smiled back at him.

"Octavio's family was quite different from the Gigliodoro clan. They were delighted that Octavio was getting married and they gave me a most effusive welcome. Octavio's mother—Señora Flores de Flores—said, 'Thank God! At long last!' and his grandmother started to pray. She said that it was a prayer in thanks for deliverance. For deliverance, Paul!"

Paul wondered if that had been a warning—but apparently not.

"There was nothing intrinsically wrong with Octavio. He was good-looking; he was intelligent; and he was faithful. That's so important, Paul—faithfulness. If you don't have that in a marriage, then what's the point of being married in the first place?"

Paul looked up at the ceiling. He did not feel strong enough to engage in debate and he wanted to hear more about Octavio. So he simply nodded and said, "Very important."

"Crucial," said Chloe. "Faithfulness is at the heart of marriage—the very heart. And Octavio never gave me cause to think that he was less than one hundred per cent faithful. And yet our marriage just didn't work. It was my fault."

"Is it helpful to talk about fault?" asked Paul.

"In some cases, yes. Octavio would still be married to me today if I hadn't brought the marriage to an end. And that was to do with his job. I couldn't abide what he did."

Paul was intrigued. "Which was what?"

"He was a bull-fight journalist," answered Chloe. "He covered bull-fighting for **El Mundo,** one of the big Madrid newspapers."

Paul was silent.

"Yes," said Chloe, her voice full of apology. "I'm afraid that's what Octavio did."

Paul felt for her. To have married a bull-fight journalist sounded like a grave error of judgement. "I'm all for cultural relativism," he said, "but . . ."

Chloe shook her head. "Well I, for one, am **not** all for cultural relativism—nor moral relativism, while we're on the subject. Some things are wrong—just plain wrong—irrespective of cultural differences. Head-hunting, for instance. Ritual murder. Slavery. All of these are wrong even if some benighted cultures may endorse them."

Chloe's tone was forceful. Paul sought to placate her. "I'd agree," he said. "Except many people would look askance at any reference to **benighted cultures.** You can't say that, you know."

"Why not?" Chloe asked indignantly.

"Because . . ." Paul shrugged. "Because there's a climate of opinion about these things. **Benighted** suggests that you think your own culture superior to somebody else's."

Chloe was silent. She looked at Paul with what seemed like genuine puzzlement. Then she said, "But it is. Not just ours—**any** culture that disagrees with slavery is superior to one that allows it." She frowned. "How can anybody—**anybody**—disagree with that?"

"It's complicated," said Paul. "Perhaps it's just a question of tact. Perhaps it's the historical context in which a remark is made. You . . ." He hesitated, but then continued, "You, you see, Chloe, are part of a culture that in the past treated many other cultures with, at best, condescension, and at worst with complete contempt. And this means that you have to be careful that what you say now—when that attitude is so strenuously rejected—does not sound condescending. Or does not sound as if it fails to value other cultures—to respect them, really."

"But I don't respect people who enslave others," said Chloe. "I don't respect people who treat other people badly in any way. I don't respect men who put women down. Why can't I say that?"

Paul sighed. "I don't want to sit here and argue with you . . . or, rather, **lie** here and argue with you."

Chloe reached out and put her hand on his brow. "No, of course not. You still have a temperature, don't you? Should I get some ice and put it on your head?"

Paul smiled. "That sounds so odd. **Should**

I get some ice and put it on your head?
How often does one have the chance to
say that?"

"Well, should I?"

"No, I'm fine. Let's get back to Octavio.
You didn't like what he did?"

Chloe shook her head. "Not in the slightest. And I suppose I should have had it out
with him right at the beginning. I should
have stopped things at the very first mention of bull-fighting. I should have said that
I couldn't have anything to do with a man
who thought that the tormenting of a poor,
frightened creature in a public ring was a
sport. How can anybody think that, Paul?
How can they?"

"Plenty of Spaniards do," said Paul.

"Then they are benighted," said Chloe.
"There is a cruel streak a mile wide in
Spanish history. Look at the **conquistadores.**
Look at them. Look at what they did
when they reached America and disposed
of the people they met. Cruelty. But that's
the past, I suppose—this was the present.
Conquistadores at least had the excuse of
being **conquistadores.** They were children
of their time—and that is always an excuse.

Aristotle would have believed in slavery, we must remind ourselves, because his time did. And Jane Austen wrote about people going off to the West Indies without saying anything about what they were doing there—running slave plantations, if we forget. She must have accepted slavery."

"So the people who go to the bull-ring today have the same excuse, wouldn't you say?" Paul was quick to add, "Not that I like the idea of bull-fighting myself. I'm just saying that the crowds who go . . ."

"Are not participating in an act of cruelty?" Chloe challenged. "Is that what you're saying?"

"No, they are," Paul conceded. "Because we can judge them by today's standards. People today should be sensitive to animal pain, to animal humiliation, because such sensitivity is part of our moral climate. It just is."

"Well, I don't disagree with that," said Chloe. "But back to Octavio—I should have been firmer. I should have spoken up."

"You said nothing?"

Chloe explained that the subject of bull-fighting had come up incidentally. "He said to me on our second date, I think it was, that he had to go off to the Plaza de Toros to write something up for the paper. I thought that he was going to interview somebody, and that this person worked near the Plaza de Toros, or something of that sort. So, when he asked me whether I would care to come with him, I said that I would. I'd fallen for him by then and I just wanted to be in his company."

"So you went off to a bull-fight?"

Chloe looked pained. "I did. But please don't be too harsh on me, Paul. There are so many things that one's younger self does that are just awful."

Paul reassured her. "I don't think the less of you for having been to a bull-fight. Don't worry. We've all done things we're ashamed of. And anybody who says they haven't . . ." He left the sentence unfinished. He was thinking of some of the things he had done.

And so was Chloe. "You must tell me sometime—you must tell me about some of your . . . how shall I put it? Indiscretions?"

"No," said Paul, smiling. "The memory of them is too painful."

Chloe returned to the bull-fight. "I

remember how it dawned on me. He had a special pass, and we were ushered into ring-side seats. I knew then, of course, where we were, but there was this awful sense of horror, I suppose, that had come over me. It was as if I was being led into a place of execution—a place where something dreadful was about to begin."

"Which it was."

Chloe agreed. "And I should have walked out right then. But I was too weak. I was too cowardly to get up and leave. I stayed there, and the whole awful show began. The ghastly, florid outfits, with those tricorn hats and the ridiculous tight trousers. The toreadors walking along in prancing discomfort, Paul, because of those stupid trousers. And the music, and then the bull coming in and looking so confused by the whole experience—wondering why he's there and what this great roar of sound is. And the poor dumb creature not realising that he **is** the show, and that this is death."

Paul closed his eyes.

"Lorca's poem," said Chloe. "Do you know it? That poem with its strange drumbeat rhythm, repeated again and again: **A las**

cinco de la tarde. I can hardly bear to think about it now. In fact, even now it makes me nauseous." She glanced at Paul. "I'm sorry, Paul—you **are** feeling nauseous, and here I am going on about **A las cinco de la tarde.**"

"What happened?" he asked.

"Nothing," said Chloe. "I sat through the whole thing and didn't act. I didn't leave. I didn't tell him how disgusting I found it. And then, I'm sorry to say, I put it out of my mind. For a long time, I didn't speak to him about his work. I pretended that it was not there. I just pretended. And that continued for several years, would you believe? Denial. That's what it was. Pure denial."

Paul waited for Chloe to continue.

"And then eventually I told him how I felt about his work. It all came out. It was quite shocking, actually, because he stood there and listened to me and his face was a picture of utter devastation. It had never occurred to him that I might find something offensive in his being a bull-fight journalist. It was his world, after all, and he had assumed that I would share it.

"His response surprised me. He announced that he was giving up the position that he

had with **El Mundo,** and that he would find
work writing about something else. There
were plenty of opportunities for journalists,
he said, although when he started to look
for something it proved more difficult than
he had imagined it would be. He eventually
ended up being offered the post of editor
of a magazine called **Poultry World.** It was
for Spanish chicken farmers and people who
bred fancy hens.

"I was very touched by the fact that he
had given up something that had meant so
much to him, and I thought that everything
would be all right. But it wasn't. After he had
been working for **Poultry World** for a few
months, he started to shrink. I don't think
I was imagining it—he just got shorter,
more hunched, thinner. He was diminished
in other ways: he used to talk loudly when
he was a bull-fight journalist; now his voice
was quieter. The absurd thought crossed my
mind that he was now sounding rather like a
chicken—a sort of low, puck-pucking—you
know the noise that chickens make.

"It was so sad—too sad, in fact, to be borne.
And so I took the decision and told him that
I couldn't bear to see him so unhappy. I said

that he should go back to his bull-fighting friends. I said that I was unhappy in Spain and that I would go back to Scotland. This wasn't completely true, but it made it easier for him, I think, and he clutched at the lifeline I had thrown him. We parted quite amicably, and he went back to his old job on the newspaper."

Chloe now stopped. Nothing was said for several minutes, and then she continued, "I remember the last time I spoke to him. I had gone home to stay with my parents for a while in Fife, and I telephoned Octavio from Scotland about something or other. I think it was a tax matter—I had to sign some papers for the Spanish tax authorities, and I needed some information from him. We spoke for a while—he sounded so cheerful. He was going to Pamplona to cover the running of the bulls. You know that festival where those ridiculous people dress themselves in white and then run through the street in front of a group of bulls? Some of them get hurt, of course, and what can they expect?"

She looked at Paul, and he knew what must be coming next.

"Oh no," he muttered.

"Yes, he went, and he never came back. Three men were gored that year—all men, of course, because few women would be so stupid. They should be ashamed of themselves—they really should. Tormenting those poor creatures like that, running in front of them like children playing a game of dare, which is what it is, of course. Octavio was unlucky. The other two were injured in the legs, but he was impaled. The bull's horn penetrated a lung and that was that."

Paul sighed. "Oh no."

"Human stupidity," said Chloe. "Cruelty and stupidity go hand in hand, don't you think?"

"I suppose they do. They . . ."

"We were still technically married," Chloe interjected. "And so I became a widow. I was also his heir in the eyes of the law, and it so happened that Octavio had inherited a fair amount of money from his grandfather's estate. I never even knew about this until I received the lawyer's letter. I had had two very profitable marriages—not that I had planned any of this. I was only twenty-something and I had an awful lot of money in the bank."

"You were lucky," said Paul. "Lots of young widows are anything but . . ."

He did not finish. There was a loud knocking on the front door. Chloe stood up and left to answer. A few minutes later she returned and announced that their visitor had been Thérèse. She had come to tell them that Audette had had her baby. The birth had taken place in the restaurant, in the kitchen. Mother and baby were now installed in the twins' house, as Audette's cottage was deemed unsuitable for a new-born baby. Claude, though, needed help to keep the restaurant going, and Annabelle was now acting as waitress. Thérèse was finding it difficult to cope with the mother and baby. Could Chloe possibly assist?

"But a baby . . ."

Chloe shook her head. "Babies may present logistical problems, Paul, but every logistical problem has a logistical solution." She paused. "Or do I mean logical?"

"Both," said Paul.

"I thought I did," said Chloe.

Paul closed his eyes. Somewhere down in his gastro-intestinal tract, the ingested toxins, the legacy of the mussels, continued their journey, proliferating in the darkness, wreaking their revenge. His raised temperature clouded his mind. He imagined young men dressed in white being pursued along a beach by a cluster of mussels, nipping at their heels.

"I shall probably go and relieve Annabelle in the restaurant," said Chloe. "In an emergency one should go where one is needed most."

Paul opened his eyes. "You? You're going to take over as waitress?"

Chloe was matter-of-fact. "Yes. Why not?"

"It's just that babies and restaurants and . . . Well, we're outsiders, Chloe. We're not even French. These people's problems are not really something we should get involved in, don't you think?"

Chloe's tone was one of reproof. "What did John Donne say, Paul? What did he say? No man is a peninsula . . ."

"Island."

"Very different," said Chloe brightly. "But the principle holds, **n'est-ce pas**?"

8

❧

Jambon des Voleurs

The birth of Audette's baby had taken place on the day after Paul's unfortunate dinner at La Table de St. Vincent. Although a few days late, the baby had arrived with extraordinary alacrity once the process had started—so much so, in fact, that there was no time to usher Audette out of the kitchen. Claude telephoned for the midwife, who arrived just in time. The restaurant was full, and he and his nephew struggled to keep a semblance of normality, with Hugo assuming the role of waiter. There was no note of who had ordered what, though, as Audette's scribbles in her notebook were intelligible only to her.

"Table four?" Hugo bent down to ask her. "Are they the fish or the meat?"

From beneath waves of labour pain, Audette grunted some response.

"She's having a baby," shouted Claude. "Leave her alone, for God's sake."

"I was only asking," protested Hugo. "You never praise what I do. I'm always wrong. You're always yelling at me."

"Because you don't ask somebody who's having a baby whether somebody ordered fish or meat," snapped Claude. "Use your brain, Hugo—for a change."

Hugo stood quite still, glaring at his uncle. Behind him, lying flat on the floor, her face contorted with the pain of labour, lay Audette.

The midwife arrived, bustling in with her air of confident competence. "Get a newspaper," she ordered Hugo.

"**Figaro** or **Libération**?" asked Hugo.

The midwife gave him a scathing look. "This is no time for jokes," she said.

Claude came to his nephew's defence. "He wasn't trying to be funny," he said. "He's just a bit unfocused, if you get my meaning."

Hugo pouted. "Unfocused? Is that what you think? Well, in that case . . ."

He took off his apron and flung it down on the ground. "There are plenty of other jobs," he spat.

The baby was now arriving. Audette let

out a scream. In the dining room, people sat at their tables, transfixed by the noises from the kitchen. When Hugo appeared from the kitchen, he addressed the nearest table. "There is a baby being born through there. Expect a delay." Without waiting for a response, he left the room. One of the diners signalled to him; another shouted out to enquire when his order would be ready. Hugo ignored both, slamming the door on his way out.

Claude appeared from the kitchen. "Mesdames and messieurs," he began. "Due to factors beyond my control, I shall have to ask you to leave."

A man asked him whether everything was under control. "Would you like us to call an ambulance, monsieur?"

Claude shook his head. "There is no need."

A further scream came from the kitchen.

"Are you sure?" asked a woman at another table.

Claude made a reassuring gesture. "Perfectly sure, madame. There is no need to disturb yourselves. Please leave without delay. There are no bills to be paid."

The diners began to make their way out. There were murmurs and anxious looks directed towards the kitchen. Before the room emptied, a baby's cry could be heard.

"Thank God," muttered a woman, one of the last customers to leave.

Claude nodded his head, in acknowledgement of the successful outcome. "Everything is under control," he said. "And I look forward to seeing you here again."

The ambulance summoned by the midwife arrived. Two young men, bearing a stretcher, brushed past Claude and entered the kitchen. There they conferred briefly with the midwife before Audette was helped onto the stretcher, the baby in her arms. Claude stood back. The midwife noticed that there were tears in his eyes. She touched him gently on the forearm.

"I'm sorry," said Claude. "I find these things very emotional. A new baby. So small— so miraculous."

The midwife smiled. "An unusual confinement," she said. "But so well handled."

The transfer of Audette from the cottage in the grounds of the twins' house into the house itself took place at the behest of the doctor. The cottage, he said, was dirty, and damp as well. That was a combination that he warned would be particularly bad for the health of the baby, let alone the mother. If Annabelle and Thérèse could see their way to allowing Audette to spend a few weeks in the main house, that would give the baby a good start and would protect the health of the mother too.

The twins needed no encouragement. Their house was large enough to accommodate the new family, and both Annabelle and Thérèse seemed to take pleasure in the work involved in the new arrangement. They were effusive in their gratitude to Chloe for relieving Annabelle of the responsibilities she had just assumed in the restaurant.

"You are so generous," said Thérèse, when the twins called round to see how Paul was faring. "You come here for peace and quiet and you take all our troubles on your shoulders. I can hardly believe it."

Annabelle was of the same mind. "Nobody in France would do that," she said. "We have become so selfish here—it's always me, me, me."

Chloe shook her head. "Not just France,"

she said. "Everywhere. Yet we have to help one another—we just have to. Otherwise . . ." She shrugged.

"Otherwise all is lost," said Thérèse.

"And anyway," Chloe continued, "I'm happy to do it. Claude is struggling. We can't let him go under."

"You're an angel," said Annabelle.

"I'm sure he'll be a very agreeable man to work with," said Chloe. And then added, "Tell me: Is he single? Is there no wife to help him out?"

This conversation took place in Paul's room, about his bed of sickness. He had been feeling slightly better, and had been thinking of something else—a problem that had arisen in one of the chapters of his book—but now he listened.

"He was married a long time ago," said Thérèse. "She came from Lyon."

"Yes," said Annabelle. "She was from Lyon. He met her there. He worked for our parents here—they were very fond of him—but after he met her he took a job over in Lyon to be near her. It was in a restaurant. I think that's where he trained."

Thérèse looked doubtful. "I don't think he was trained. I think he was some sort of kitchen porter. That's different." She paused. "They were married only five years, I think. She left him, and then we let him have the restaurant. Not free, of course—he's always paid rent."

"Not much," said Annabelle. "He doesn't make enough to pay much rent. And anyway, rents are low out here in the country. Some buildings you can't get a tenant for even if you charge next to nothing."

"Or nothing itself," said Thérèse. "We're useless landlords, Chloe. Audette lives rent-free. Claude pays a pittance."

"She could never afford to pay anything," Annabelle explained.

"Poor man," said Chloe. "Losing his wife like that."

"Very sad," agreed Thérèse. "I think he's lonely."

"There is no need for any man to feel lonely," muttered Chloe.

Paul looked at her. She had done so much, he thought, to combat loneliness in men.

Perhaps he should say something to her. Perhaps he should say, **You have made so**

many men less lonely . . . No, he could not say that; it would be misunderstood. And it was also possible, of course, that Chloe had made many men **unhappy** and even made them lonelier when she was no longer in their lives. She described the end of her marriages as amicable, but was that because that was the way she needed to think of her past? Had she left all those husbands, or had they left her? It was all very well saying **We drifted apart,** but somebody had to start the drift. Some people who said that they drifted actually set sail, full steam ahead . . .

Chloe did not feel Paul's eyes upon her. She looked briefly at Thérèse before turning away. "And since then?" she asked.

The question hung in the air for a few moments. Paul saw Thérèse glance at Annabelle. He found himself thinking: **Why does Claude pay hardly any rent?**

It was Annabelle who answered Chloe's question. "He's still single."

"He would be a good catch," mused Chloe. "He's a good-looking man."

"Very," said Annabelle.

Thérèse sniffed. "Looks are nothing.

France is full of good-looking men who are very bad for women."

"Or so useless," said Annabelle. "Like . . ."

Thérèse looked at her sister sharply. The conversation, it seemed to Paul, was straying into painful territory. Who was so useless?

"Like Philippe?" Thérèse said. She glanced forbiddingly at her sister, as if to foreclose any further discussion, and then continued, to Chloe, "Philippe is my ex-husband."

"I wasn't talking about him," snapped Annabelle.

"Well, who were you thinking of, then?" Thérèse challenged. "Your Antoine?"

Annabelle gave her sister a venomous look. Paul noticed this; he had known a pair of twins who were just like that: they were inseparable but still occasionally exchanged barbed comments and looks of pure hatred. He waited for more, but Annabelle now merely shrugged. "Nobody in particular. I was making a general remark about men, and the number of useless men there are. Most women could make a list—if you asked them."

Thérèse sighed. "Philippe **was** useless. I've never been one to deny that."

Chloe sought to defuse the situation. "I've known many useless men," she said. "The ranks of useless men are ... are ..." She waved a hand in the air. "Multitudinous."

Paul laughed. "Are you aware of my presence?" he asked. "I am, after all, a man, and men have feelings, you know." Women resented men talking about them in a disparaging way—and they were right to resent that, thought Paul—but they were not always consistent: men could be run down, it seemed, with relative impunity.

Chloe looked at him fondly. "Oh, darling, you're not useless. No, no, no! You're a **new** man. We're talking about unreconstructed men."

So that, thought Paul, is the great divide. Men who think like women are acceptable, but men who think differently—in the way in which men might think if not persuaded otherwise—can be dismissed. Of course, aeons of misogyny had brought this all about, he told himself, and men could hardly complain about a long overdue adjustment. Yet how long would the period of rectification last?

Annabelle was apologetic. "We've been very rude. We must leave you to your recovery. It's good to see you looking better."

"We shall bring you some food," said Thérèse. "After an episode of this nature, you will need soup. Weak soup."

"Vegetable soup," said Annabelle.

"And then you must come and see the baby," said Thérèse. "And Audette too. She was asking after you. I think you made an impression on her."

Paul sank back in his bed. He was feeling stronger, but he wondered whether he would find the energy to continue with all this. He had a book to write, and the tranquillity he had sought to help him in that task seemed to be eluding him. Then there was this food poisoning. Add to that Chloe, who, although he enjoyed her company, and although he admired her, could only be described as full-on. And now there were the complicated affairs of the village—the baby, Audette, the twins, Claude, the nephew Hugo, and, somewhere in the background, Philippe and Antoine. Life, it seemed, was like a skein of abandoned wool—you pulled at a thread and out came yard after yard.

. . .

Claude embraced Chloe, kissing her on each cheek, and then, for good measure, repeated the gesture. She smelled garlic, and something else too: Apples? She did not mind. **I like men who smell of garlic,** she said to herself. Her first two husbands had come from garlicky backgrounds, and there was something exciting about that. Husband number three had not had that smell about him; he smelled of **office,** she thought, that strange combination of stale air and paper and flat, uninteresting coffee served in plastic mugs.

Annabelle had told the chef after only one day's work that Chloe had offered to replace her. At first, he was alarmed. "But this woman, this Chloe person, is English. How can an English person do a job like this? I don't want to be too sceptical, but . . . but how?"

"She's a Scotswoman," Annabelle corrected him. "They are quite different."

Claude was unconvinced. "I only say that because I'm worried. It is very good of her to take on this job at such short notice." He paused; some things were **contra naturam.**

"In general, British people do not like to wait on tables. They employ others to do that."

Annabelle liked the British, just as she liked the Americans, and would defend them against what she saw as superior Gallic remarks. It was only too easy to be condescending, if you were French. "Oh, I don't know about that. British people are not **that** lazy."

Claude hummed. "I'm not saying they're lazy, I'm saying they don't like to wait on tables. That is an art. Perhaps they have not got it in quite the same measure as proper French waiters have. Not that I'm saying they don't have other things . . ." He paused. "Forgive me, Annabelle, I am being very rude. We French people sometimes appear rude but are not really intending to be rude. It is because . . ." He shrugged. "Perhaps it's something to do with our language. French may sound a bit arrogant sometimes. As if it's God talking, perhaps. You know how God talks. French suits him very well, I think."

Annabelle laughed. "The English used to say that God spoke English. But we knew he spoke French all along."

"President Mitterrand," mused Claude.

"Remember? People called him God, didn't they? So apt."

Annabelle smiled. Mitterrand was an age away, sufficiently distant to encourage feelings of nostalgia.

"He sounded like God when God was feeling a bit grumpy, or disappointed," Claude continued. "De Gaulle, of course, could carry that off. He **looked** like God, after all."

"Ah! And would God drive a Citroën?" As a child, she had had a school history book, **Our France,** with photographs of General de Gaulle emerging from a low-slung black official Citroën.

Claude laughed at the thought. "De Gaulle had a driver—as would God. Anyway, have you discussed the pay with her? I hope she isn't expecting too much."

Annabelle had already discussed this with Chloe. "Too much? She's expecting nothing. She's doing this to help us . . . to help you. She told me that she doesn't need to be paid."

Claude let out a whistle of surprise. "Nothing?"

"She is well off, I believe. She has had many

husbands, I'm told, and if you have many husbands you can acquire assets." She smiled. "Just as the husbands lose assets, of course. But then if men insist on having all the money, they can hardly complain when they have to hand some of it over."

And now, Claude thought as Chloe presented herself in the restaurant, **here is this Englishwoman—or Scotswoman, should I say—proposing to help me in my little restaurant, and I shall have to show her how to do things. What if she resents being told? What if she thinks she knows how to do it already? What if she drops things? Or spills them over the customers? As if I didn't have enough to cope with, what with those mussels and that poor man being so ill; and the doctor speaking to me about his having to report me to the public health people the next time it happens; and the only-too-regular failure of my soufflés when I try so hard to get them right . . .**

Because I am a failure. I am just a failure. I've tried and tried. I've worked so hard to get things right, but none of it seems to make any difference, and I

end up scraping a living, just. And there are all those chefs who find it so easy, so effortless. They bask in the adulation of their public. They win awards. They write books. And here am I in this wretched little restaurant in the middle of nowhere, where most of my trade is passing, and hardly ever returns, and where people complain that things don't taste as good as they would like them to taste, that there is too much salt, or too little, and where the sauce has curdled or the cheese is too dry and stale.

"You're very kind," he said to Chloe. "With Audette tied up with her baby and my nephew . . ." He waved a hand in the air, to signify evaporating smoke.

"You don't have to thank me. I'm happy to help."

He showed her the kitchen. It was mid-morning, and it was already late to be start-ing the preparations for lunch. He seethed at the selfishness of Hugo, going off like that, flouncing out because of some imag-ined slight. That was because . . . It made the back of his neck feel warm. That was be-cause Hugo needed to be toughened up. His parents had let him sit about the kitchen too much. It was not their fault, of course, after what had happened, but a boy needed to be taught what was what if he were to make anything of his life. Claude himself had tried to take him in hand, but had not got very far. He had taken Hugo with him when he went hunting with his friends, but had eventually had to give up on that. He had tried and tried, but the boy seemed completely uninterested. It was the times, of course. So many boys these days were encouraged to behave like girls.

"My nephew," he said to Chloe, "is not cut out for this work. He's too sensitive. Handling the public is not always easy." He looked at her; he intended this as a warning of what she might expect—indirect, yes, but a warning nonetheless. Customers could be demanding; they could be rude. The waiting staff were the lightning conductor for rudeness.

"I have had a lot of experience," Chloe replied. It was true: she had had a lot of experience, although she had never been a waitress. But there could not be much to it, she thought, and as for handling the public, a firm hand was needed—that was all. Chloe had never had any trouble with the public.

She cast an eye around the kitchen. It was untidy, she thought. The saucepans were all over the place. The cooker looked greasy. The crockery was stacked in a haphazard fashion, rather than according to the circumference of the plates. The cooking oils, in bottles on a shelf above the sink, appeared cloudy. She looked at Claude, too, allowing her gaze to linger while he went off to find the day's menu that he had written out, by hand, on a single sheet of paper. He was undoubtedly handsome, and he had not let himself run to fat, as so many chefs did.

He returned with the menu. "There are no specials today," he said.

"Then that should be easy enough to remember. I shall simply say, 'There are no specials.'"

He gave her a sideways glance. "That's deliberate, you see."

She read the list. "It looks delicious."

Again, he glanced at her, as if uncertain as to whether she was being sarcastic. She intercepted this glance and said, hurriedly, "I mean it. This Normandy ham, for instance, with blackcurrant sauce. That'll be very tasty. I can't resist ham. I feel that . . ." Her voice trailed away. She had seen the small pile of packets, and realised, from the label, that this was the Normandy ham, with its ready-made sauce.

Claude saw what she was looking at. He became defensive. "It's very good," he said. "Audette found it for me."

Chloe remembered that Audette had had another part-time job—in a supermarket— and that she stole all her food from there. So the Normandy ham, with blackcurrant sauce, was not only pre-prepared, but stolen too.

"We could call it **jambon des voleurs**," she said. "Thieves' ham."

She made the remark without thinking, and immediately regretted it. But Claude was busy now, and seemed not to notice.

Chloe saw a pile of unwashed potatoes lying loose on a shelf. Potatoes **dauphinoises** were on the menu.

She pointed to the potatoes. "I could wash and peel those," she offered.

Defensiveness turned to gratitude. "Could

you? That would be so helpful. I have the sardines to prepare."

She did not look for cans of sardines, but they were there, she suspected—and saw them later, when she saw Claude drain them of their oil as he began the process of rendering them Portuguese. She had the chance to look at one of the empty tins and saw that they were North African. **Geography,** she thought, smiling to herself; **countries are not always where you want them to be.**

9

Bleu

Over the following five days, Paul saw very little of Chloe—or of anybody else, for that matter. Chloe appeared to be thriving in her new role as waitress at La Table de St. Vincent, going off to the restaurant after breakfast and staying there until mid-afternoon, when she returned to the house for a siesta. Then she would go back to the restaurant at six, ready for the evening shift, and would only return after Paul had gone to bed. The sisters seemed similarly absorbed in their role as carers for Audette—Chloe had seen them and reported to Paul over breakfast one morning that they were doting on the baby and spoiling Audette, who did very little but read brightly illustrated fashion magazines and watch Brazilian soap operas dubbed into French.

The comparative isolation of his circumstances gave Paul time for his work, and it
was once again going well. A chapter entitled
"Food as Gift" was proving lengthier than he
had imagined because there was so much to
say about what it was to give another food.
He had come across an account of the dropping into Holland of food supplies during
the period of German occupation. He had
read of the feelings of the aircrew as they jet-
tisoned their sacks of food in a low pass over
a field, and of how the Resistance receiving
it below had spelled out, in pieces of white
material laid on the ground, the two words
Thank you, although this was a perilous
thing to do. The pilots had cried; they admitted it. They had survived so much, and
yet that small gesture meant more than anything else to them. They had no tears to shed
for those underneath their bombing path—
who could afford such a luxury at that time?
But they had tears to shed over those two
small words.

He wanted to say something about that,
and he wanted, too, to write about how
Greek monasteries are bound to a rule of

hospitality by which they must provide every visitor with a meal. He wrote about breaking bread with another, and about the obligations that followed upon that simple act of sharing. Eating with others was different from just talking to them—it was an act of commitment, a recognition of shared humanity. We all share these physical needs, it said; we are brothers and sisters in our vulnerability. He liked that, and underlined the phrase: **we are brothers and sisters in our vulnerability.** Yes, we were. That was exactly what we were. That insight was followed by reflections on commensality—the notion of eating with another—and the idea that there was a moral choice to be made **before** you sat down at the table with another person, whether as the host or as a guest. Should you decline to eat with somebody on the grounds of moral disapproval, or could you sit there, relying on mental reservation to protect you against guilt by association?

"Are you enjoying yourself, Chloe?" he asked at breakfast one morning.

She told him she was. But then added, "Although I feel so bad about leaving you to fend for yourself."

He assured her that she need not be concerned. His book was growing by the day. It was a respectable manuscript now, not just a few slender pages.

She was relieved to hear that. Did that mean, she wondered, whether he might have a bit of time to spare?

Paul was cautious. "Possibly. Not much, but possibly a little."

Chloe did not hesitate. "You see, Paul, dear Claude—and he **is** such a dear man—is a terrifically keen chef, as you know, but . . ." She looked at Paul with appeal in her eyes. "But his cooking skills, alas, leave a great deal to be desired. In fact, they leave everything to be desired."

He said that he had formed the impression that she did not rate him too badly as a chef.

"No," said Chloe. "I've been trying to be positive. And I still am trying. But it's difficult. We had a table of three walk out yesterday. I almost came to blows with them. Stuck-up food prigs."

Paul waited.

"They complained about everything—absolutely everything, starting with the cutlery, which they sent back even before they started their meal. They said that it was dirty."

"And was it?"

Chloe looked at Paul reproachfully, as if he were inappropriately **parti pris.** "A dishwasher doesn't always do the job properly—unless it's German. German dishwashers go on forever and get everything spotlessly clean. Other . . . well, other dishwashing machines are human, and they can't always get everything. How can they?"

She seemed to be waiting for an answer.

"I don't suppose they can," Paul conceded.

"Well, there you are. You understand. That table of three did not. And it went downhill from there. The soup was greasy, they said."

"And was it?"

There was a further look of reproach, but then, "A bit. In fact, quite a lot. But that was because the stock had too much grease in it. And was incompatible. The soup was a beef consommé, but the stock was fish-based."

Paul's eyes widened. "That's impossible," he said. "The essence of a beef consommé is the stock itself. That's what consommé really is. Stock, and a good dose of dry sherry."

"I know," said Chloe. "I tried to tell Claude

that, but he seems so defeated by everything. He just sighed, and said that he tried to get things right, but they didn't always work."

"And the table of three? That was too much for them?"

Chloe shook her head. "Something else happened, but I didn't think I needed to involve you in that."

Her mood changed. Now she was brisk. "I'm sure that a few lessons from you, Paul—master-classes, shall we call them—a few of those would make such a difference. Just show him where he's going wrong. I can do the rest."

Paul was puzzled. "The rest?"

"The follow-up," explained Chloe. "I'll consolidate. I'll help him regain his confidence." She paused. "I'm fond of him, Paul. He's a good man. A good man with a bad restaurant."

Paul made a mental note. **A good man with a bad restaurant.** It could be a chapter title, because there were all sorts of questions it provoked. **Why do bad restaurants happen to good people?** Or possibly, **Do we get the restaurants we deserve?**

He looked at Chloe. He had to agree. She

was a conspicuously generous person and it would seem churlish if he declined. France was making him a gift, conferring on him the benison of its peaceful countryside, its quiet. He could very easily put something back, especially since he was writing about that precise subject, about food, about sharing and giving.

He nodded his agreement.

"I knew that you would," enthused Chloe. "Just an hour or two a day. No more than that."

"Starting?"

"Tomorrow."

"Will he accept it?" asked Paul. This was, he thought, a fundamental question. One did not simply barge in and tell a chef—and a French chef at that—how to do things.

"He will," said Chloe.

"How can you be so confident?"

Chloe gave the answer. "The poor man is in love with me," she said. "He'll do anything I ask." She paused. "Just like you."

"Chloe," said Paul, "I am not in love with you."

"That's not what I meant."

"Nor will I do anything you ask."

She looked surprised. "But I thought you would. How very disappointing."

"You're incorrigible."

"And you're delectable, Paul."

Paul shook a disapproving finger. "Flattery will get you nowhere, Chloe."

"I have no desire to get anywhere," said Chloe. "I am one of those who have no inclination to go anywhere other than where they are—metaphorically speaking, of course."

"In other words, you're a conservative."

Chloe was animated in her denial. "Far from it. I don't accept the contemporary orthodoxy, the repetition of clichés and the slavish adherence to the received view." She paused. "But enough of that, Paul. The important thing is that you've agreed to help Claude. He will be a willing disciple, you mark my words."

"I'll try. But I'm not sure that it's going to work."

"I am," said Chloe. "It will all work very well. It'll be the best of all possible worlds."

The quotation from Voltaire hung in the air. "Pangloss," muttered Paul.

Chloe looked almost coy. "Did you know,

Paul, I was married to a Dr. Pangloss? Did I ever tell you?"

"A real Dr. Pangloss?"

"That was his name."

Paul struggled with the implications of this unexpected disclosure. "So you were at some point actually Mrs. Pangloss?"

"People laughed," said Chloe.

"Can you blame them?"

Chloe looked thoughtful. "No, probably not. But still . . ." She looked at her watch. "Claude's expecting me back at the restaurant. I mustn't disappoint him."

Paul realised that there was something he needed to ask her. "You said . . ."

"Yes, I said that he . . ."

". . . is in love with you. Were you serious?"

"Yes," she replied. "I imagine he wants to marry me."

Paul felt a sudden stab of alarm. "But, Chloe, you barely know him. You can't possibly . . ."

"Don't worry," said Chloe. "I have no intention of acquiring yet another husband. I'm not impetuous in these matters, Paul— credit me with that."

"If you did marry him," asked Paul, "what number would he be? Six?"

Chloe frowned. "Do you count annulments? Because technically an annulment means that you were never married in the first place. That's a matter of canon law."

"Count them," said Paul.

"In that case, darling, yes, six. But it's not going to happen, as I've told you."

"Six, including Mr. Pangloss?"

"Including him. And he was actually Dr. Pangloss," said Chloe. "He had a Ph.D. So many people do these days."

"In what?"

Chloe looked vague. "Byzantine frescoes," she answered, adding, "I think."

Paul looked away, suddenly unsettled. How could you possibly live with somebody and not know the subject of his Ph.D.? You could not, because if there was one thing that people wanted to talk about, it was their Ph.D., and you would never fail to mention that to your spouse. You just wouldn't.

The thought disturbed him because as it occurred to him he reached that most painful of conclusions—that somebody close to you was not the person you imagined her to be. There was still a possibility that Chloe was being deliberately disingenuous in claiming not to know anything about her ex-husband's Ph.D., but it was also possible, he felt, that she had made up a lot of what she had said to him. These doubts, once planted in his mind, grew rapidly. The Dr. Pangloss story was just too good to be true, and if that were the case, then the same might be true of other stories Chloe had told him. What about Antonio Gigliodoro and the bull-fight journalist—latterly of **Poultry World**—Octavio something or other? Could it be that Chloe had made them up too? She had often expressed a horror of a dull life, and for such a person, a whole series of colourful, but invented, husbands could be attractive. This meant that Chloe might never have had a husband—not a single one—and that all this talk of these men was no more than wish-fulfilment. If children created imaginary friends for themselves, then might adults not do the same?

But why would somebody like Chloe have to do that? The articulation of the possibility—even the mere thinking of it—made him feel disloyal. It was tantamount to an accusation of deliberate lying on Chloe's part, and that was a step far beyond anything he would have contemplated doing. Besides, he liked Chloe—he admired her—and he did not like the thought that she had been so mendacious. And yet Dr. Pangloss . . . that was surely pushing the boundaries of the believable.

Or perhaps she had been speaking in jest, not expecting him to take her seriously. That was a possibility, but it was also, he thought, clutching at straws. The more likely conclusion was the uncomfortable one that Chloe was a fantasist who had deliberately misled him about her fictitious past.

But why should somebody as sophisticated as Chloe find pleasure in such a pointless and ultimately counterproductive deception? What on earth could she have been thinking of?

Chloe's request was not the only one that Paul received that day. While he was still reflecting, with a mixture of hurt and puzzlement, on Chloe's apparent fantasising, Annabelle called to see him. She came straight to the point.

"Would you mind helping us with something this afternoon?"

Paul could hardly refuse—at least in principle. "If I can."

Annabelle took that as agreement. "Good. Audette needs to go to the supermarket. She has no car at the moment and so somebody needs to drive her."

She looked at him expectantly. Paul wanted to sigh, but stopped himself.

"The baby can't go," Annabelle continued, "and so somebody has to stay behind and look after him. Thérèse can't manage that by herself—she gets anxious that the baby will stop breathing—which means I'll have to stay with her. Which means there's nobody to take Audette shopping."

Paul pointed out he had no means of transport. "I'm not sure if I'm insured for Chloe's car. I could find out, if you like."

Annabelle said there was no need. "You can use our car, if you wish. It's insured for all drivers."

She waited, and Paul knew that there was only one answer he could give. He liked the twins, and he wanted to be helpful. "I suppose I can do that. When?"

They agreed a time, and, after a relatively fruitless couple of hours at his desk, Paul walked the short distance to Thérèse and Annabelle's house. Thérèse answered the door, signalling to him to be quiet because, as she explained in whispered tones, the baby was asleep.

Audette was in the kitchen, dressed in a faded pink housecoat and smoking a cigarette. When Paul entered the room, she stubbed out the cigarette in a saucer before rising to her feet.

"I'm ready," she said to the room at large.

Annabelle produced the keys of the car. "The gears can be awkward," she said, handing them to Paul. "I'm going to get the gearbox seen to, but you know how it is. But you'll be all right."

"Time," said Thérèse. "There's never any time to do a thing."

"Tell me about it," said Audette. "I can't even buy cigarettes."

"The baby," Thérèse explained to Paul.

"Yes," said Audette. "I've had my baby, you know."

"I'd heard that," said Paul.

Audette was gathering a few things she needed for the trip to the supermarket.

"Have you got money?" asked Annabelle.

Audette did not answer directly, but made a dismissive gesture. "I have a list," she said, tapping her head with a finger. "Up here."

"We need bread," said Thérèse. "I've asked Monsieur André to keep a couple of loaves."

"Pah!" said Audette.

Annabelle caught Paul's eye. "Audette and Monsieur André have their differences," she whispered.

"We all do," said Paul tactfully.

Audette had overheard. She looked at him with interest. "So you share my view of that **mec**?"

"He didn't say that," Annabelle snapped. And then, as if to mollify Audette's feelings, she added, "He sometimes has strong views, but his heart's in the right place."

"Pah!" said Audette. "He's a Le Pen man."

"Bakers should be judged on their bread, not their politics," said Thérèse.

Paul frowned. There was something fundamentally wrong with that, he felt, because the grounds of judgement had to be specified. He should talk about it in his book. There could be a section called "Our Daily Bread" . . . A good baker could be a bad man—and a bad man could be a good baker. One might decline to buy the bread of a good baker on the grounds that he was a bad man, but that was perhaps easier said than done, especially in a small village. And there were bigger issues too. Should we boycott food produced by countries with bad governments? Such attitudes might make people feel virtuous, but the people punished on the ground might be innocent farmers. That introduced complications that could be debated at greater length if he ever got that far with his book, which was beginning to look doubtful.

"There are many fascists in the village," said Thérèse. "They meet for coffee every Wednesday."

Paul sighed. "Why do people not remember?"

"Remember what?" asked Thérèse.

"The last time," Paul replied. "The nineteen thirties."

"Because they're ignorant," said Thérèse. "Ordinary people are ignorant of history. Their education is full of slogans and superficialities. They've been made stupid by their teachers." She looked down at the ground. "France used to be such a beautiful place.

Peaceful. Ordered. Now . . . there's an ugliness. We're strangers to one another. We don't know who our neighbours are."

Audette had lost interest. Turning to Paul, she said, "We must go. We can collect the bread on the way back. Come on."

The car had been parked outside, and Annabelle now explained the gear shift to Paul while Audette lowered herself into the passenger seat. "Ouf!" she said, and then, "Oh!"

Annabelle finished her explanation of the gear shift. She had done this while sitting in the driver's seat, with Paul looking on through the open door. Now, as she prepared to yield the seat to Paul, she said goodbye to Audette. "Be careful," she said, and leaned over and kissed her. The kiss lasted more than a few seconds; it was lingering. Paul instinctively looked away. Once freed from Annabelle's embrace, Audette started to adjust her safety belt. "I'm still too fat," she muttered. "You have a baby and you think you'll be lighter immediately. It doesn't work that way."

"No," said Paul. "I'm sure it doesn't."

"You haven't had a baby," observed Audette.

Paul was taken aback. "I never said I had."

"So you don't know, then," said Audette. "No man knows."

"I think I can imagine it," said Paul mildly, struggling with the reluctant gear lever.

"I don't think so," Audette retorted.

Paul did not respond.

"Do you think men should be allowed to marry one another?" asked Audette.

"I don't see why not," Paul replied evenly. "If that's what will make them happy."

Audette turned in her seat to fix him with an intense stare. "You think it's all right for two men to try to have a baby?"

"I don't think that's what they're doing," said Paul.

"You think that?" challenged Audette.

They moved slowly out onto the public road. "I do," said Paul.

"Would you marry another man?" asked Audette.

"Some men prefer their own sex, as do some women." He kept his gaze on the road ahead, but he felt her eyes upon him.

"Why do you say that?" asked Audette. Once again there was a note of challenge in her voice. "Why do you say that about women?"

"I was talking about men—and you asked me, didn't you? I was just pointing out that what I said about men applied to women too."

Audette turned away. "Men don't understand," she said, and lapsed into silence.

It was a drive of twenty minutes. A few miles down the road, with the fields of ripening wheat stretching out on either side, the road dipped down to a bridge over a sluggish river. A small creature—a ferret, perhaps— dashed out in front of the car, causing Paul to brake sharply. The animal disappeared into the undergrowth, delivered by whatever rural divinity it is that hedges such lives, and the journey was resumed. But the incident had jolted Audette out of her silence.

"I'm very happy with my baby," she said. "I didn't think I would be."

"That's good," said Paul. "It would be difficult otherwise, I suppose."

"Bleu said at first I shouldn't have him," she went on. "He said that there were too many babies already. He shouted a lot."

Paul was tactful. "Bleu? He's your . . . your partner?"

Audette snorted. "**Quel imbécile!** Some partner."

"Ah well. Then you're best without him."

Audette nodded. "Except that . . ." She did not complete the sentence. Paul waited.

"Except?"

"Except he wants the baby. He heard that he'd been born. Now he wants him."

"To take him from you? He seriously wants to take him from you?"

Audette wound down the window and spat outside. Paul swerved slightly, but recovered.

"Yes. He said since it's a boy and he's the father he has the right to him. He says that's the way it is with his people."

Paul asked who his people were. Something had been said about horse thieves, he seemed to recall.

"They're scum," said Audette. "Scum. Those people are scum."

"What do they do?"

"Steal things. Cars, mostly, these days. It used to be horses, but there aren't so many around now. They'll take a horse if they find one, but usually it's cars. And motorbikes. They steal motorbikes down here and take them up to Paris to sell them in the **banlieues.** The police never find them because they're afraid to go in there." She paused. "The police are cowards. All of them."

Paul said that he did not think anybody could take a baby from his mother. "Surely, nobody would allow that. You could go to court, couldn't you?"

Audette shrugged. "Bleu doesn't care about that. He'll still try." She fixed Paul with a mournful stare. "He's not like you. He's a pig."

Paul raised an eyebrow. "Oh well, I wouldn't worry."

"You see, you're a gentleman, aren't you?"

He laughed. "You flatter me."

"No, I mean it. You never hit anybody, did you? You don't do that sort of thing. You wouldn't raise your hand to a woman."

"No. I wouldn't. To anybody, I suppose. Violence doesn't solve anything."

"Tell that to Bleu," said Audette, her voice heavy with bitterness. She lowered her gaze, and suddenly, without warning, placed her hand lightly on his thigh. She looked up, as if to gauge his reaction.

Paul glanced down. The pressure on his

thigh was increased. He said the first thing that came to mind. "I don't think so. Sorry."

She did not take her hand away. "You don't like me?"

"Of course I like you. I just don't think that there's going to be anything like that between us."

Her hand moved away.

"Thank you," said Paul.

"I wondered," she said.

"Wondered what?"

She looked out of the window. "I wondered whether you were interested, you see. So now I know you're not."

Paul frowned. "I'm not." And then he realised that this might be misunderstood; but it was too late.

"Men like you—considerate men—often aren't. I don't mind. People should be allowed to do what they want to do. Boys, girls—does it matter? Same thing, really."

"I'm not," Paul protested. "It's not that."

Audette shook her head. "You don't need to say anything else. Who cares these days?"

They had reached a large sign advertising the presence ahead of the supermarket. "We go in here," said Audette. "You can park round the back. There's a special place there. You wait while I go inside."

Paul felt he had to correct her impression. "I think you should know something—" he began.

Audette interrupted him. "I told you. I don't care."

"But—"

She was not listening, and he had to park the car.

"You wait," she said. "I won't be long."

10

❧

Soupe à l'oignon

*C*hloe's eyes opened wide. "She did what?" she exclaimed.

They were at breakfast together, Paul having returned from his morning trip to the **boulangerie.** Four fresh croissants, glowing buttery, were in a small bread basket in front of them. Milky coffee steamed in the wide drinking bowls; a newspaper, which neither would look at until later in the day, lay folded at the far end of the table. The front-page headline, though, could be made out: **Rail strike in third day—President warns . . .**

Chloe had not come in from the restaurant until late the previous night, well after Paul had gone to bed. Now he told her about his trip to the supermarket with Audette.

"She stole the lot," he said. "Or at least I think she did. I didn't go inside. I didn't see the actual stealing."

"You waited in the car?"

"Yes. She said that she had to see one of her former workmates. So I sat and listened to the radio until she came out again only about ten minutes later. She was carrying a large box."

"And it was all in there?"

"Yes, everything. She went back in for two more boxes—there were three in all. Baby supplies. Cans of food. Washing powder. Everything.

"I helped her to load the boxes in the car, and then I drove her back. I didn't know at that stage, of course—it was only on the way back that it all came out. It was as if she didn't care who knew. She was brazen."

Chloe rolled her eyes. Paul, watching her, thought: **I must have been wrong. I misunderstood. Dr. Pangloss was a joke, perhaps, not intended to be taken seriously.**

"How did she put it?" Chloe asked.

"I asked her whether she was going back to work in the supermarket once the baby was a bit older. She said she was not—she had handed in her notice, she said. It would cost her, she went on to say, because food was getting no cheaper and that was one of the perks of the job."

"That's one way of putting it," Chloe said wryly.

"Yes. I asked if she got a discount as an employee, and she laughed. She said the discount was one hundred per cent. And then she said that everybody enjoyed the same discount. I asked her if the management minded, and she made one of those monosyllabic sounds the French love. **Bof,** I think. Or **pfff.** Or something similar. Then she said that all that was required was discretion. If people didn't abuse the system and take too much, then the management turned a blind eye."

Chloe took a sip of her coffee, momentarily closing her eyes with pleasure. "Divine," she said. "Warm morning sun. This coffee. And look out there." She pointed out of the window to where a line of poplars marked the end of the garden. Beyond the trees, a field of hay had recently been cut, the grass now stacked in orderly sheaves. A small flight of pigeons, three or four birds, described a low, erratic arc across the sky.

"You can forgive anything in a place like this, Paul. Or at least I can. It's all very different here, don't you think?"

He knew what she meant. Moral probity, perhaps, was a northern concept—a concomitant of a Protestant conscience and a Protestant landscape. Soft hills, warmth, thyme-scented air made a nonsense of the diktats of probity. Relax. Don't worry too much. Rules are an effort that need be neither observed nor sustained.

But something within him rebelled against this, no matter how persuasive were the temptations of the south. And in this mood he said, although he had not planned to do so, "This Dr. Pangloss . . . did he exist?"

Chloe put down her bowl of coffee. He noticed that she spilled a small amount. A shaking of the hand? He looked away, embarrassed.

She took time to answer, and when her reply came it was in measured tones. "Did you take me seriously? Oh, I'm sorry. I thought that you would see the joke."

He snatched a glance at her, and then quickly looked away again. "Of course I saw the joke. But then I thought: Well, maybe there really was a Dr. Pangloss. I see now that I was wrong."

There was an almost immediate draining away of tension. Chloe visibly relaxed, and took another sip of coffee. Her hands were steady now. "I did know somebody who was a bit of a Pangloss," she said. "He was an optimist. His name was Macintyre, but I always called him Pangloss." She paused and directed a smile at Paul. "I didn't marry him."

"Then you never were Mrs. Pangloss," said Paul.

"Of course not," said Chloe. "Had I been, I would have hung on to the name. How could one resist? It would be delicious. Imagine having one's name called out at an airport. **Will Mrs. Pangloss kindly report to the ticketing desk?** Imagine."

"Except that nobody these days would recognise the reference," said Paul. "Nobody reads **Candide** any longer."

Chloe's response was tossed off quickly. "I don't expect them to. But I thought the definition of an educated person was one who at least knows what's in the great books he or she hasn't read."

This was a return of Chloe to form, and Paul smiled as he helped himself to a croissant and a refreshed bowl of coffee. The action of putting jam on the croissant, and the tearing of it into bite-sized pieces, gave him the opportunity to think. He felt relief. It had been an absurd suspicion on his part, and he felt ashamed of himself. Chloe had been nothing but kind to him. She had lent him the flat in Edinburgh and now she was sharing with him her house here in France. She had not even asked for a contribution to the housekeeping expenses; Paul had already tried to pay his share, and had been rebuffed; now he was planning to press the money on her. He should not have doubted her.

That morning Paul gave Claude the first of his promised master-classes. Chloe was there, half listening to what was said, but for the most part busying herself with what she described as a deep cleaning of the kitchen. Cupboards were opened, contents taken out, sniffed, and in some cases tasted before being replaced or peremptorily tossed into the bin. Paul was struck by Claude's acceptance of this gross interference in his kitchen by one who was no more than a temporary, unqualified waitress—and a volunteer at that. He found it difficult to imagine a French chef of any standing tolerating such behaviour, but then he reminded himself that Claude was not a chef of any standing at all—he ran what, after all, was known locally as the second-worst restaurant in France; he was on notice from the local doctor that he might be reported to the health authorities; and his kitchen had only recently doubled up as a maternity ward. In such circumstances he was in no position to resist.

From the cupboards, Chloe moved on to the saucepans. These were of some antiquity, bought from the kitchens of some crumbling and unloved chateau, made of copper, and hung on pegs along one wall. Taken down, they were stacked in the sink while Chloe methodically scrubbed each one before returning it to its peg.

"How dirt accumulates," she said cheerfully, peering into the largest of these pans. "Whole generations of bacteria here. Look, Paul. Take a look. This might explain your recent discomfort."

Paul was embarrassed at Chloe's apparent lack of concern for Claude's feelings. He himself had glossed over the debacle with the mussels when Claude had repeated his apology. It was not helpful, he thought, to bring up the issue afresh.

Once again, Claude seemed to accept the criticism without demur. "You're right," he muttered. "I must be more careful about that sort of thing."

"Yes," said Chloe. "You must. It's probably that pretty little boy of yours."

"My nephew," began Claude. "Yes . . ."

"His **nephew,**" Paul whispered to Chloe. "His **nephew,** Chloe."

"I know that," snapped Chloe. "But that's no excuse."

"I'll speak to him," promised Claude.

Paul scrutinised Claude's expression. There was no resentment that he could see, which fitted, he felt, with Chloe's supposition that Claude was in love with her. And looking at him now, Paul thought that this was probably true. The chef's eyes were fixed on Chloe, and whenever she glanced in his direction, they lit up. It was strange, Paul thought, how there was light behind the eyes, and how ready was that light to shine when confronted with an object of desire. Yes, Claude had fallen for Chloe—that was utterly apparent—and she . . . well, that was more difficult to read. She clearly liked Claude, although her treatment of him now seemed to be inspired by something akin to tough love. A man might be admitted to the circle of her affection, it would seem, but only if his copper saucepans passed muster. That, Paul thought, had not yet happened.

While Chloe continued with her cleaning mission, Paul, with one eye on the clock, went over the proposed lunchtime menu with Claude. They did not have much time, it already being ten o'clock, and the first customers for lunch being likely to arrive shortly after twelve. Claude had various courses in mind, including a mushroom quiche he had made the previous day. This was examined and quickly condemned.

"The pastry," said Paul, "is inadequately cooked. It's soggy."

Claude looked crestfallen. "One does not want pastry to be too dry and crumbly," he said.

"Nor raw," said Paul, prising a small

section off the edge of the quiche. "Look. This is sticking to my fingers."

Attention passed to the soup, which was onion-based, and which had been made three days earlier. The bread that can accompany such a soup had been put into the pot at the time of initial preparation, with the result that it had now totally disintegrated, joining at the bottom of the liquid the cheese that had been transformed into a glutinous mass. For some reason that Paul could not fathom, this soup, which should have been brown, was of a curious green colour.

"We have the time to begin again," Paul said as he laid down the spoon used to taste the soup. He tried but did not entirely succeed in suppressing an expression of shock on registering the taste of the curious green offering.

"You don't like it?" asked Claude. He leaned forward nervously to examine his own creation.

"It's not that I don't like it," said Paul hurriedly. "It's just that it's somewhat unusual—for **soupe à l'oignon.**"

Seeing Claude's crestfallen look, Paul added, "There are different views about this sort of soup, you know. Some people make it without beer and wine. Some people even leave out the vinegar."

Claude looked panicky. "Beer? Wine?"

"Let me show you," said Paul. "Where are your onions?"

Chloe, who had caught some of this exchange, replied from the other side of the kitchen. "I think you might be looking for these," she said, producing a few undernourished onions, most of which, having been picked too early, were still green. Paul took them and examined them. "I'm afraid these won't do," he said. "This soup is onion-based. Onions are at the heart of it."

Claude looked at his watch. "Could you give me ten minutes?"

Paul was doubtful. "We don't have much time."

"Just ten minutes," Claude insisted. "My sister—Hugo's mother. She lives in the village. She always has onions."

"And a few bottles of beer?" asked Paul. "Dark beer? Amber's best."

Claude nodded. "Her larder is always well stocked."

Once Claude had slipped out, Chloe gave

Paul a thumbs-up sign. "He just needs a little encouragement," she said. "Cooking's a question of confidence, don't you think?"

"Confidence and the right ingredients," Paul replied. "These onions . . ." He gestured hopelessly to the small and bedraggled pile.

Chloe returned to her cleaning tasks. Now it was the turn of the chopping boards, which she began to scrub energetically in soapy water. That task took longer than she had imagined, as years of fat had been worked into the wood. This now emerged like the lower layers of a palimpsest, to be scoured off and washed away. Paul watched with the fascination of distaste, but was impressed by Chloe's non-judgemental cheerfulness. He felt proud of her, and of her no-nonsense willingness to roll up her sleeves and tackle so potentially dispiriting a task. And he was impressed, too, that the goal was the benefit of others, and not personal gain of any sort.

Paul tackled the grating of cheese and the slicing of garlic. By the time Claude returned, everything was ready for the softening of the onions in one of the newly cleaned pans—a process that Paul intended that

Claude should perform under close supervision. It was an elementary skill, but such was his lack of confidence in Claude's ability that he wanted to ascertain that he knew enough to distinguish between caramelisation and the state of being burned. He found it hard to believe that anybody could be so inept and still be in business; perhaps local opinion was right—perhaps this really was the second-worst restaurant in France.

Claude was not away long. He had found a good supply of onions—four long strings of them, in fact, neatly plaited in the way of the Breton countryside, in perfect condition and ready for use. But he had also found his nephew, who was now with him, holding a couple of these onion strings and taking in, with visible astonishment, the transformation that was being effected in the kitchen.

"My nephew is back," announced Claude, nodding towards the young man. "He has thought things through."

Smiling, Paul offered a handshake. "Would you care to help us?" he said. "We're working on a couple of dishes for lunch."

Hugo nodded, and went to retrieve an apron hung on the back of a door. This brought a shaking of Chloe's finger. "That apron's filthy," she said. "Here." She extracted a freshly laundered white apron from a bag she had brought with her. Hugo took it and donned it with satisfaction.

"Better?" asked Chloe.

"Much better," muttered Hugo.

"It's all a question of attitude," said Chloe. Turning to Paul, she suggested that the master-class resume. "Make large quantities of that soup," she said. "There'll be plenty of takers, and we can all have a bowl ourselves for our own lunch before people arrive."

Paul began. He noticed that although Claude was participating, his attention was wandering and was focused, he thought, more on Chloe than on the master-class. In contrast, Hugo was watching his every move with rapt attention. After a while, it was Hugo to whom he addressed his remarks; Claude appeared not to mind, and slowly distanced himself, drifting over towards Chloe to help her with one of her cleaning tasks.

The young man showed himself to be a responsive pupil. The **soupe à l'oignon** was not an unduly complicated dish, even according to the more intricate traditional recipe that Paul was following, and it was soon prepared and ready for serving. The other dishes planned for lunch were a wild mushroom roulade, made with ceps that Paul had acquired at the market the previous day, guineafowl with a red wine **jus,** and sole served with **sauce Dugléré.**

The **sole Dugléré** that Paul proposed brought a reaction from Hugo. **"Dugléré,"** said Hugo. "Adolphe Dugléré was a very great chef."

Paul looked at him with interest. "You know about him?"

Hugo nodded. "Yes. I've read about him." Then he added, "I prefer **sole Véronique,** though."

Paul could barely conceal his astonishment. "You do, do you?"

"Yes. And we have grapes outside that we could use for that. They've been growing against the wall back there. They're ready."

Paul looked thoughtful. "Are you interested in the great chefs?"

Hugo nodded. "Yes, of course. I have books about some of them."

"Sole Véronique?" asked Paul.

"Auguste Escoffier," answered Hugo. "He

invented that. It was something to do with an opera called **Véronique,** I think. But it may have been different."

"Oh yes?"

"There are some who say that Mallet, who was chef at the Ritz in Paris, invented it and named it after another chef's new daughter."

Paul smiled. "I didn't know that."

Hugo glanced at his uncle, now on the other side of the room. "Uncle was never really interested in that sort of thing. He's always said that food is just food." He paused. "I don't think that way, monsieur. I think it's a whole lot more."

"Well, you're absolutely right," said Paul.

"I wanted to work at one of the big restaurants," Hugo continued. "That restaurant in Vienne, for instance, the one where Monsieur Point was chef. He was a great man."

Paul knew about that. "A very great man," he said. "But why didn't you get a job somewhere like that?"

Hugo looked down at his hands. "My father's blind," he said. "We have an orchard. My mother can't cope with it. She needs to look after my father, and I have to help her. I can't get away."

"I'm very sorry," said Paul. "Has he . . . Has he been like that for long?"

"Four years," said Hugo. "I was sixteen when it happened. He was cutting a branch of a tree with a chainsaw when the chain broke. It snapped back across his face."

Paul winced.

"They couldn't save his eyes. They tried, but they couldn't. So now he's blind." He paused. "Uncle gave me a job so that I could stay here. I shouldn't have left the other day, but I was just so fed up. He never let me do the cooking. He had to do it all the time. I was just to be his assistant."

"I see."

"My mother told me to apologise and come back," Hugo continued. "That's why I'm here."

While this exchange was taking place, Claude appeared to have given up all pretence of being involved in the master-class and was busy helping Chloe to open, assess, and then rearrange jars of preserves. They were sampling a chutney and discussing the results. Chloe shook her head, and the jar was unceremoniously tipped into the bin.

"Look at Uncle," muttered Hugo. "He doesn't care."

"Doesn't care about what?"

"About cooking. He doesn't like it. He likes all the fussy bits—writing out the menus and so on. And he doesn't mind serving—he likes it because he can talk to the customers. He's a show-off, you see. He enjoys going to market too—he's fond of bargaining." There was a pause. Hugo now looked almost apologetic, as if ashamed of his disloyalty. "The truth of the matter," he continued, "is that Uncle is really . . ." There was another pause, briefer this time. "He's a really useless chef. Some people just are."

Paul said nothing; he was deep in thought. Sometimes, it seemed to him, people were in the wrong job. They believed they had to do one thing when they should be doing another. And if you showed them that there was somebody who could do their job— somebody who perhaps had been watching them all along—and that they could do another job perfectly well, then they were much happier and much more fulfilled. All they had to do was to make the switch.

11

❧

Some Men Suffer Too

"We don't like the thought of you sitting there alone," Annabelle said over the telephone. "Sitting there and thinking about this book of yours. No. You must have dinner with us."

Paul accepted without demur. Chloe was working in the restaurant and the house would seem empty without her; he had nothing to read; and the ancient television set in the sitting room seemed to have lost its ability to transmit sound. Paul had turned it on shortly before Annabelle's call and had spent twenty minutes watching a discussion programme consisting entirely of talking, but silent, heads—over which a caption proclaimed **CRISE IMMINENTE.** The expression of the participants was grave—as befitted those who were debating an imminent crisis; after a while, though, the tenor appeared to change, and expressions of concern were replaced with smiles and silent laughter. Perhaps the crisis had abated, Paul thought; perhaps the imminence of threatened disaster had diminished and good humour could return.

The surrealism of his watching this silent debate suddenly came home to Paul. As he switched off the defective television, a smell of overheated plastic, laced with notes of burning rubber, drifted up from the defunct set. Reaching down behind it, he took the plug out of the wall socket and thought, at that moment, of the electricity thief. There had been an electricity thief, somewhere . . . and it came back to him. Bleu, whom he had never met, had been the electricity thief. Bleu, lover of Audette and putative father of her baby.

He had a few hours in hand before he was due to go for dinner. These he spent toying with his manuscript. He was now writing about food as offering, and it was slow going. Why did the ancient Greeks burn meat as a sacrifice to the gods? Perhaps the answer was simple: the gods, like everybody else, enjoyed the wafting smell of sizzling steaks. **The Greek gods, after all,** he wrote,

were only human . . . No, that would not do. The Greek gods were **not** human . . . or were they human in their essence, and yet immortal? Was immortality the sole defining characteristic of a god in ancient Greece? The Greek gods were human in so far as they showed human emotions: they were ambitious, truculent, vindictive, and often strikingly petty. All of those were human characteristics which proper, monotheistic gods unambiguously eschewed. And yet, he thought, the monotheists' gods still had susceptibility to flattery attributed to them: they liked their praises to be sung; they liked to be remembered in ritual; they encouraged references to their abiding wisdom.

By the time he left the house he had added a grand total of ten sentences to his manuscript, scrapped three, and significantly altered two others. At this rate, he thought, he would finish **The Philosophy of Food** at the end of the following year, eighteen months beyond the deadline agreed with his publisher. Of course, publishers' deadlines were rarely meant to be taken seriously—or so he had suggested to Gloria. "They factor in a delay," he said. "Everybody knows that.

They have a different calendar, rather like the Julian calendar, or is it the . . ."

"No," she said. "They don't. They usually mean what they say. They're odd that way."

The thought of his lack of progress made him feel downcast. He was not at all sure that he still wanted to write **The Philosophy of Food.** He had begun to feel that there was something excessively ambitious about the whole endeavour. He may have studied philosophy at university, but he never progressed beyond the introductory undergraduate courses, and did that entitle him to write on such matters? There were already people who had written books on the subject— serious books that, unlike his, had no recipes in them. There was Julian Baggini, who had talked about the moral implications of what we ate, and Harry Eyres, who wrote about Horace, and Horatian pleasures of the table. Then, of course, Roger Scruton devoted a whole book to the philosophy of wine. **I drink, therefore I am . . . ,** Scruton had said, a haunting phrase which Paul felt he would never be able to match. **I eat, therefore I am** was a pale Cartesian reference by comparison, probably because **eat** did not rhyme with **think** and the play on words was lost. And that, he decided, was the problem. His whole enterprise was doomed to failure. This was the wrong thing to be doing. **I am a charlatan,** he thought. And then he thought again: **No, I am not a charlatan because no real charlatan ever says "I am a charlatan."** The point about charlatans was that they never acknowledged their meretriciousness. And psychopaths, Paul suddenly asked himself. Did a psychopath ever say "I'm a psychopath"? Or did that admission require an insight that psychopaths simply would not have? If you are always in the right—as psychopaths must feel they are—then the whole concept of psychopathy would be inconceivable.

Annabelle greeted him at the front door. "Audette has returned to her cottage, as perhaps you know, and Thérèse is cooking tonight," she said. "Our tastes are very simple and she was worried that somebody like you might feel . . ." She looked at him quizzically.

"I'm happy with anything," he said. "The simpler the better."

"My view too," she said. "The more you add, the more there is to go wrong."

"As in life," said Paul. He thought of **The Philosophy of Food.** He should not have said yes. It was his own fault.

As she led him towards the kitchen, Annabelle warmed to the theme. "Every so often you should just clear everything out," she said. "Clear your diary. Throw the clutter away—the papers, the letters, the books— all the things you keep that you really don't need to hang on to. It's like going on a diet— one of those detoxifying ones. You feel all cleaned out."

Paul nodded his agreement. He did not feel all cleaned out—quite the opposite, in fact. His life was cluttered by one overwhelming burden, **The Philosophy of Food.** If that were not there, then he would feel free again. He could get up in the morning without a brooding sense of obligation to an omni-present, reproachful taskmaster: a taskmaster composed of Gloria, his publisher, and his readership—a trinity of expectations and potential reproach.

They were halfway down the corridor lead-ing to the twins' kitchen. On the wall at that point was a framed engraving of the carriage scene from "Boule de Suif," with the nuns and Boule de Suif herself, with her picnic basket of delicacies. The eyes of the bourgeois travellers are drawn to the delights of the basket, while the aristocratic members of the party, as hungry as they are, struggle to maintain their haughty demeanour.

He stopped, staring at the picture in the dim light of the corridor.

"Maupassant," explained Annabelle. "It was my mother's favourite. Maupassant and Balzac. These days . . ." She shrugged. "These days people don't want to read about that sort of France."

Paul only half heard what Annabelle had to say. He was examining the picnic basket more closely. There were pies and cold meats—a ham, a string of sausages—there were upturned puddings, which surely would not have kept their shape so well in real life; there was a jar of preserved fruit. And in the midst of this examination, he made up his mind: he would stop writing about the philosophy of food. He would write instead about a village in France that has a restaurant that needs improving. He would write about a man and woman who come to the village and find that all is not quite as it seems. It would be a book about rescue—about how something that was failing was made to succeed.

He was brought back to the present moment by Annabelle. "We'll go through here," she said. "This is where we sit when we have visitors."

In the formal sitting room—the **salon**—Thérèse rose to greet him. From a table beside the piano, she took an already opened bottle of wine and poured Paul a glass and then one for her sister.

"Our neighbour's wine," she said, lifting her glass in a toast. "He's inordinately proud of it."

"It's all right," said Annabelle. "It's not as good as he claims, perhaps, but it passes muster—just. Claude uses it as his house wine in the restaurant."

"People accuse him of watering it down," said Thérèse. "But you know what people are like. They'll look for any excuse to run others down."

Annabelle shook her head sadly. "It's such a big problem in the country. It results from people not having enough to do. If you don't have things to keep you busy, you end up starting fights with your neighbours."

Paul said that he found the wine pleasant enough.

Annabelle smiled. "I'll tell him. He loves to hear about people liking his wine." She paused. "Your cousin . . . What a kind woman she must be."

"Yes," said Thérèse. "To help Claude out like that! How many women would do that sort of thing for no other motive than the desire to help . . ." She left the sentence unfinished. Paul felt that there was an ominous note to it—as if a real desire to help was the very last motive she suspected.

"She is a generous-spirited person," he said firmly.

"Of course," said Thérèse quickly. "I wouldn't suggest otherwise . . . not for a moment." Again, the words came out with the opposite implication.

Annabelle took a sip of her wine. "Your cousin," she said, "has been married before?"

Paul looked up at the ceiling. "Yes," he said. It would be simplest, he felt, to avoid saying too much.

"Just once?" asked Annabelle.

The question was too casually put. **They know,** thought Paul; **they know.**

He affected nonchalance. "Actually, more than once."

"Twice?" said Thérèse.

This was followed by silence.

Paul thought quickly. Technically it would be correct to say that Chloe had been married twice—because she had. She had also been married three times, and then four times, and then . . . But this, he realised, was pure sophistry.

"Five times," said Paul, adding, "I'm sorry to say."

Thérèse let out a brief cry of alarm. "Five times!"

Annabelle pursed her lips. "There are some who make rather a lot of mistakes . . . in this department."

"But five times," repeated Thérèse. "Five times is surely a little bit—how shall I put it?—greedy?"

"There are not enough men to go round," said Annabelle. "And in times of scarcity, to have five husbands is perhaps a little bit . . . just a touch . . . greedy." She looked at Paul anxiously, and then added, "Not that I'm accusing your cousin of greed. Perish the thought."

"Well, you are," said Thérèse bluntly. "And it is, I think. Five husbands—five! When the rest of us struggle to get one."

"And as often as not, that one may not be much good," interjected Annabelle.

Thérèse looked pained. "Exactly," she said. "Philippe, alas, comes to mind in this context." She looked at Paul. "Have I spoken of him before?"

"You may have," answered Paul. "But . . ." He did not want to rake over old coals, and he felt slightly embarrassed to be discussing husbands with these women he barely knew.

"He was a very boring man," Annabelle interjected. "I've met dull men before in my time, but Philippe . . ." She rolled her eyes.

"I regret to say that my sister is right," said Thérèse.

"I'm surprised you married him," said Annabelle. "I wouldn't have."

"And I wouldn't have married Antoine," Thérèse retorted.

"No, possibly not."

They looked at one another, united in regret. Paul tried to think of something to say. **I should not say "Which one was worse?"** he thought.

Thérèse looked out of the window. "Yes," she said, "Philippe was extremely dull. And yet, you know, I had no inkling of it at first. I had no idea—no idea at all."

Annabelle nodded. "That's right. It was only later that she discovered how dull he was."

"Perhaps I should have detected it earlier. I sometimes wonder if I was—"

Annabelle interrupted her. "No, my dear, you mustn't reproach yourself." She turned to Paul. "It was model railways, you see. He concealed his model railways from her to begin with."

Paul struggled to conceal his surprise. "He was a model railway enthusiast?"

"Fanatic," said Thérèse.

"Obsessive," added Annabelle.

Thérèse sighed. "He built model railway systems. It began in a spare room we had, and then he acquired an old storeroom somewhere and set up a system there. He had a few friends who did this. They had a timetable."

"And kept the trains running according to a schedule," explained Annabelle. "The trains ran more or less twenty-four hours a day. One of them was always on duty."

Paul drew in his breath.

"Yes," said Thérèse. "It was that bad."

"I see," said Paul.

"Poor Thérèse," said Annabelle. "How could one compete with that sort of thing?" She answered her own question. "It was impossible—quite impossible."

"I issued him with an ultimatum," Thérèse said. "It was me or the model railways."

There was silence. Eventually Paul said, "I'm very sorry."

"It was for the best," said Thérèse. "These things are often for the best."

"I sometimes wonder if he's happy," said Annabelle.

Thérèse did not hesitate. "He is. He's very happy. For some men, model railways are enough."

"Well," said Paul, "that's something, isn't it?"

"And I'm happy," said Thérèse. She paused,

looking expectantly at her sister. "And there was Antoine."

Paul waited.

"I met Antoine when we were both twenty-two," said Annabelle. "It's too young, that. It didn't used to be, but it is these days."

"Our parents met at about that age," said Thérèse. "They were both students in Paris. It was 1968."

"Ah," said Paul. **"Sous les pavés, la plage."**

Thérèse smiled. "Exactly. 1968."

Annabelle sipped at her wine. "They hated de Gaulle, you know. They thought that he stood for everything that was wrong with the world. Authority. The past."

Her eyes narrowed. "They listened to people like Sartre. Sartre and de Beauvoir. They hung on every word they uttered." She shook her head in disbelief. "Sartre actually idolised Mao. And then, lo and behold, Mao turns out to be a mass murderer, like all the other mass murderers. Stalin. Hitler. Pol Pot."

"Our parents were very naïve," Thérèse remarked. "Babes in the wood."

"It was chic," said Paul. "Mao and Che Guevara. They were symbols of resistance to the tyranny of the middle-aged."

Annabelle looked at him challengingly. "Do the middle-aged perpetuate a tyranny?"

Paul explained that he did not consider it a tyranny himself—but some did.

"Pah!" snorted Annabelle dismissively, and then returned to the subject of Antoine. He had been chronically unfaithful, she said. "He couldn't resist women. He tried, I think, but it was just too much for him. I grew tired of his deceptions."

"You had a terrible time," said Thérèse.

Annabelle shrugged. "There are so many women about whom one would say that."

She looked at Paul, perhaps a bit reproachfully, he thought. **Should I apologise?** he wondered. But Thérèse now said, "And men too."

Paul nodded. "Some men suffer too," he said.

"Possibly," Annabelle conceded. "Possibly." She offered to fill Paul's glass, and he accepted.

Thérèse looked at him over her wine glass. "Your cousin . . ."

"Yes?"

Thérèse exchanged a glance with Annabelle before continuing. It was clear to Paul that whatever was to come had been rehearsed by the two sisters beforehand.

"Your cousin," continued Thérèse, "has become very friendly with Claude. Very close."

Annabelle was watching his reaction.

"I've noticed," he said. "My cousin is . . . well, she enjoys the company of men."

The two Frenchwomen regarded him impassively. Eventually Annabelle said, "The company of men?"

"Yes," said Paul. "There are some women who enjoy that. They like having men friends."

Annabelle looked away. Then, turning to face Paul again, she said, "Young Hugo feels that the situation requires our attention."

Paul frowned. "In what sense?"

Annabelle seemed embarrassed. "He feels that his uncle may be in danger."

It took Paul a few moments to react. Then he laughed. "Oh, I see. He thinks that my cousin has her eye on his uncle? So it's a case of the nephew protecting the uncle from a voracious woman?"

"No," said Thérèse. "From a dangerous woman."

Paul shook his head. "Forgive me," he

said. "It's possible that I don't understand you properly. Sometimes, when you're having a conversation in a foreign language, you don't get things right. This may be happening here. Forgive me. Dangerous? Are you suggesting she's some sort of **femme fatale,** intent on **seducing** Claude? Is that the idea?"

"No," said Annabelle. "We're not suggesting that. It's just that Hugo has uncovered something that raises questions about your cousin's . . . well, raises questions about her identity. She may not be who she claims to be. That's the issue, I'm afraid."

Paul felt the urge to laugh. This was ridiculous. It was perfectly possible that Chloe might be conducting an affair with Claude—after all, she did have form in that respect—but to suggest that she was in some way a threat to the chef seemed to be fanciful, to say the least.

"I can see that you don't believe us," said Thérèse.

Paul smiled. "I admit that my cousin has a bit of a past. But there are plenty of people who have a chequered history when it comes to men—or women. They just do."

Thérèse listened, but was clearly not convinced. "Then why does she have a false passport?" she asked.

Paul looked puzzled.

"Hugo found it," Annabelle said. "It was in a bag in the kitchen. He did not know that the bag belonged to your cousin. He was looking for something else and he came across a passport that appeared to belong to your cousin. It was probably a fake."

Paul was polite. Annabelle's tone had turned accusatory. Yet he was still their guest, and one did not accuse one's guests—or their cousins—of bearing false documents. "May I ask why?"

"Because it had her photograph in it," said Thérèse. "But the name was different. It was not the name she had given earlier on, nor the name on her credit card. They'd seen that, you know. On the credit card she is Mrs. Chloe Jameson. In the passport she is Mrs. Chloe Pangloss. And it was a French passport, by the way."

Paul felt his heart leap. **Pangloss!**

"Yes," said Annabelle. "I'm not surprised that you are astonished. Pangloss is a very unusual name. It's the name of the doctor in **Candide.** But . . ." She hesitated. "It's the name, too, of somebody who lived not far from here a few years ago. A certain Dr. Pangloss."

Paul stared at them mutely.

"Who disappeared," Annabelle continued.

"And was never found," said Thérèse. "Never seen again."

There now followed a period in which nobody said anything. A few minutes after the beginning of this silence, there was a knock, followed by the sound of footsteps in the hall. Thérèse put down her wine glass and went to investigate. A minute or two later she returned, and Audette was at her side, her baby in her arms.

The baby seemed motionless, and Paul gasped with alarm. And then he realised that the infant was clearly awake, and was waving its arms.

"Bleu has returned," blurted out Audette. "He's come back."

12

❧

Griotte Cherry Clafoutis

The dinner with Annabelle and Thérèse had been abruptly cancelled—"suspended" was how Thérèse put it—when Audette had arrived with the news of Bleu's return. Paul did not stay long, as it seemed to him there was no place for him in the ensuing discussion. Thérèse fussed over the baby, Annabelle hovered on the edge of tears, and Audette herself alternated between bouts of vengeful swearing and hysterical sobbing. He was able, though, to put together a picture of what had happened. Bleu, the electricity thief and former lover of Audette, had presented himself at Audette's door that evening, along with a woman called Gigi—a woman of the very worst calibre, said Thérèse, who had seen her photograph in the local paper: a member of a well-known family of pickpockets and

itinerant prostitutes, she was regularly pros-
ecuted for handbag-snatching on the railway
platforms at Poitiers. Bleu, it appeared, was
living with this woman in a caravan parked
in one of the fields of a local alcoholic pig-
farmer. "Fleecing him, no doubt," said
Thérèse. "Plying him with alcohol."

Audette had tried to prevent Bleu from
entering the house, but he and Gigi had
pushed past her.

"They marched right in," she said. "Right
in. Stood there and made their demands."

Annabelle had enquired what these were.

"My baby," said Audette.

This had brought a sharp gasp from
Annabelle. "Kidnapping!"

Thérèse frowned. "Well, not quite. They
didn't take him, did they?"

"No," said Audette. "I wouldn't have let
that happen."

"Good," said Thérèse. "So they went away?"

"Yes."

Annabelle pressed Audette for more information. "Why would they want the baby?"

Audette hesitated before she gave her answer. "He says he is the father."

"Hah!" said Thérèse. "What nonsense."

Audette looked at the floor. Annabelle raised an eyebrow.

"Even if he is the father," said Thérèse, "he would have no right to the child. You are the mother."

"Yes, I'm the mother," said Audette. "But he has been to a lawyer. These people . . . people like him—they have money. They can afford a lawyer. The lawyer told him that if the judge hears that I have been—" She broke off.

Thérèse sighed. "Your prison sentences?"

That was new to Paul. But now nothing would surprise him. Audette nodded. "He said that Bleu would get custody of the child. The lawyer assured him of that."

Annabelle had begun to cry, and Paul, sensing that his continued presence would add little to the evening, had thanked the twins and slipped away. As he left, Thérèse had come out to whisper to him.

"Can you stand by?" she asked.

"Well, yes. Obviously if there's anything I can do . . ." He regretted his words immediately, but he had said them.

"Good," said Thérèse. "I'm worried about

her staying where she is. Not with that man around. The poor girl is terrified."

He understood. "Of course. It must be a nightmare."

"She can stay here tonight, of course," said Thérèse. "We're perfectly happy to look after her—for a night or two."

Paul waited.

Thérèse lowered her voice yet further. "But beyond that . . . The problem, you see, is that Bleu will guess she's with us. After all, her house is in our grounds."

Paul nodded. "Yes, I imagine he'll work that out. But what about the police? Can't you get the police to have a word with him?"

Thérèse raised her hands in despair. "The police? Worse than useless, I'm afraid. They're afraid of those people. They won't touch them."

Paul was shocked. This was France. This was the European Union. This was today. "No?"

"No. France is full of no-go areas, you know. Outsiders don't realise it. This is one. These people—these travellers—pay no taxes, observe no laws, and are left to get on with it by the police. It's easier that way."

Paul was not sure whether to believe her.

Gypsies had always been at the bottom of the social pecking order—accused of any- and everything. Yet could they really operate with such impunity? He doubted it.

"So," continued Thérèse, "I think it might be best if Audette and the baby come to stay with you for a while. Would you mind very much? They'd be much safer, as this Bleu person would not know where they were. They could lie low, so to speak."

Paul opened his mouth to speak, but was interrupted. "It's very kind of you," said Thérèse quickly. "But I'd better get back in there. My sister is very emotional, as you've probably observed." She smiled. "But we love her for all that, don't we? We do."

"But what about Chloe?" he stuttered. "I'm just staying with her. I'm a guest. She's the one you'll need to ask."

Thérèse brushed off his concerns. "She'll be fine. Don't worry about her."

With that, she ushered him out into the dark. As he walked back down the village high street, Paul reflected on the events of the past few days. The peaceful sojourn he had planned in rural France was proving to be anything but that. He had become involved with the affairs of a failing, if not failed, restaurant; he had convinced himself of the futility of a project for which he had already signed a contract; and now he had agreed—or it had **been agreed**—that he would look after a woman and baby on the run from a psychopath. And, to add to the mixture, having only recently exonerated Chloe from suspicion, he had now discovered that his fears about her had some foundation. If she was Mrs. Pangloss after all, then why had she denied it? And who was the Dr. Pangloss who had disappeared so mysteriously? Suddenly it occurred to Paul that those who have spouse after spouse have sometimes been known to dispose of them.

The thought sent a chill up his spine. Was he sharing a house with a woman who had been responsible for disposing of a husband? Where? In a quarry, perhaps? There were disused quarries nearby—he had seen them—and he had noticed that one of them was filled with water. He had walked past it and peered down into its green depths. Oddly enough, at the time it had crossed his mind that this was exactly the sort of place where a killer might choose to dump a victim. Wrapped in chains, or lead weights, or whatever it was that such people used to dispose of their victims, a corpse would sink in the sure and certain knowledge of never being disturbed. Was this the watery grave of Dr. Pangloss?

With Chloe still in the restaurant, the house was in darkness when he returned, a dark shape, crouching upon the earth; the bushes shadows; the horizon a distant line where the land merged with a sky to which a few stars, and the stronger planets, added pinpricks of light.

He knew it was irrational—that a house at night was no more than a darkened version of a house by day. But now, as he let himself in the front door, he felt a stab of fear. His life in Edinburgh had been an ordered, secure one in which concern for safety played no part at all. The world into which Chloe had taken him was different: this was a place of real conflict, it seemed, where things might go unpredictably and badly wrong.

He reached for the switch beside the front door. This was the switch that would turn on the lights in the hall and in the corridor beyond. With those illuminated, he could light the kitchen and, if he chose, the court-yard at the rear of the house. He thought he might put as many lights on as possible, to dispel these ridiculous fears of his.

The switch did not work. He tried it again, to no effect. Making his way into the dark-ness of the hall, he crossed to where he knew he would find a table lamp. Feeling for the switch on this, he flicked it into the on posi-tion. Nothing happened.

Paul stood quite still. They had been warned about power cuts, but he had been told that they tended not to last very long. They were, it was said, on a different, older circuit from many of the other houses in the village, and therefore they might lose electricity when others still had it. Peering out of the win-dow, he saw now that this was exactly what seemed to be happening: across the fields, on the other side of the village, lights blazed from the windows of several houses.

It did not take long for Paul to make up his mind. He would go to the restaurant and warn Chloe about the power cut. He would then wait there until he could accompany

her back to the house. She had said something about candles, but he had no idea
where they were. She could find them.

He left the house, feeling somewhat relieved to be out of it. Then, walking as briskly
as he could, but resisting the temptation to
break into a run, he made his way back across
the village to La Table de St. Vincent.

There were very few people in the restaurant. Claude, in a waiter's apron, was conversing with the diners at one of the tables,
while the others busied themselves with their
meals. From a quick glance round the room,
Paul formed the impression that in spite of
the empty tables, things were going well—
Chloe's intervention, whatever it was, was
clearly having its effect.

Claude smiled at him and indicated with a
toss of the head that Chloe was to be found
in the kitchen. Paul went through the swing
door, to see Chloe and Hugo bending over
a baking tray. Hugo looked up and smiled
warmly. "Clafoutis," he announced. "Griotte
Cherry Clafoutis. About to be served for the
first time."

"And it's superb," said Chloe. "Here, taste
a tiny slice."

Paul inspected the soft flan. He noted the red juice of the cherries seeping out into the surrounding mixture, just as it should do in a good clafoutis. He commented on the fact, and Hugo beamed with pleasure.

"You've been doing all the cooking tonight?" Paul asked. "What about Uncle?" He nodded in the direction of the dining room.

Chloe answered on Hugo's behalf. "Claude has been very happy looking after the front of house," she said. "And doing the waiting."

Paul smiled at Hugo. The young man was looking at him with bright, expectant eyes. "So you've done everything back here?"

Hugo bit his lip. "I hope it's been all right."

"They looked happy out there," said Paul. "You can always tell."

Chloe now passed him a slice of the clafoutis. Paul tasted it, and looked appreciatively at Hugo. "Where did you pick that up?"

The young man squirmed with pleasure. "I read about it. I used Joël Robuchon's recipe. He used it at the Jamin."

Paul smiled. "Robuchon? You know that I met him once?"

Hugo's eyes widened. "You met him? You talked to him?"

"Yes. He was . . . well, he was like anybody else, I suppose. Very down to earth. Very helpful. He wore the tricolour on the collar of his chef's tunic."

"Very patriotic," said Chloe. Turning to Hugo, she said, "And the other dessert, Hugo. Tell Paul about that."

Hugo gestured to a large dish in which several light concoctions had been placed. Each looked like a tiny, circular mousse, topped with foam. "Marcona Almond Cream," he said proudly. "I've made eight, and so I hope that some people will go for the clafoutis."

Paul examined the desserts.

"You could try one," said Hugo. "Please try one."

"And then there'll be seven," said Paul.

"I want you to." There was something pleading about the young man's tone. Paul glanced at him; the young chef was looking at him almost with longing. **Had anybody ever been nice to this boy?** Paul found himself thinking.

He reached for a spoon. "What are the ingredients?" he asked.

"Almond paste, sugar, yoghurt, cream, and gelatin sheets."

"Ah, gelatin. It keeps everything together."

Hugo nodded. "I love using it. I'd put it on everything if I could."

"Stick to the rules," said Paul. "And one of those rules is: never add another ingredient. Take things away, but never add to a recipe."

Hugo looked anxious. "Always?"

"Always," affirmed Paul.

He tasted the almond cream, licking the spoon clean. Hugo watched him attentively, waiting for the verdict.

"Transcendent," said Paul.

Hugo frowned. "Which means?"

"Which means that it's better than everything," said Chloe. "It leaps over everything."

"Really?" asked Hugo.

"Yes," said Paul. "That's what it means. Well done, Hugo."

He turned to Chloe. "There's bad news," he said.

Chloe listened in silence as he told her of the evening's events. As he reached the end of his account, she started to untie her apron. "I shall have to go and see what's going on," she said. "Paul, can you stay and help Hugo with the rest of the evening?"

Paul shrugged. "I suppose so. We still have Claude."

"No," said Chloe. "I think that Claude will probably want to come with me."

"We'll be all right," said Hugo. "There aren't many guests. We'll be all right."

"There you are," said Chloe. "You stay, Paul. Claude and I shall go and see what's happening." She paused. "He will be very upset."

The last of the diners left. There were effusive remarks. "I've been here before," said one. "People have said . . . well, they've not been particularly complimentary."

"That's putting it mildly," said another.

"They called it the second—"

Hugo interrupted. "The second-worst restaurant in France. Yes, I know. But we try, you know."

"It isn't," said one of the diners. "Not now. Definitely not."

Back in the kitchen, Paul helped Hugo to stack the remaining plates in the dishwasher and to soak the pans. Claude and Chloe had not returned, and so it would be left to the two of them to close up for the night.

Hugo had not eaten and was hungry, as was Paul.

"I could make an omelette," he said. "It's the best thing to have late at night. It's easy on the stomach."

"Perfect," said Paul.

"Mushrooms? Cheese, with some truffle?"

"I can't resist truffles," said Paul.

"Then it will be truffle," said Hugo, reaching for a jar from a shelf.

Paul watched as the young chef prepared the omelette, shaving the truffle onto the fluffy surface of the egg. There was a deftness to his movements, a confidence, that told him that his earlier instinct had been correct: this was a natural cook.

They sat down at the small table near the kitchen window. Hugo had produced a bottle of wine, and had poured a glass for Paul and one for himself. "Chinon," he said. "One of my favourites."

Paul raised the glass to his nose. "Yes," he said. "Yes."

"Tuffeau limestone," said Hugo, and

304 The Second-Worst Restaurant in France

then, as if embarrassed at his knowledge, added, "The soil, you see. It makes the wine like this."

"It's good that you know these things, Hugo," said Paul. "You don't have to apologise. Not to me."

"You're the one who knows. You've written all these books."

"I know for a short time." Paul laughed. "Then I forget. A real chef remembers in his bones." He raised his glass to Hugo. "To La Table de Saint Vincent—and its distinguished future."

Hugo cast his eyes down. "If there is one."

"There should be."

Hugo was looking at him intently, as if there was something more that he wanted to say. He had not begun to eat his omelette.

"Don't let that get cold," said Paul.

"No, I won't."

But he did not lift his knife and fork.

"Anything wrong?" asked Paul.

Hugo shook his head. Then he said, his words half mumbled, "When are you going back to Scotland?"

Paul shrugged. "I haven't decided. Perhaps in a month or two."

Hugo lowered his gaze. "A month or two," he echoed, with regret. He paused, and then, lifting up his fork, he plunged it into the omelette. It was a gesture of disappointment; it was the way in which an omelette would be attacked by one who was not happy with the world.

"I have a life to lead at home," said Paul. "I have to work, you know."

"You could work here."

"In France?"

"Yes. Right here." Hugo made a gesture that encompassed the whole kitchen. "We could run this place. We could make something really great of it." He hesitated. "Together. You and me. Without Uncle. He's lost interest."

Paul began to laugh before he realised that laughter was not the right response. Hugo was entirely serious. He stopped himself. "I'm sorry."

"I meant what I said."

"I know you did," said Paul, quickly. "And I shouldn't have laughed."

"Then why not?"

"Because I have a life elsewhere." He paused. "And because I think you could do this by yourself. You could, you know."

Hugo looked at Paul in disbelief. "Me? Run this place?"

"Why not?"

"Do you think I could?"

Paul smiled. "I think you have the makings of a great chef."

Hugo said nothing for a few moments. Then he asked, "Do you really think I could?"

Paul said he did think that.

"But Uncle?"

"Let's see what happens," said Paul.

13

✦

Stranger Things Have Happened

When Paul made his way into the kitchen the next morning, Chloe was already up. She had brewed coffee and the smell of the freshly ground beans wafted over from the stove. Paul sniffed at the air appreciatively. He glanced towards the window, under which the morning sun was basting the flagstones with buttery yellow. This was the difference, he thought; this was the difference between France and home, between this place, with its soft southern sunshine, and Scotland, with its attenuated, pale blue light. Scotland seemed so far away—in every sense. It had its moments, of course—everywhere did; but they were radically different from the French drama into which he had wandered—or been thrust, perhaps. He glanced at Chloe; if he had not had that lunch with her back in Edinburgh, then he would not have found himself here, immersed in this full-dress rural opera. He smiled at the thought. We imagined that we planned our lives; but we did not, or only rarely. We felt our way through them. We lurched. Our lives were not like a Swiss railway timetable—ordered, predictable, and running along predetermined lines. Our lives were . . . the metaphor escaped him, and he sniffed at the coffee again. **Time to smell the coffee . . .** Or was it roses?

Chloe looked at him in a businesslike way. "Everything is arranged," she said. "You were asleep when I came back last night. I didn't want to wake you."

"I helped to tidy things up at the restaurant. I was tired."

"Yes, of course."

He thought he should apologise. "Thérèse asked me about Audette's coming here," he said. "She presented it as a **fait accompli,** I'm afraid. I told her she'd have to ask you, but she was in full flow. I'm not sure that she took it in."

Chloe was unconcerned. "Oh, she asked. Well, sort of. Some people ask in such a way as to make it impossible to say anything but yes. It's what I call an ask-demand."

"She made an ask-demand?"

Chloe chuckled. "Of the most classic variety. But there we are. **Ibi sumus,** as my Latin teacher used to say—if I had a Latin teacher, which I can't quite remember. There was somebody who was described as the Latin teacher, but I'm not sure that she actually taught any Latin. She was very fond of putting her arm about you—quite respectably, of course—and saying, 'You must read Catullus one day, my dear. He wrote such charming love poems.' Such teachers are so **inspirational,** aren't they?"

"Times have changed, Chloe."

"Of course they have. You don't have to tell me that, Paul." She gave Paul a disapproving look, as if he, single-handed, had been responsible for a seismic shift in social mores. "There are so few inspirational teachers left, aren't there? They're all busy filling in forms and meeting targets and so on. And fending off their ill-disciplined charges." She paused for long enough to shoot another disapproving look in Paul's direction. "Do you realise, Paul, how much teachers have to put up with these days? Do you realise that the children actually swear at them? And then the teachers are told not to respond because it's elitist—elitist!—to discourage everyday language. The view is taken that if that is how people talk, then that is how they talk. It's not for us to tell others how to express themselves."

Paul sighed. "Stupidity."

"Stupidity on stilts, Paul!" Now she frowned. "That was Bentham, wasn't it? Or John Stuart Mill? I confuse the two of them—I always have. Those two and Epicurus. For some reason I think of Epicurus as being in their company, but he wasn't really, was he?"

"You were thinking of Jeremy Bentham," said Paul. "And he said **Nonsense on stilts** about natural rights."

Chloe nodded. "Oh well, there you are. And he's the one they keep in a cupboard at UCL, isn't he? Have you seen him?"

Paul had. He had been taken to the cupboard by a friend at the university, who had pointed out the wax head placed on the actual skeleton of the philosopher. The clothes, stuffed with hay, gave shape to the bones. "They take him to faculty meetings," the friend had explained, "and record him as being present but not voting. It's bizarre, but they consider it great fun. You know how odd the English are."

"We shouldn't be talking about Bentham," said Chloe. "We should be talking about Audette and the baby, since they are coming to stay in . . ." She looked at her watch. "In exactly thirty minutes—if they're punctual, which they won't be."

"Has the baby got a name?" asked Paul.

"He's called Aramis, apparently."

"One of the Three Musketeers—remember? Athos, Porthos, and Aramis. I loved that story as a boy."

Chloe waved a hand airily. "It meant less to me. In fact, it meant nothing. But that's what the baby's called—somewhat surprisingly. I don't immediately associate Audette with French literature. Or any literature, for that matter."

Paul thought of something. "There's a perfume of that name, isn't there? **Aramis.** You see it at airports, in the duty-free."

"So there is," said Chloe. She poured herself a cup of coffee, topping it up with milk she had heated on the stove. "Milky, white, not all that hot—**café au lait,** or is it a **café noisette**? Or do they say **caffè latte,** like everybody else? It's so confusing, Paul—life, that is."

"**Café au lait** is coffee with lots of warm milk," said Paul. "And **café noisette** is coffee with lots of milk, but maybe not quite so much. It's meant to look the colour of a hazelnut."

"And you needed a bowl for **café au lait**?"

"Traditionally," said Paul. "And it was really for breakfast."

"This is such a wonderful country," said Chloe. "What can we do but admire a culture that encourages people to sit in pavement cafés and drink milky coffee from bowls."

"Audette and Aramis," Paul reminded her.

"Yes. Them. Well." Chloe became business-like once more. "We must give them sanctuary. They are Mary and the blessed infant seeking a stable. We cannot turn them away. And this wicked Bleu, this **voleur d'électricité,** is Herod—on the rampage. We shall not allow him to find our little family."

Paul looked at Chloe in astonishment. "There are some analogies one should not push too far," he said.

"Oh, Paul, don't take me so literally. We

are **Homo ludens** as well as **sapiens,** remember. We must have our fun."

He thought: **And our deceptions, or,
perhaps, our fantasies, Mrs. Pangloss?**

"I've already prepared a room for them,"
Chloe continued. "It's the one next door
to yours. I've put out the towels and bowls
and things that will undoubtedly be needed.
Babies require such a large support system,
don't they? Endless bottles and pads and dis-
infectants and the like. The room looks to
all intents and purposes like a hospital ward."

Paul was thinking of the implications of
having a baby living in the next-door room.
"How long will they be staying?" He added
hurriedly, "Not that they're unwelcome."

Chloe shrugged. "I suspect that they will
be here for a few days. By then the danger
should have receded, I hope."

Paul thought that unduly optimistic.
"What about the lawyer? What about his
custody claim? Those things grind on and
on. They take ages. That means that our
friend Bleu will be here for some time."

Chloe conceded that the law moved slowly,
but seemed unconcerned. "True, he might
prove tenacious, even if his legal claim is

weak. However, that might not be too much of a danger for us. Bleu might have bitten off more than he can chew."

"I don't see that."

"Bleu might find it necessary to make himself scarce," Chloe said. "He might think it wiser to move on—**sans Aramis,** which one might translate, roughly, of course, as **unperfumed.**"

Paul blinked at the joke. "You're very clever, Chloe," he said.

"Thank you. It was just a thought—a little wordplay to relieve us of the gloom that might otherwise descend. Levity, you know, is always the best cure for gloom. A spot of levity and the clouds lift—usually quite miraculously."

"But why would he move on?"

Chloe, who had been standing near the window during this exchange, now sat down at the pine table that dominated the centre of the kitchen. "Because," she said, "there are times when people like that encounter, well, people like that. And they don't like it."

Paul struggled to make sense of this. "I'm sorry, I don't quite . . ."

Chloe raised a hand. "It's best not to

discuss these things too much, Paul. That's what I've learned in my career."

Paul frowned. "Learned in what career?"

Chloe ignored this, but Paul continued, "What career, Chloe? You've never spoken about a career."

Chloe turned to look at him directly. Her voice became colder. "Don't underestimate me, Paul. And don't condescend, either. Women don't like male condescension."

"I'm not condescending," Paul replied. "And I certainly don't underestimate you. I was just wondering what you meant by 'my career.' You never said anything about it." He did not say what he was thinking—which was that having that many husbands could in itself amount to a career. He assumed she did not mean that.

"Sometimes we sound metaphorical, Paul. Surely you know that. We live by metaphors." Her voice had become warm again— almost coquettish. And what other woman, Paul said to himself, could sound coquettish when talking about metaphor?

"So **career** is a synonym for **life,**" said Paul.

"It could be," agreed Chloe. "Or possibly not. It's contextual, I should say."

Paul took a sip of his coffee. "Oh well."

"My thoughts exactly," said Chloe. "Oh well." She put down her cup and wiped her lips with the corner of a handkerchief. "The plan, Paul, is as follows. They—that is, Audette and **le petit Aramis**—come here. Annabelle and Thérèse will provide back-up. They'll cook and so on while I go off to Paris for a few days. I shall take Claude with me."

Paul was unprepared for this. Chloe had said nothing about Paris. "What? You're going off?"

"Yes," said Chloe. "It is necessary for me to go up to Paris for a brief visit. I shall not be away for any longer than is necessary."

"But in the middle of all this?" Paul protested. "Do you have to? Can't you go when things are a bit more settled?"

Chloe's reply was brief and unambiguous. "No. Can't." Then she went on. "And since Claude will be away too, do you think that you could possibly help Hugo in the restaurant? You two will have a lot of fun." She paused, but only for a few seconds, before continuing. "That's so kind of you, Paul. You really are a very kind man, you know."

She was concerned about his book. "Of

course, you shouldn't forget that you're writing a book. Don't let that slip."

"**Was** writing one," said Paul.

He told Chloe of his decision to abandon
The Philosophy of Food. "The whole thing
was inauthentic. I didn't really believe—"

"Let me stop you there," said Chloe.
"You're absolutely right to abandon the whole
thing. If you feel inauthentic, then the book's
inauthentic—beyond a shadow of doubt."

"I haven't told them yet," said Paul. The
thought appalled him. He would have to
speak to Gloria, and she had already arranged matters with the publisher; all of that
would have to be unstitched. What would
she think? What had Gloria done to deserve
all that?

" 'Them'?"

"My editor, Gloria. She'll tell the publishers."

"Because you can't face them?"

Paul felt miserable. Chloe was right; it was
cowardice that was preventing his telling the
publisher that **The Philosophy of Food**
would never be. "I know what I have to do,"
he said. "And I shall do it. I'll e-mail Gloria
later today."

"Phone," said Chloe.

He looked at her. She had no right to tell him what to do. What was wrong with breaking the news to Gloria by e-mail? He silently posed the question, and immediately answered it himself. E-mail was the easy way out. Talking directly to somebody was more morally courageous than merely sending a message.

"You're right," he said. "I'll call her. It would be . . ."

"More courteous."

He nodded his assent.

"When?" she asked.

"This afternoon," he began. But Chloe had produced her mobile telephone from the pocket of her jeans and passed it to him.

Gloria was slow to answer and Paul was about to ring off—not without relief—when she eventually picked up the phone. She seemed pleased to hear from him. "I've been thinking about you," she said.

He had been thinking about her too, he reflected. Not constantly, as one may think about a lover, but certainly every day, at odd hours and unexpected times. He did not say this, but said instead, "Me too."

This seemed to please her. "I meant to phone you. I'm sorry."

"Me too."

There was a brief silence, during which Chloe looked expectantly at Paul. Then Gloria said, "The book? Is everything going well?"

There was another silence.

"Paul?"

"Yes, I'm still here. France is still here. The book . . ."

"Is there a problem?"

"You might say that."

Silence.

"Paul?"

He took a deep breath. "I don't want to write it. I hate it. I hate **The Philosophy of Food.** It's rubbish."

From the other side of the room, Chloe raised an eyebrow.

Then Gloria said, "Well, it's funny you should say that, because you know what? I never liked the idea."

Paul stopped her. "What? You never liked it? Never?"

"Yes, yes," said Gloria. "I know I encouraged you, but that was because **you** wanted to write it, and it seemed to me that I should support you in what you wanted to do. And then when I went to the publishers they said 'Great idea,' but I could tell that they weren't **thinking** 'Great idea.' "

"You could tell?"

"Yes. When people say 'Great idea' in a flat sort of way you know that they don't think it's a great idea. English is more of a tonal language than we think, Paul."

Paul felt a great surge of relief. Chloe, who could hear much of this, made a thumbs-up sign.

"So, you want to call off?" asked Gloria. "Because it seems to me that nobody wants **The Philosophy of Food.** You don't. I don't. The publishers don't. And that leaves the public."

"They don't want it," said Paul. "You develop a sort of sixth sense about what will run and what won't. And my sixth sense tells me that the public thinks: **The Philosophy of Food? No, bad idea.** That's what the public is thinking, Gloria."

Gloria agreed. "What the public wants is books about French people eating really nice food. They like to read about that, and they like to see that on television."

Paul looked up at the ceiling as he spoke. "Television?"

"Yes. We've had an approach. The people who did your last series. Some of them have hived off and started a new company to make documentaries and so on. The usual stuff. Anyway, they—these hived-off people—have been in touch with me about you."

"About me?"

"Yes. They were very polite about you, actually. They said that the ratings for your last series were pretty good and now it's being rebroadcast all over the place. Lots of repeat fees, Paul. Lots."

"And?"

"And they said, 'Do you think Paul might be interested in doing something about French people eating nice food?' Well, those weren't their actual words, of course, but that was the gist of it. So I said, 'He might be—I can ask. At the moment he's writing a book about the philosophy of food.' And you know what, Paul? There was a long silence . . . That didn't press the right button with them. But they said, 'Come back to us if he changes his mind.' And I said I would."

Paul said nothing for a few moments. His thoughts were inchoate, but rapid.

"Paul?"

"Yes, I'm thinking. I've had an idea, Gloria."

"Oh good. That's what we need, Paul. Ideas . . ."

"No, just listen. How about . . . how about a television series that follows the progress of a young man—a really good-looking young chef—not me, of course, but a young Frenchman called Hugo, for instance—who works in this really awful restaurant run by his uncle."

"Called?"

"The uncle would be called Claude. And I would be there, but only in the background, as narrator, so to speak. Anyway, this restaurant they have is failing badly. People are calling it the second-worst restaurant in France."

"No! That could be the title of the series. **The Second-Worst Restaurant in France.**"

"It could be. So we follow the fortunes of this young chef and his efforts to pull the place up by its bootstraps. We go to market with him and see all the . . ."

"Mushrooms," said Gloria. "People love looking at mushrooms on television. Put a mushroom into anything and the ratings go north. No, I'm not joking. I heard that from somebody. They said everybody in television knows that."

"All right. The camera lingers on the mushrooms. And Hugo picks up mushrooms and sniffs at them. The viewers will love that. And then we see him in the kitchen making a dessert, perhaps. A clafoutis."

"What's that?"

"It's a sort of flan. You put cherries in it and the cherry juice seeps out into the flanny bit."

"Oh my God, Paul. I can see that, I can see the juice seeping out."

"Can you? All right. They'll love that. Then we see him tasting the clafoutis. Putting it into his mouth . . ."

"His mouth?"

"Yes. And then we see the diners in the restaurant and hear what they have to say. Maybe we learn a bit more about them.

Where they come from, and so on. We see Hugo discussing the dishes with them. And so on, and so on, until the inspector from Michelin drops by and says, 'You're not doing too badly, young man.'"

"Oh, Paul, this is good. Really good. They'll leap at it. I know they will. And there'll be the book to accompany the series. You can do that, can't you? I take it you actually want to write this one."

He told her he did.

"In that case, Paul, we're in business." She paused. "But Paul, can you actually instruct the Michelin people to drop by? If this is a proper documentary we can't use actors, you know."

"This will be real, Gloria. Authentic. And no, you can't instruct the Michelin people to do anything. We'll just have to hope."

"Because that would be a great ending, wouldn't it? A Michelin rosette."

"Stranger things have happened," said Paul.

14

⚜

France, France

Aramis arrived in a Moses basket that was elaborately decorated with antique Normandy lace. This lace had been retrieved from an attic by Thérèse, washed, ironed, and lovingly tacked around the edge of the basket. In addition to the basket, there were bundles of sheets and towelling, and a whole box of soaps, lotions, and bottles of various descriptions. Paul watched as the house that he and Chloe had been occupying so comfortably was converted into an infant's caravanserai. Annabelle and Thérèse were clearly in charge, directing Audette, who seemed to accept their authority meekly and without question. They showed her the room she would occupy; they demonstrated how the eccentric taps in the bathroom preferred to be operated; they identified the cupboards in the kitchen in which she could stack her stolen food, relegating some of Chloe's provisions to a back shelf in the process; they pointed out where, in the garden, she might sit and not be observed by anybody from the village.

"Nobody need know you're here," said Thérèse, "as long as you don't go out. Paul can go to the village for you, if you need anything. You can do that, can't you, Paul."

Paul did not object. And nor did Chloe, who might have been expected to be bemused—at the least—by the way in which the house that she had, after all, rented was being taken over, mid-lease, by its owners. She was preoccupied, though, with her own plans, which involved, Paul noted, lengthy and somewhat furtive telephone conversations. She gave no explanation for these, and Paul did not presume to ask. Nothing was being revealed about her trip to Paris, although Claude, who appeared shortly after Audette had moved in, was given a full briefing in the courtyard. Paul watched him being spoken to by Chloe, and saw the nodding of his head in agreement, and other signs of his thraldom.

"Is Claude driving you to Paris?" Paul asked.

"He is," said Chloe.

He waited for her to venture more information.

"You couldn't have gone by train?"

She shook her head. "Not this time," she said.

By ten o'clock Chloe was ready. The car was packed and a picnic, prepared by Claude, was loaded. Annabelle and Thérèse were still fussing over Audette and Artemis, and Paul, having waved goodbye to Chloe and Claude as they made their way down the drive, set off for the restaurant. He had spoken to Hugo on the phone and had promised him that he would be available for preparations for both lunch and dinner. Hugo had found a friend to help out as waiter, leaving Paul free to help him in the kitchen. They would go to the market at Montmorillon, too, before they started getting ready for lunch.

Hugo was in the kitchen when Paul arrived. Several books, annotated and stained, in the way of well-used recipe books, were open on the table. He greeted Paul effusively, pointing to one of the recipes in front of him.

"This will do for tonight," he said. "If

we can get good artichokes and some sheep's-milk cheese. What do you think, Monsieur Paul?"

Paul looked at the recipe. It was elaborate, by any standards. He glanced at the book's title page. "Escoffier?"

Hugo nodded. "I bought it from a book dealer. He said it had belonged to a well-known chef. You'll see the notes on the sides—and the dates he made some of the dishes." His finger went to a cluster of pencilled notes in the margin. "You see. March fourth, 1938. July third, 1939. And then nothing until 1946."

Paul gazed at the tiny handwriting. There had been a war. Rations must have been tight, even in the natural larder of France. Food had been commandeered to feed Germany.

"It's hard to imagine now," he said.

"What is?"

"Occupation. Or Vichy. Being frightened. Being hungry." He flicked a page. "Particularly being frightened."

He looked at Hugo. He looked at his bright eyes. Something made him ask, "Have you been frightened, Hugo?"

The young man moved away from the

table. He opened a window, busying himself with the tasks of preparing the kitchen. "Me? Frightened?"

"Yes."

Hugo hesitated. He looked outside, past the fringe of creeper intruding upon the window; past the sign that said **La Table de St. Vincent.** "Possibly. Now and then. But who isn't?"

"Hardly anybody," answered Paul. "Well, there may be a few big heroes here and there. But most of us . . . no, we've been frightened at some stage of our lives."

"Yes," said Hugo. "We have."

"And then we discover that we don't need to be frightened. We switch on a light, you could say, and the light shows us that there was nothing to be frightened about."

Hugo was silent. Paul saw that he was fiddling with the strap of his watch. He met the young man's gaze and held it.

"So," Paul continued. "Who is it, Hugo? Who are you frightened of? Your uncle? Is that it?"

The corner of Hugo's mouth twitched. It was all the confirmation Paul needed.

"Why don't you speak to him?"

Hugo shook his head. "No. I can't. All my life he's been trying to make me something that I'm not. I can't go and tell him now. Not now."

"You can't tell him to his face that you don't want to be like him?"

Hugo nodded.

"You can't tell him now that you don't want to have anything to do with his hunting, and all that outdoors stuff? Or his politics?"

Again there was mute confirmation.

"You can, you know. Or, if you like . . ." Paul had not thought it through, but he pressed on. "If you like, I can speak to him. Sometimes it's easier that way." He paused. "Sometimes other people can do the things that we find it too hard to do."

Hugo took a step backwards, and for a moment Paul thought he was going to run away. But then he stood still. He wiped his hands on the apron he was wearing. Then he examined them.

"All right. If you don't mind. But . . ." His voice betrayed his anxiety. "But what are you going to say to him?"

"To let you go. To let you be yourself."

"He won't do that."

"I think he might. I suspect that he actually loves you, you know, but has an odd way of showing it. I think he also needs to let himself go. He needs to . . ."

". . . stop trying to cook," Hugo interjected, and then grinned. Paul laughed.

Hugo drove Paul to the market in his small van. They wandered along the stalls, gradually filling the two large bags they had brought with them. At one stall that sold mushrooms, Paul asked Hugo to pick one or two out of the tray and sniff at them. "I'd like to take a photograph of you doing that," he said.

"Like this?"

"Just like that. Perfect."

Over coffee, their provisions bought, he sent the image to Gloria. **Here we are,** he wrote in the accompanying text. **This is Hugo, and this is a mushroom in the Montmorillon market. What do you think?**

The reply came quickly. **Perfect mushroom. Perfect young man. Love, G.**

"What are you doing?" asked Hugo.

"I'm writing to my editor," Paul explained. "And by the way, Hugo, what would you say to being part of a story?"

Hugo shrugged. "I don't mind, I suppose. You'd like to use me in one of your books?"

"Yes, as the main character. It would be a story about the second-worst restaurant in France and how it's transformed into one of the best restaurants in the country. It'll be a sort of rags-to-riches story—for restaurants."

Hugo smiled. "With a happy ending?"

"Of course."

"Then that's fine with me."

Paul reached out to shake his hand.

It was three days before Chloe and Claude returned from Paris. It was a time of unremitting hard work for Paul. In the mornings he accompanied Hugo to market or to one of the farms from whom he bought supplies directly. There were trips to the **charcutier** and to a cheesemaker who lived at the end of a remote and inaccessible track. In the afternoons, once lunch was served, he helped him prepare the evening menu. Hugo knew more than Paul had imagined he would, and he found himself learning as much from the young man as Hugo learned from him.

The day before Chloe returned, they went to the market together earlier than usual. There were things to be had, Hugo explained, that disappeared quickly. In particular, the oyster van would not stay long, and if you did not get there early you might miss the best of the oysters. And the same thing went for some of the green vegetables. "They put the best out at the beginning," Hugo said. "They know that the people who go to market early know what they're looking for. The best. You'll see."

They parked outside one of the churches above the town square, and walked down the narrow street that wound its way towards the river. Although it was barely eight o'clock, the town was already active. In the square, most of the stalls were already erected, and the traders were busy covering trestle tables with the day's offerings. Paul spotted the oyster van, an ancient Citroën with a pull-down panel on one side. This provided a surface on which large trays of ice had been laid out. The oysters were displayed on these like little dishes with corrugated edges.

They bought a cup of coffee from one of the cafés before they began on their purchases. The smell of the coffee mingled with that of freshly baked bread from the **boulangerie** next door. Paul closed his eyes and remembered how he had sat in his kitchen back in Edinburgh with just such a cup of coffee before him, and had tried to be mindful, as his friend had recommended. That seemed like a long time ago—in a place that seemed very far away. Now he closed his eyes again, just for a few moments, and filled his lungs as deeply as he could. Coffee, bread, a whiff of diesel fumes from a passing vehicle, stone, the river . . . a palette of smells that, if called up later, would bring him unerringly back to this moment, standing in the coffee bar, close to the door, and feeling the sun now on his face.

Hugo had finished his coffee and was agitating to go. Paul drained the last few drops from his cup and replaced it on the counter. The woman behind the bar smiled and nodded.

They had jointly made a list, and they worked through it in order. The last item, after the oysters, was olive oil.

"There's a place on the other side of the bridge," Hugo said. "They only sell olive oil. But wait until you taste it."

"Good?"

"It's the best. The best you can get in France. Italy's another matter. I don't know much about their oil, although I know it's pretty good."

"I can tell you about all that," said Paul. "I tried hundreds of their Tuscan oils last year. Well, not hundreds, but a lot. The Tuscan ones are the best. They're the lightest."

Paul noticed that Hugo was looking wistful. He regretted mentioning his familiarity with Tuscany. To those who had never gone anywhere—and he presumed Hugo was one such—the mention of elsewhere might simply emphasise the limits of their world.

"It's Provence for us," said Hugo. "You can always tell." Then he added, "I've never been there."

"You've plenty of time," said Paul.

"It's hard to leave."

Of course; of course. The father. The accident.

Then Hugo said, "They'd like to meet you, you know—my people. They know all about you. That's what the village is like, of course. Everybody knows everything." He paused. "We could go there after this."

"I'd like that."

And now, confronted with rows of bottles of olive oil, they dipped small fragments of bread into tasting dishes. Hugo seemed to know the man who was attending the stall and he replied at some length to his queries about the health of his father. Paul concentrated on his tasting.

The man turned to Paul. "You know where that's from, monsieur?"

Paul shook his head. "I'm not an expert."

The man smiled. "You could spend a whole lifetime becoming an expert on olive oil. And even then, you'd not have the time to taste half of them."

He reached for an unlabelled bottle of oil and poured a small amount into a spoon. "Here," he said, passing the spoon to Paul. "Try this one."

Paul noticed the colour. "It's very dark," he said.

"As it should be," said the man.

Paul raised the spoon to sniff at it.

"Pepper?" said the man.

Yes, there was pepper. And something else. Dust? The sky? Heat?

"The trees are very old," said the man. "You won't get that from new trees."

Paul took a sip of the oil. He shut his lips and allowed the oil to move around within his mouth, coating it with . . . He tried to place the taste, and eventually alighted on artichoke.

"Precisely," said the man. "Well done, monsieur. That's exactly what I get from that oil myself. Artichoke."

"You see," said Hugo. "You see. You've only been with us for a short time, and you're becoming an expert."

"Beginner's luck," said Paul.

"Ah, you're too modest, monsieur. You've been singled out by somebody." The man pointed skywards. "They decide up there who will be able to appreciate olive oil as it should be. It's not up to us at all."

"We should take some of that stuff," said Hugo. "Four litres."

"Les Mées," said the man. "That's where that's from. The cultivar's pure Aglandau olives. From the plains. Oils from a hill are different."

"They're clearer," said Hugo. "The hill oils are much clearer. It's the soil."

The stallholder was impressed. "You know what you're talking about, young man," he said.

Paul noticed how the compliment seemed to boost Hugo. Claude had crushed him, he thought; he might not have meant to, but the older man must not understand that although people might be guided in a particular direction, they should not be forced. There was a fragility about Hugo that meant that he needed encouragement. Claude had thought, perhaps, that this fragility might be buttressed by exposure to male outdoor pursuits; but he was wrong. It needed something far subtler than that.

They went straight back to the restaurant to offload their purchases and prepare lunch. There were few customers, and they were able to spend more time than usual preparing the dishes.

"How does your uncle Claude prepare his oysters?" asked Paul.

Hugo shrugged. "He opens them. Takes them out and then heats them under the grill."

Paul winced. "That's all?"

"He puts garlic on them. Quite a lot of garlic."

Paul winced again. "Would you like me to show you?"

Hugo looked keen. "Of course."

Paul asked him if he knew how to make a **béchamel.** Hugo did, although he said that his uncle rarely bothered. He had a ready-mix version that came frozen in bags. "He uses that," he said. "It doesn't taste good."

"It should be a criminal offence," muttered Paul.

Hugo laughed. "He's always talking about law and order."

"Let's make our **béchamel** and then take it from there," said Paul. "We'll add cream and cheese."

"Gruyère?" asked Hugo.

Paul looked surprised. "You know how to make a Mornay?"

"I've read about it. I've hardly ever done it."

"Well, this time we'll use Parmesan rather than Gruyère. It goes better with oysters, I think."

Hugo made the sauce under supervision. "Make it thick," said Paul. "Really thick—so that it sticks to the spoon. Twice as thick as a **béchamel.**"

They had the sauce ready, but the customers, when they came, declined the offer of **Huîtres Mornay.** They wanted sea bass on fennel, or steak tartare, the two alternative special offerings. When the last of the customers had gone, and Hugo and Paul were tidying the kitchen, Paul had an idea. "Do your parents like oysters?"

Hugo nodded. "I think so."

"Why don't we take these oysters to their place and give them a treat?"

$\mathscr{H}$ugo went off into the orchard with his father—pressing business with a leaking stand pipe that would not be turned off. Paul offered to deal with the oysters, which left him alone with Hugo's mother in the kitchen. He laid out the oysters on a baking tray. She watched him, and then lifted her eyes to his face and smiled.

"He's wanted to do this ever since he was a small boy," she said. "It's a calling, isn't it, monsieur?"

"It is, madame. I think—"

She stopped him. "You should call me Adèle. And my husband is Jean. They won't be long out there—my husband sees very little; he needs Hugo's help."

"I'm sure he's very helpful. I've seen what a hard worker he is."

She thanked him. Her manner was friendly in a way that reminded him of rural Scotland. It was a country characteristic— a directness and a lack of pretense that one encountered in places where not much happened, and where people still treated strangers as people, rather than as a threat.

"My brother-in-law has been a chef for many years, but somehow he never seemed . . ." She trailed off.

Paul was tactful. "It's not for everyone," he said. "But for those who love it, it's all they want to do."

Adèle inclined her head towards the window and the orchard outside. "I think he has that in him—our son."

"He does," said Paul. "I really think he does."

She sighed. "But I'm not sure that Claude sees it that way. He holds him back. He doesn't encourage him."

"No. I've guessed that."

She went over to the window and gazed out to where Paul could make out the figure of Hugo bent over a recalcitrant piece of piping. "Claude has a rather restricted view of the world," she said. "I know that we're nothing special—we're just ordinary people—but our views are . . ." She hesitated. "Less rigid . . . yes, perhaps less old-fashioned than his."

She glanced at Paul, as if to ascertain whether he had picked up the point she wanted to make.

"Perhaps he has an idea of what young men should be," he ventured. "Hugo mentioned hunting."

She rolled her eyes, leaving him in no doubt as to her views. "He can't understand why Hugo doesn't want to join him in that syndicate of his. They have the rights to the shooting in a large wood over that way. He offered to take him in on that—Claude has no son, you see. His wife left him. I suspect she couldn't stand it."

"I see."

"She was quite artistic, you know. She was a dressmaker—a very creative one."

"Oh."

"She ended up in Montpellier. She had a brother down there, a doctor. A pathologist. He was single and she kept house for him. It suited them both. I think they were happy enough."

"Which is the most that any of us can wish for," said Paul.

She looked at him thoughtfully. "Yes, that's right." She paused. "And which is what we want for our children, don't you think? Just that. Just that would be enough."

Paul waited. She was looking at him in a way that presaged a request. And now it came.

"Do you think you could do anything to help him, monsieur?"

"Paul, please."

"Paul. Could you?"

He wondered what he could possibly do. Speak to Claude, who would tell him to mind his own business? Try to find Hugo a job somewhere? There were restaurants in Scotland that would take him if he recommended him. But Hugo was needed here, he thought, so that was not an option.

"I'll think," he replied.

She looked at him gratefully. "He's a good boy."

"I can tell that."

The door opened and Hugo came in from the orchard, his father following him. Hugo guided him towards a chair at the kitchen

table. "We fixed it," he said. "A washer—
that's all. A little washer goes and you have
a big flood."

He looked at the oysters, ready now to be
put under the grill, and came and inspected
them. A fresh Mornay was prepared.

Hugo's father spoke to Paul from the table.
He asked about Scotland and about what
fruit they grew there. He asked about whisky
and distilleries. Had Paul been to that island
where there were—what?—six or eight distilleries; just one small island with all those
distilleries. Did Paul like Calvados?

At the cooker, Hugo glanced at Paul. Paul
picked up the anxiety behind the glance.
This was where the young man was from;
this was his world, and it was so different
from the larger world that Paul inhabited.

Paul said quietly, "What a nice place."

"You think so?"

"Of course."

The young man retrieved the tray from
the grill and sprinkled breadcrumbs over the
oysters in their sauce. When he turned
round, Paul could see the pleasure written
over his face. "Here's your treat," he said to
his parents.

They all sat at the table. A bottle of wine was produced from the fridge and they toasted one another. Paul watched as Hugo guided his father's fork to the shells. "Six of them, Father," he said. "Six on your plate."

They talked about Annabelle and Thérèse. "We were happy when they came back here," said Adèle. "They have been good for the village."

"Villages are dying," Hugo's father said. "Poor France."

"Not altogether," said Paul. "France is still very strong. Things will get better."

"I hope you're right," said Adèle.

They did not stay long. Hugo had to get back to the restaurant to prepare for the evening. Nothing was said about it, but Paul knew that he would help him. How quickly, he thought, did one become part of the world of others, with all that that entailed— the need to help them, and, more importantly, the desire to do so.

In the early evening Thérèse telephoned the restaurant to let Paul know that Chloe had returned to the house and wanted to see him.

"I won't be long," he said to Hugo. "I'll have a word with her and then I'll be back."

"I can cope," said Hugo. There was defeat in his voice.

"Listen," said Paul. "Remember what I said. Just remember it."

Hugo nodded mutely.

Back at the house, Aramis was being fed in the kitchen. Audette barely looked up when Paul entered, but continued to chat on her mobile phone while allowing the baby to suckle. Chloe was seated opposite her and rose to embrace Paul when he came in. At her side was a bulky man somewhere in his late forties, his hair cut short in military style. If one saw him in the street, thought Paul, one would put him down as a paratrooper. Now he rose to his feet and extended a hand to Paul.

"This is my friend Marc," said Chloe.

Paul felt his hand almost crushed in Marc's grip.

"Paul speaks very good French," Chloe said to Marc.

Marc nodded and parted his lips in a thin smile. "That's good," he said, and then added, somewhat darkly, Paul thought, "Some people don't speak French. None at all."

It was not an observation that could be argued with, Paul said to himself.

"No," said Chloe, glancing at Paul as she spoke. "There are people like that. But there we are."

Paul thought that he understood the message behind Chloe's glance. It said, **Don't disagree with him: this is not for discussion.**

Chloe and Marc sat down. Paul found a chair next to Audette. She looked at him briefly, and then continued her telephone conversation.

"What a pretty baby," said Paul.

Audette looked at Aramis, as if noticing for the first time that he was there. "He's a boy," she said curtly.

"Yes, I know. Aramis. After the musketeer."

Audette stared at him uncomprehendingly. "What?"

"Aramis is a musketeer. You know, **The Three Musketeers.**"

"It's a perfume," she said scornfully.

Paul suppressed a smile. It was true: she had named him after the perfume. He looked across the table at Chloe, but she was talking to Marc and had not heard his exchange with Audette. For her part, Audette had returned to her telephone conversation, and so Paul waited until he had Chloe's attention.

"Do you and Marc go back a long way?" he asked.

It was, he thought, an innocent question, and yet the reaction, from Marc at least, was a frown and a worried glance in Chloe's direction. **An ex-husband?** Paul wondered.

Chloe answered calmly. "A bit. We've known one another for some years, haven't we, Marc?"

Marc nodded. "A few."

"And you live in Paris?" Paul asked, directing the question to Marc.

Again, there was a prickliness in the other man's demeanour.

"Marc lives in different places," Chloe said. "Sometimes Paris, sometimes elsewhere."

"That's right," said Marc, his tone surly. "Not always Paris. It depends. Some people live in different places."

Well, thought Paul, one couldn't argue with that. And he realised he was not going to find out much more from Marc and his Delphic observations. He looked at his watch. "I should get back to the restaurant,"

he said. "I take it that Claude will be returning to work now."

"Not tonight," said Chloe quickly. "Maybe
tomorrow. Not tonight."

Paul felt a momentary irritation. He had
agreed to help while Claude was away, but it
seemed to him that there should be no call
for his assistance now that Claude was back.

"What's he doing tonight?" he asked.

Marc bristled. "Probably sleeping," he
said. "People sleep at night."

Chloe answered Paul's question. "Nothing,"
she said. "But I don't think he'll be able to get
back to work until tomorrow."

"Nothing," said Marc. "He's doing nothing."

It was obvious to Paul that if Claude was
doing nothing that evening, then he would
be doing it with Chloe and Marc. But he
did not give voice to his suspicions. "Tell
him that I can't spend my entire day tomorrow working in the restaurant. Tell him that
we're going to have to talk about that."

Chloe looked concerned. "I'm sure he'll
sort something out," she said.

Marc was on his feet now. "Good to meet
you, Paul," he said. "See you later maybe."

"Yes, of course." Paul held Marc's gaze.

It had that challenging, slightly threatening quality of the short-fused—the man capable of being tipped over into violence in an instant.

Chloe accompanied him out into the courtyard.

"Your friend's very charming," said Paul.

She gripped his arm. "Now, Paul, there's no need for sarcasm. Marc may not be everybody's cup of tea, but he's a good man at heart."

Emboldened, Paul asked her about her connection with him. "Is he a lover, Chloe?"

Chloe giggled. "Marc? Please! I don't go in for rough. No, no, Paul. You're barking up the wrong tree there."

"Then what? Why's he here?"

"Business," said Chloe. "A bit of business." She began to walk, her arm now linked in Paul's. "I wanted to talk to you about Claude," she continued. "I've had a long discussion with him."

"And is **he** a lover?" asked Paul.

"You are a very suspicious young man, Paul. You see lovers behind every tree. Just as they did in Haile Selassie's garden in Addis

Ababa. Apparently, there were spies behind every tree. Visitors saw them hiding."

"Can you blame me for being suspicious? You wouldn't tell me why you were going to Paris. You won't answer half my questions."

She smiled. "Yes, perhaps you have grounds for suspicion. Wrong, of course, but grounded, which is a different department, isn't it? And Claude and I, yes, we have become close. He's very keen to come back with me to Scotland for a while—when I eventually return. In a couple of weeks' time, I think."

"Are you going to marry him, Chloe?"

She stopped. Now there was reproach in her voice. "You have no right to ask a question like that. You're very impudent. You may be my cousin, but I am considerably older than you, and you don't ask senior relatives whether they're going to marry any Tom, Dick, or Harry."

"Well, are you, Chloe?"

"The answer, as it happens, is no. However, that does not preclude our spending some time together. I find him attractive, in an odd, rather Gallic, rural sort of way. But I couldn't marry somebody like him, poor dear. You know me, Paul—there's not an intellectually snobbish bone in my body, not one . . . but what would we talk about?"

Paul was thinking ahead. "And his restaurant?"

"Claude is tired. He'll be happy to hand it over to Hugo."

Paul allowed himself a sigh of relief.

Chloe heard it. "Yes, my reaction too. I realised at an early stage that this is what must happen and it was merely a question of planting the thought in his mind. It did not take much to do that. He was very responsive. Claude actually owns a farm in the Auvergne. He inherited it from his grandfather. He's keen to get back there."

"I'm glad," said Paul. "I was going to speak to him about it. I also wanted to speak to him about how he treats Hugo."

"Oh, I've already done that," said Chloe. "I gave him a very long lecture on that subject as we drove up to Paris. He had to listen. Men are at their best when they have to listen because they can't get out. He was in that position. And he agreed that he had not been very kind to that young man."

"Good."

"Yes. He said that Hugo had always been a disappointment to him. That he had hoped for something different. I told him off about that, and I think he came round to seeing it from my point of view. Eventually. The poor man hangs on my every word, you know. It's so appealing. He promised me he would say sorry to Hugo and let him be."

"Let him be himself."

"Precisely. Which is always the best thing to be, wouldn't you say, Paul? Be yourself." She waved a hand in the air. **"This above all: to thine own self be true.** Polonius, wasn't it? To young Laertes."

Paul could easily have demanded: **And who are you, Chloe?** but he did not, because they had reached the courtyard and had come across Annabelle collecting heads of lavender.

"Lavender is very calming for babies," said Annabelle. "Snip, snip."

"Yes," said Chloe. "Snip, snip." She turned to Paul. "Be careful, Paul."

He looked up sharply. What did that mean?

"Snip, snip," repeated Chloe, and turned on her heel, to go back into the house.

. . .

$\mathcal{P}$aul went to Alphonse's bakery the next morning with a larger-than-usual order for croissants. "Guests?" asked the baker, as he lifted the freshly baked rolls off their tray.

"Yes," replied Paul, and then remembered. "I mean no."

Alphonse raised an eyebrow. "A dozen croissants, though. You'll be putting on weight, monsieur."

"Your fault," said Paul, laughing.

A woman whom Paul did not recognise came in behind him. The bell linked to the door gave its familiar jangling warning.

"Madame," said Paul politely, allowing her to pass.

She did not greet him, but immediately addressed Alphonse.

"You heard?" she asked.

"Heard what, Louise?"

She leaned over the counter towards the baker. "Blown up. That caravan. The one that's been on Bernard's field."

Paul remembered who Bernard was—the alcoholic pig-farmer, whose pigs, themselves said to be drunk, had famously broken out of their enclosure and disturbed a Bastille Day picnic in a village garden.

The baker let out a whistle. "Where Bleu's been staying? Blown up?"

"Destroyed. The police have come in from Montmorillon. Almost nothing left. All blown up."

The baker lowered his voice. "Anybody hurt? Bleu?"

The woman shook her head. "They were out. They came back to find it. They say he's disappeared. And her too. That . . ." She looked over her shoulder at Paul, watching her language in the presence of a stranger.

"These people have their feuds," she whispered to the baker. "If you cross one of them, they never forget it, and they set fire to your barn. That happened down at Albert's place—remember? They argued with him about something or other and set fire to his stable. It's what they do."

Paul, having paid for the croissants, thanked the baker and left. His heart was racing. This was no accident—he was sure of that. He paused outside, uncertain as to whether to go directly home or to visit the scene of the crime. For that, he thought, was what it was—a crime—and it had been perpetrated, beyond any doubt, he felt, by Chloe and Marc. And possibly by Claude, too, the helpless lover in thrall to a dominant mastermind. The thought appalled him. You did not blow up other people's caravans, no matter the provocation, no matter how much you felt they deserved to be blown up. How dare Chloe? How dare she? And he could be implicated because he was living under her roof. If she were to be arrested, then he would be taken in too— the police were never going to discriminate between an innocent cousin and a criminal plotter. For a moment he imagined a shoot-out, with the police, in those black uniforms of theirs, sniping at the house before storming it. **Les flics** were tough and would not hesitate to use force. Was Chloe **armed**? The possibility had not occurred to him before, but now it did.

A police car shot past him in the street. It was heading in the direction of the pig farm, and he did not follow it, but turned back towards the house.

· · ·

Chloe was in the courtyard when he returned. Marc was with her, dressed in a tight-fitting black T-shirt that accentuated his muscular build. He was loading a small suitcase into the back seat as Paul appeared.

"I'm taking our guest back," said Chloe brightly when she saw Paul. "He cannot stay for breakfast."

"A train," Marc grunted. "Poitiers."

Paul glanced at him and then looked back at Chloe. "There's been an explosion," he said.

Chloe put her hand to her mouth. It was an exaggerated, unconvincing piece of acting, thought Paul. It was almost risible. "No!" she exclaimed. "An explosion!"

Marc shrugged. "Gas cylinders," he said. "Caravans have gas cylinders. They're always exploding."

Paul stared at him. "Why would you think it's a caravan?" He thought: **How elementary. How absolutely elementary.**

Chloe spoke quickly. "We need to leave for the station. I'll be back late morning, Paul." She paused. "I know—I'll come for lunch at the restaurant. You'll be working there, won't you, darling? We can have a nice little chat."

Paul said nothing. Chloe and Marc got into the car, slammed their doors, and set off. Chloe took a hand off the wheel briefly to give Paul a wave, and then they were gone. **Escaping,** thought Paul.

He went inside. Annabelle and Thérèse had arrived while he was at the baker. They received the croissants with expressions of appreciation, and put them into the oven to warm. Audette was in her dressing gown at the table, smoking a cigarette. Aramis was in his basket, apparently sound asleep.

"You've heard the news," Thérèse said. "Bang! The whole thing went up."

"Bleu was very lucky," Annabelle said. "They say that he and that woman were off with his people somewhere—a wedding, I believe."

"Those people are always getting married," said Thérèse.

Annabelle nodded. "Yes, they are. Anyway, they were extremely lucky they weren't there."

Audette had not said anything. Now she said, "Pity."

Paul glared at her. "Pity what?" he snapped. "That they weren't there? Is that what you're saying?"

Audette drew on her cigarette. "Why would I say that? No, I meant it's a pity their caravan's been blown up. They've had a narrow escape." She smiled up at Paul. "See?"

Aramis awoke, and was immediately picked up by Thérèse. "He needs his bottle."

Annabelle said, "Poor Audette is finding it difficult to feed him."

This information was for Paul, and he acknowledged it with a glance at Audette, who shrugged. "Sore," she said.

Annabelle took the croissants out of the oven and placed them on plates. Paul sat down at the table.

"Well," said Annabelle. "What a start to the day."

Paul's mobile gave its characteristic, intrusive ping. He fished it out of his pocket and switched it on. There was a message from Gloria.

Snap decision. They want to send somebody to scout it all out. Not in the bag yet, but initial sounds are very positive. I think this is going ahead. We're on our way, Paul. Love, Gloria. xx

.   .   .

Claude had left Hugo in charge in the kitchen, and was concentrating on the customers. In the kitchen, Hugo showed Paul what he had prepared. "This," he said. "See this. And this. How about that? Smell this. Yes, go on."

"Wonderful," said Paul. "They're going to love this." He paused. "And Uncle out there?"

"He told me to get on with it. He's going into town to meet his friends. They were in the army together. They drink beer."

"They'll be happy," said Paul.

Hugo frowned. "I suppose so."

"Are you all right?" asked Paul. "Do you need any help?"

"Maybe this evening."

"I'll be here," said Paul. "And there's good news. That television show I told you about."

Hugo grinned. "I can go and have a shower. Smarten myself up."

"Unnecessary," said Paul. "This is fly-on-the-wall stuff. Now, can you give me that table near the window? I'd like to have lunch with my cousin."

"Of course."

. . .

Oh dear, Paul," said Chloe. "I can see that you're upset about something. Tell me, darling. Tell Chloe."

Paul closed his eyes briefly. He would not be distracted by feminine wiles. She could flutter her eyelids as much as she wanted, and act the **ingénue,** but he would not be distracted. He opened his eyes. "Chloe, did you and that friend of yours . . ."

"Marc?"

"Yes, Marc. Did you and Marc blow up Bleu's caravan?"

He had expected a florid, expressive denial. He had expected injured innocence and reproach at the very thought. But what came was quite different.

"We thought about it," she said.

Paul gasped. "You mean to tell me that you planned to blow up a caravan? Is that what you're saying?"

Chloe was calm. "Keep your voice down, Paul. You don't want to enliven people's lunch with **lurid** accusations! Heavens no!"

"Well, did you?" Paul hissed.

"No, we did not. We had decided not to do anything quite that dramatic. Marc was going to get the message across rather differently."

Paul frowned. "With violence?"

"Not necessarily. Sometimes the prospect of violence—the threat—is more effective than actual force." She spoke as if she were furnishing an explanation of simple physics. "So, Marc had a word with this Bleu in town yesterday evening—earlier on, well before the explosion. He made the situation quite clear. Bleu was to leave the neighbourhood. People like that—like Bleu—understand that message. Whether or not he would have complied, who knows? But when he came back to find the caravan in pieces, I think he put two and two together."

Paul shook his head in disbelief. "Chloe, who exactly is your friend Marc?"

She replied without hesitation. "French security. A specialised branch of it. The French are—how can one put it?—robust about these things."

For a few moments Paul was silent. At a nearby table, a middle-aged couple scrutinised the menu in silence. Then Paul asked, "Chloe, who exactly are you?"

"Your cousin, Paul. You know that."

"Mrs. Pangloss? Amongst other identities, perhaps."

Chloe studied him in silence. "All right," she said at last. "That's one of them."

"Are you a . . . a criminal?"

He saw that Chloe's reaction to this was unfeigned. "A criminal?" Her voice was full of reproach. "A criminal, Paul? Is that what you think?"

"Well, you don't give me much of an alternative."

She shook her head. "Oh, Paul, what a conclusion to reach. No, darling, I am **not** a criminal. I am a helper."

"Whose helper?"

"The authorities. I shouldn't have to spell it out. And I'm not meant to, anyway. But for years my career has been—on an on-and-off basis—with British intelligence services, with occasional bits of work for our American friends. And the French. We're all meant to be on the same side, Paul. A bit of a bourgeois club, I suppose, but there we are. You make do with what you get in life."

He searched for words, but found none.

"Marc and I have worked together in the past. He's a very persuasive man, you see, and so I thought he was just the fellow to sort out this awkward Bleu customer. And he was. But by complete coincidence— and I mean this, Paul—by complete coincidence on the evening that he had a word with Bleu, their wretched caravan blew up. Convenient, of course, because it under-lined the message to Bleu, and these people understand that sort of thing. So he's away, and Audette will hear no more about the custody of **le petit Aramis.** That name, Paul. Aramis!"

"It's the perfume," said Paul. "She told me."

"How priceless," said Chloe. She looked at Paul—fondly. "All forgiven?"

He struggled with his feelings. What had Chloe done? She had resorted to threats and force to achieve what was probably the right result—and yet, and yet . . . means and ends: it was the same debate, endlessly rehearsed, endlessly unended. As a boy he had par-ticipated in a school debate: **Does the end justify the means?** He was fifteen, and it was all new to him then; but it was very old, he realised, and it would get older yet. Audette was, in her very particular way, awful, but she was not as awful as Bleu. Aramis would be better off with her than with his father, and he would have Annabelle and Thérèse to help him through life. They clearly loved him, and they had no children of their own, what with their unfaithful and model-railway-obsessed husbands.

And then there was Claude, who would no doubt enjoy his dalliance with Chloe and would probably be hurt when it came to an end, as it most certainly would. But he wanted a change, and a change is what he would get. Which left Hugo, who was going to be left to get on with the thing that he seemed to love above all else.

Paul sighed. "I suppose everything's worked out for the best."

"The best of all possible worlds," said Chloe. "Now, who said that, Paul?"

"Voltaire. Candide's companion, Dr. . . ."

"Of course. Of course."

Paul looked at her. This, he thought, was the moment when he would know whether she was telling the truth. "Was there a Dr. Pangloss? I mean, a real Pangloss, who lived somewhere near here? Somebody said something, you see—I think it was Annabelle or Thérèse. They said there had been . . ."

He stopped. Chloe was shaking her head.

"I have no idea," she said. "Absolutely none. Perhaps there was. **Somebody** must be called Pangloss."

He watched her. He watched her eyes.

She said, "Don't you believe me, Paul?"

Paul hesitated.

Chloe stared at him reproachfully. "You must, you know." And then, "I've never lied to you, Paul. Never. I told you, didn't I? I was joking about being Mrs. Pangloss. That joke had nothing to do with my false passport—or, shall I say, my passport of convenience. That was work. All officially approved."

Wine arrived and Paul poured each of them a glass. "White Burgundy," said Paul as he lifted his glass. He saw Chloe through the wine, a shifting form, blurred. "Let's not talk about it any more. **Fini.**"

Chloe raised her glass. "How lovely. You know, this restaurant seems to be improving."

He told her about the imminent arrival of the television producer. "Nothing's decided yet, but somebody's coming to scout it out. I gather they like the idea of doing a programme about a restaurant that is made into something special."

"From being pretty awful?"

"Yes. Although . . ." Paul sounded tentative. "Although, do you think this place was really that bad? Even when Claude was through there in the kitchen?"

Chloe took a sip of the wine. "They called it the second-worst restaurant in France—as you know. I thought that was a bit unkind. Possibly the third- or fourth-worst might have been more fitting."

Paul savoured the description. He was not sure. "The fourth-worst restaurant in France? I'm not convinced that has the right cachet."

"You think if you're going to be bad, be really bad?"

"Perhaps."

"Yes," said Chloe. "I think you're right."

"For the purposes of the programme—if they make it—they'll need to show it as it was. They'll need to get Claude back—and show some of his creations. That green onion soup, for instance."

"The toxic mussels."

Paul shuddered. "Don't talk about those."

"So, you think they really will make the programme?" asked Chloe.

"I don't see why not. It's a good story, isn't

it? People like a rags-to-riches tale. They love to see things turned around. You may have seen some of those programmes where they give people a makeover. They sort out their hair and their apartments and so on. They make their life better. Or different, should one say. It's not always clear that things are better afterwards."

"How perfectly wonderful," said Chloe. "Do you think there might be a part for me in this film? Just a tiny part? **Comme ça.**" She held up a tiny gap between thumb and forefinger.

"No," said Paul. "I don't."

"Oh well," said Chloe. "I just thought I'd ask."

"No harm in asking," said Paul, and reached across the table and took her hand.

"Dear Chloe," he said. "You know that we used to call you Remarkable Cousin Chloe."

She smiled. "Did you really? Well, well."

"It was a compliment, you know. We admired you."

"Well, that's good to know."

"Of course, we had no idea that you . . . that you did the things you do. This career of yours . . ."

"Oh, that," said Chloe. "It was largely part-time. And I was always on the right side."

"Of course. The right side."

Her expression was serious. "Oh, there is a right side, Paul. Don't ever be mistaken about that. The right side is the side that, by and large, is kind to people. I know that sounds terribly simple—childish, even. But it's ultimately the only test. There are kind countries and there are unkind countries. There are countries that hold people down, and those that don't. Kindness, Paul, operates at every level of our lives—up there at state level, and down there, amongst ordinary people doing ordinary things."

"And freedom?" asked Paul.

"Oh, that's part of it, too. As a general rule, making other people happy is one of the few things we can do with utter certainty that what we're doing is the right thing. And I think we have happy outcomes to our little sojourn in France, wouldn't you say?"

Paul said that he thought Chloe was right.

"And now," said Chloe, "you have these people who want to make a film about the restaurant and its fate. Will that be a film with a happy ending, do you think?"

"Yes," said Paul. "I'm certain of it."

"Then, good. I'm glad." Chloe looked thoughtful. "And Gloria? What about her?"

"She remains a friend. A colleague too."

Chloe stared at him. "Do you love her?"

Paul looked out of the window. **How does one find the answer to that question?** he asked himself. **How do you?**

"Remember one thing," said Chloe. "The human heart has many chambers."

"What do you mean by that?" asked Paul.

"Exactly what I said," replied Chloe. And then she added, "Be kind to her, Paul."

Paul sat quite still.

"Did you hear what I said?" asked Chloe.

"Yes," he said. "I did."

The following morning Paul went to the market with Hugo. The young man had a long list of things he intended to buy, and they moved from stall to stall, examining produce, talking to the stallholders, and sampling wares. When they had everything they needed, they sat down at a table of the café near the church and ordered two **cafés au lait.**

Hugo was keen to talk about the menus

he had planned. "I've found this book," he said. "It's a reprint of a book of recipes by a chef who wasn't very well known except in this area. But he had a real following round here."

"A local following is sometimes best," said Paul. "Anybody can be famous if you put him on television—but what counts is the opinion of the people down the street."

Hugo sipped at his coffee. "This book you're doing—this film—about our place."

"Yes?"

"Will it make our restaurant famous?"

Paul nodded. "For a while. But you know something, that sort of fame doesn't last. People will talk about it for a few months—maybe for a year or so. But then they'll forget. You'll have to carry on looking after the ordinary people who come to your restaurant from not too far away. Or passing trade—the people who see that sign on the road, the one that says, what is it?"

"Highly Recommended."

Paul laughed. "Yes, that one. Perhaps it should say something different."

"Very highly recommended?"

Paul thought for a moment. "No, not that.

How about **The Second-Best Restaurant in France**? How about that?"

Hugo grinned. "It would give me something to work for."

"Yes, we all need that, don't we?" He paused. "Although some of us already have it—and don't know that we do."

Hugo stared at him.

Paul looked up. The morning sky was blue and empty, and wide as any ocean. France, France. A swallow dipped and swerved, in pursuit of invisible prey, some tiny flying insect, or simply because the wind was in its wings and the air all about it was warm and buoyant. France.

ALEXANDER MCCALL SMITH is the author of the No. 1 Ladies' Detective Agency novels and a number of other series and stand-alone books. His works have been translated into more than forty languages and have been bestsellers throughout the world. He lives in Scotland.

RECEIVED JUL -- -- 20